An Andy Holliday Travel Mystery

Murder By Bay Breezes

John Elvin

Dedication:

To Neil Marr

Chapter One

There are sun-drenched days when hunting herons stand stock still in the coastal shallows as tufted brown marsh reeds dance to the tune of the breeze. Cloaked in a broad electric blue sky, the lower eastern shore of the Chesapeake Bay beckons, inviting the visitor to share its ancient and enduring natural secrets.

Of course, I hadn't actually made it to that out-of-the-way corner of the Chesapeake Bay yet. I was just going by pictures in the guidebook.

It's an old habit, starting work on a story as soon as I've got the assignment. Sort of like guessing where puzzle parts go when you first open the box, and then there are changes as you progress.

For instance, I later learned that not every tall, stick-figure bird in Bay country is a heron. It might be an egret. And there are even a couple of different kinds of egret.

Well, I had a lot to learn.

Including the answer to a dangerous question, one that few people wanted to ask: Who killed Sammy Sanchez?

But I'll begin at what was for me a new beginning.

I was in the offices of Here & There, the Family Travel Magazine, a glossy monthly given away in hotels, motels and restaurant entryways.

It wasn't the sort of job I wanted, but at that point I was more beggar than chooser, sliding the slippery slope, rapidly maxing out credit cards. Have you ever applied the brakes only to find you are on black ice? That was how my life was going at that point.

Besides, travel-writer, how bad could it be? Luxury suites, gourmet meals, swimming pools trimmed with gorgeous women in eye-catching states of revelation. I could handle that.

Chin up, shoulders back.

The brass nameplate read: Karl von Klonk, Editor.

I marched past the nameplate.

Sitting at a desk was a large – frog? How about: *froglodyte*. Just the sort of invention that an editor, savaging through my clever efforts, would strike. Toad will do for editors, this one certainly. At the very least a gnome, with the complexion of an unbaked biscuit, thinning hair slicked back, brown suit, brown tie and, no doubt, brown shoes and socks. His mere presence might frighten small children and domesticated animals. It was even a bit unnerving to a brave man of the world like me.

"Take a seat." That was it. No word of greeting or offered handshake.

The visitor chairs were, of course, lower to the floor than his own, so you had to look up. I felt like I was in a vintage war movie, playing a captive in a military interrogation room. But von Klonk seemed in no great hurry to make me talk.

There were little cannons on his desk. Several little brass cannons, and a host of miniature soldiers in antique regalia, some with muskets, some with sabers.

I don't mean to be judgmental or paranoid but could I have taken a wrong turn? Was I maybe in the rec room of some weird asylum? No, I'd seen the brass plate on the door, a serious credential. "Who's winning?"

"I am, as usual." He hardly glanced up, only as needed to acknowledge my presence. It was just as well, his froggy eyes discouraged contact. "This is pretty much an entry level job. Our applicants are usually ... younger."

"It's not as though I had to fight my way through a crowd."

"Point taken. You look the role, anyway."

"That's encouraging."

"The role is important. These kids…" He glanced toward the outer office where there were no kids, nor elders, nor infants. "We might try you; some maturity … in appearance, anyway … might just do."

Sure. It comes in kit form, the travel-writer job interview kit. And what was in his kit, this pond-dweller dressed for a reunion of Stasi agents? I waited him out.

"Shirt's kind of rumpled."

Sorry, the laundress is on holiday. "Irish linen. No starch. Has that tendency."

"It's rumpled."

"Never stopped me getting into the Jockey Club." These days I couldn't even afford parking at a fancy restaurant but playing the status card had the desired effect. It rated actual eye contact, met deadpan. Like any seasoned reporter, I could ask, say or hear just about anything with the impassivity of a rock.

"I spoke with someone who worked with you. Said you're a regular Don Quixote."

Don Quixote. What was wrong with that? Not exactly Sherlock Holmes but a kindred spirit, righting wrongs in his own peculiar way. I stared at the military array on von Klonk's desktop. "We all have our quirks, I suppose."

"Yes. Said your career was headed for the crapper. That right? And you made a foolhardy attempt to revive it?"

"It wasn't any sort of foolhardy attempt at anything. I was ambushed."

He nodded in mock agreement, tossing in an upside-down

smirk for good measure. "Everyone saw your story shredded on *60 Minutes*. The sources you claimed don't even exist."

The problem is, it would take forever to explain. If I had an explanation, which, unfortunately, I didn't. "I was set up by some very clever people."

"The way I heard it, you bought into a bunch of gossip. We don't need a gossip columnist. Can you write features?"

"You name it. If it's news business, I can handle it." That was reasonably true. I'd worked most desks on my way up the ladder, learning fast or bluffing in unfamiliar territory. Features? Hadn't I won the Northern Virginia Garden Club's *Best Flower Feature of the Year* award in my younger days? I'd played poet with posies. I thought about sharing that, then reconsidered.

Von Klonk slowly moved four foot soldiers forward of the brass cannons. "Fine. For the purposes of *Here & There*, a good feature story is basically a lengthy photo caption, light and lively, rich in descriptive fluff. Got that? Travel isn't reality, it's fantasy. Any problem with that?"

"I don't imagine so."

"No imagining. Yes or no?"

"No problem."

"No gossip, no intrigue, no scoops, just wholesome all-American hype."

"Mom, baseball and apple pie, my specialties."

"No comedy either. I'm giving you a chance. Thirty days, we'll see where it goes from there."

I said I'd have a look at some back issues, get a better idea of how he wanted stories handled.

"Skip that. I'll tweak your stuff in the direction we want to go, don't worry. We have something cooking down on the Chesapeake Bay, what they call the Eastern Shore. Lower Eastern Shore, that is. Don't look so thrilled."

"I was thinking maybe Paris or Rio…"

"Been done. The ad department sees the Lower Shore as untapped territory, ripe for plucking. The local tourism guy is getting back to me shortly."

"Lower Shore? That would be Chincoteague, Assateague?"

"No. Off limits! The boss has that reserved. His wife likes to feed the wild ponies."

"That's illegal, isn't it?"

"Sure it is. He pays the fines, writes the whole thing off on taxes."

All right, I give up. I'm supposed to pull a travel story out of thin air? "Those are the attractions, as far as I know. What else is there? What's the focus?"

"The focus is advertising. First, last and always. It's our lifeblood; so your mission is to scout out and spotlight potential advertisers, simple as that. That's the bottom line. Also the top line, middle line, only line."

"I see."

"You'd better. Another thing: I think your byline might prove a liability, so you'll be known as Andy Holliday. Problem?"

The problem was it was ridiculous. "Not so long as I can cash the checks."

At the flick of his finger an antique infantryman fell over. "Yes, well, there is one more thing." He spun one of the little cannons around so that it pointed directly at me. "Watch your expenses, Holliday. Gas is going over a buck and a quarter gallon. That's robbery. How much gas you figure it will take, getting down there and all?"

He didn't mention getting back. "I have no idea. It wouldn't be like, say, driving to Cleveland."

"Yeah, very perceptive. I'm going to bill the advertising department for gas. It's their idea, anyway. What a fiasco. Or maybe we can handle it by phone. Could you do that?"

"It's my favorite instrument."

"Hang on."

I hung. He stabbed a couple of digits on his touch-tone phone. He talked. He was quiet, his face reddening. He smashed the phone down like he was killing a bug.

"Mr High-and-Mighty, the ad director. We have to have someone on the ground down there, break the ice for the sales guys. What can I do when he's got his nose half a mile up the boss's ass?"

I got the impression von Klonk would like to trade noses with Mr High-and-Mighty. He treated me to his entry – quite possibly a winner – in the Sour Face Contest. "You will be a guest of the Tourist Bureau. Make the most of it. You get my drift?"

"Your drift is my drift."

His reply was mumbles and grumbles. I suppose that's one way to indicate an interview is terminated; ignore the interviewee. He noticed me again. "I'm giving you a chance, so don't blow it. Just do the job, no fancy footwork, no theatrics."

"I'll give it my mature best."

He swished me away with a hand signal. "Go see bookkeeping."

Don't click your heels, don't give a Nazi salute, just quietly take your leave, Andy Holliday. Like the fortune cookie said: *A drowning man isn't picky about who throws him a rope.*

I filled out forms, swore I'd told the whole truth and nothing but the truth, amen, then inspected my so-called workstation.

Like several other unoccupied cubicles in the large room outside of von Klonk's office, it came equipped with a word processor and telephone. The desk drawers were as empty as what used to be my bank account.

Von Klonk buzzed me to say that no formal itinerary would be provided. I was to rendezvous with a representative of the Tourist Bureau late the following afternoon.

"And, listen, Holliday, I've got a headline for you. *Bay Country: A Fine Place For Family Frolic.* How's that grab you?"

"I'm giddy."

"What's that?"

"I said *I'm ready.*"

"Good. Now go put some legs under that headline. And be quick about it. Time is money."

Tell it to Einstein. Didn't that poor guy spend half his life trying to figure out *time*? And all along, he could have just asked von Klonk.

Well, I was back in the game.

Yes, the weedy sandlot and not the big leagues anymore. And I wasn't even me, I was Andy Holliday. But I'd landed on my feet again — not a bad trick when you are too, well, *mature* to start over and too young to quit. I had a job!

Lucky me! Or so I imagined as I set off for the far reaches of the Chesapeake Bay.

Chapter Two

I felt like a lost sailor who'd sighted land, though what I'd sighted was Washington in the rear view mirror.

It was a day for feeling good, bright with spring's promise. A grand day for travel. Though, according to the guidebook, I was headed for a place where blue skies and sunshine could quickly somersault into gothic fog and mist.

I left Our Nation's Capital to the latest invading herd of pinstriped polecats and the new Chief Skunk, Ronald Reagan, who had recently proved his staying power by surviving an assassination attempt.

Oh, I liked Reagan well enough. He put on a good Presidential show. But he and his gang were no different from any of the others, there to pick the Treasury Department lock.

Yes, Washington under Reagan would certainly provide plenty of investigative opportunities. The problem was that I had been benched, sidelined, fairly much booted off the field. Gone now were the glory days when the high and mighty developed intestinal trouble when my byline appeared.

All right, no brooding.

On a good day — meaning one with little beach traffic — it's an easy hour's drive, maybe a little less, a straight shot out of the city to the Bay Bridge.

Actually there are two bridges spanning the Chesapeake, side-by-side, each channeling traffic in an alternate direction for five or so up-up-up and *down* miles.

Those sky-rise steel peaks have instilled terror in so many motorists that for-hire drivers are on call to help the reluctant get across.

Just before the bridge I blew by Annapolis, home of the US Naval Academy and developing as a suburb of Washington. Fond memories tried to lure me to stop because, at least once upon a time, you could find real crabcakes in Annapolis, not those crappy crumb-filled inland concoctions – in Annapolis, in those good old days, crabcakes were made of crabmeat, with just a dab of egg, mayo and a little pinch of Old Bay spice.

It was an amusing touristy town then, a snuggled waterfront mix of faux and genuine colonial homes and quaint shops. And more if you knew your way around. But that was then.

Ah well, onward.

Across the bridge, on the peninsula known as the Eastern Shore, it's only a short northward run to the turn-off for the ocean beaches. And veering south off that, at Salisbury, is a less traveled road toward my destination.

Along the way to the Salisbury turn, I passed not far from the quiet, manicured estates of St Michaels, the posh Bayside community where Washington's rich and famous find shelter in their dotage. Then Easton, then Cambridge, once proud bastions of tidewater maritime and plantation society, now caught in the standardizing stream of progress – cookie-cutter strip malls, fast food franchises, homely apartments and featureless tract housing. To see any reminders of yesteryear would require a trip off the beaten path, and I had no time for it.

Then gradually the look of the land shifts to truly rural, here an antique shop and there a farm-stand, and, turning south at Salisbury, where most go on toward the ocean beaches, farmland and woods fill the miles as you search for the next small town.

I'd promised no brooding, but that didn't mean I couldn't

mull. Why ever, in the early days when I had choices, did I decide to focus on writing about mischief in government and politics? There were reporters making perfectly good money covering subjects with real meaning and substance: archaeology, anthropology, geography, history. Although, from what I'd seen from my journalistic observation post, you can't really get away from the political, all fields have it. But in Washington you get the double dose, the politics of politics.

Ah well, not my problem on this day. I'd tumbled into travel writing, hadn't I? And not exactly the top tier. As for the assignment, what could be simpler? It would be a sleep-walk; just grab a handful of brochures at the Tourist Bureau, whip together a glowing yarn about hidden beauty, long lost heritage, recreational wonders – I'd skimmed the guidebook, hadn't I?

One intriguing insight I'd picked up from the guidebook is that the Eastern Shore hides many vast estates, hidden plantations with mansions invisible from any distant public roadway, owned by old-line migrants from the exclusive Delaware Valley or the odd Saudi oil baron. Soon, I assured myself, I'd be in the company of captains of industry, sportsmen known the world over, wealthy sorts, duPonts, Chryslers, Mellons, Rockefellers, and legions of rich divorcees or widows anxious to add a bon vivant travel-writer to their menageries.

Dream on – what was that name again? – Andy Holliday.

My timing was good and the restaurant easy to find, but in fact most any commercial establishment would be easy to find on the Lower Eastern Shore, there being only one busy road, Route 13, touted as *The Ocean Gateway*.

The restaurant was decorated as though it had been around a while, with rustic booths and, on the walls, murals depicting a romantic fountains-and-nymphs place that existed only in the painter's dreams.

I surveyed the diners scattered among the booths and tables. No one among the baseball caps, bald heads and burr cuts leapt up to greet me. I asked the girl behind the front counter if she knew Barney Cole.

"Barney? Sure. You're the guy he's supposed to meet? He called to say he'd be a little late. Car trouble."

A little late. I didn't like the sound of it, and it turned out I had a good ear. I sat in my car and read the guidebook, and I'd faded to sleepy boredom when I spotted a suit headed for the door of the restaurant.

"That you, Holliday? Terribly sorry. Car's in the shop. I hit a deer the other night, then the rental car broke down, it's been like that."

"Hit a deer? You're okay?"

"Sure. Happens all the time around here. They wait in ambush. Nature's suicide bombers. Their way of getting back at us for hunting them."

"Is that a fact?"

"Pure speculation. Don't quote me, the locals will think I'm on the side of the deer."

Cole looked familiar, but it may have been generic. He glistened, probably bathed in suntan oil. If I'd been casting him it might be as proprietor of a resort gallery stocked with forged old master paintings and hallmarked British silver services fresh off the boat from China.

Cole led the way to a booth. "Well, here you are. Welcome to Delmarva, Holliday. Obvious, I suppose, that's Delaware,

Maryland and Virginia."

"Sounds as though it could be a state in its own right."

"Maybe. The Delaware and Maryland parts might go along with it. The Virginia section is somewhat a place apart, maybe a bit resentful, as though it got robbed of the northern peninsula. There were battles over that, way back when. Or it could just be that Maryland and Delaware have the big cash cow resorts. But Chincoteague is coming along."

"Well, I've been warned off of Chincoteague, unfortunately. But generally it seems I'm assigned to the central area, a bit north and a bit south of where Maryland and Virginia meet."

"That's my turf, and you're my guest. Too bad about Chincoteague, of course. That would be a hot spot for you."

"Well, I guess I'll have to make the best of East Westerly."

Did I pick up a slight roll of the eyes? If so, in a flash Cole was back in character. "Hope you're hungry? This place serves two meals and calls it one. The food's not bad. I mean, it's okay. Glass of wine? Cold beer?" He spoke with a careful and practiced delicacy, as if addressing students in an English class for foreigners.

"I'll skip the booze, thanks. Iced tea would be fine."

"Careful with it, sweet tea around here is like drinking cane syrup."

Yes, I suppose I've neglected to mention: I don't drink alcohol.

It's like this: When I got into the news business, a reporter who didn't drink, and I mean *drink*, was a freak and soon an outcast. I became a very good reporter, a remarkably functional drunk.

The party lasted for years, but a time came when it was over and I was one of a few who hadn't wised up and gone home. Suffice it to say that life ultimately handed me a bloody shape up or ship out notice, and unlike a few diehard buddies, I took the former option. Better late than never.

But back to Cole, and my feeling that I knew him from somewhere. I asked if I'd seen him on TV. "It's as though I know you, not personally but somehow or other."

He looked for his reflection in the fingernails of his left hand. "No. I was behind the scenes. Might have been a picture in one of those show-biz magazines. I was in LA, Hollywood, the big time. But… here I am, here we are."

I was well aware of the feeling.

Cole seemed surprised when our waitress appeared, a young blonde with a warm smile and a second-look figure. "Hi Angie, where's Serena?"

"She didn't show up today. We've had to share her tables."

"She's had a hard time of it."

"They said she's not answering her phone." The waitress took our orders and headed for the kitchen.

The Athenian pizza sounded ok, feta and spinach is pretty hard to screw up. I opted for that. Much as I love Italian food, the sauces are often made with wine and I don't knowingly get even that close to alcohol.

Cole answered a question I hadn't asked. "This is Serena Sanchez's section usually. She's tops, works days out where you'll be staying and most evenings here as well, never misses her shift. But she's dealing with a tragedy. Her son died a couple of weeks back."

"Died?"

"Oh, can't say it was surprising. He was a weird kid, always snooping around."

"He died of weirdness?"

"That's a good one. No, he was poking around where he didn't belong, fell into an old refrigerator and got trapped. Probably playing one of his detective games, spying. Might never have found him but the fridge got hauled to the scrapyard."

Was it just me, or was Cole being dismissive of the kid's death? It bothered me enough that I checked it out. "Are you saying he got what he deserved? Rubbed you the wrong way, this kid?"

"It's nothing." He shrugged, gave it a moment's thought. "Just a little something."

"So his mother's a friend? Do you need to find out why she's not here?"

"I don't think so. She's Mexican."

"That explains it."

"Well, I mean, people talk."

"They talk about Mexicans?"

"Never mind. Let me tell you about where you'll be staying. It's in a little village called East Westerly, out in the country a ways."

I hadn't stopped for so much as a snack on the way down and had no trouble making short work of the Athenian pizza. Not bad, though personally I would have cranked up the greens and cut back on the feta. "There are hotels out there?"

"It's not exactly a hotel. It's a bed and breakfast. Will be, anyway, when Miss Worple gets done with the renovations. See, the problem is there's not much open this time of year. We had to take what we could get."

"I don't mind a motel."

"There aren't any that belong to the Lower Eastern Shore Tourism Association, just yet. The association is a work in progress, Holliday. I'm in the process of building it up. There aren't too many members at the moment, but Miss Worple signed on."

I didn't like the sound of it. "How many members do you have?"

I thought maybe he was going to do a count on his manicured fingernails. Instead he just grimaced slightly. "I don't have the figures with me. Anyway, your article's going to do us a world of good, Holliday. Counting on you to spread the word. You were asking about Miss Worple's place …"

"Is East Westerly on the map? I don't really know my way around here."

"Not sure. It would be on the old ones, of course. There was a time there was a lot more to it. The population is greatly, well, diminished. Not too many people out that way at the moment, some watermen, farmers, a few old-timers, lots of, umm, lots of, you might say, ruins. Part of the charm, of course. The nostalgia factor, right?"

"I'm not sure what you mean by nostalgia factor."

He was back at his fingernail fascination, carefully studying the dainty collection, buffed to a high gloss. People send a lot of different signals with hands and fingers, what was his? I settled for smugness but decided I'd ask a shrink next time I got caught in that net. Cole continued: "Oh, you know, 'I beheld the legendary site of the daring sea rescue,' or 'here once was baked the world's largest strawberry pie,' or 'said to be haunted by pirate ghosts.' There's just no end to good old days angles around here."

"Great. But you're just fabricating. Got anything I can actually use?"

"Tell you what, Holliday, why don't I just do up a draft for you? And then you put it in your own style, you know … make your job a lot easier wouldn't it?"

Mentally, I mounted my high horse. There was a time when that would have been the end of the conversation, I would have walked away in a professional huff. It was going to be my story, not Cole's. "Generous of you. But I've got to kill some time down here, might as well spend it researching and writing. I'll get with you later about filling in the blanks."

"Right, suit yourself. I'm sure you intend to run the article by me before you go to press, just for the sake of accuracy."

How about, just for the sake of seeing if I said what you want me to say? It's not so much that I'm a man a principle as I am a man of limits. I mean, I don't know what my rules are until I sense someone breaking them. But I let it drop and went over the directions again with him. The route seemed simple enough, just a few turns, but a long drive. I had reservations and they weren't the kind Barney Cole had made for me. "Is there a notation on the map, *beyond this point are monsters?*"

"Funny thing, they do have a monster out there, it's called Chessie. I mention some sightings in my brochure."

"So you're sending me to the edge of the Earth."

"Well, you might think so after a storm or an unusually high tide, but in those cases you can't get there from here –- unless you wade five miles of water. Turns into an island."

"Strange that people would want to live like that."

Cole played the professor card. "There was a time, Holliday, everyone around here traveled by boat. You're about twenty miles by auto but only ten by boat. People built along the water to get their crops and catches to market, at least in the days before the railroads."

"There are trains through here?"

"Used to be. You can still see where the tracks ran, though the rails and timbers have been salvaged. Like I said, a lot of things around here aren't here anymore, but of course there's a romantic angle in that."

"Romantic. Goes hand in hand with nostalgic?"

"Well, I mean there are great opportunities for using your imagination."

Red flag. Von Klonk's image loomed up in my mind, warning against the imaginative.

I asked Cole if he had any tips on writing about the people and places hereabouts.

"Hmmm. Well, a lot of the watermen are from the islands, Smith and Tangier, they have their own way of talking. An old way, brought over from England. So if you're down along the water and talking to someone you can understand, they're probably not from the islands."

"I'll need a translator?"

"Just listen real close, you'll pick it up. I mean, it's the same language we speak, just spoken differently."

"Sort of like New Hampshire Yankee, or Alabama Southern?"

"No. You need to think in terms of centuries, not geography."

Cole shuffled around in his seat like he was chasing a bug. "Goodness, I seem to have left my wallet back at the shop. Would you cover this, Holliday, and I'll square it with you next time?"

Chapter Three

It was difficult not to drift into imaginings given the monotony. There were fields and forests, and then came forests and fields.

Anybody can make a mistake, right? I could have gone for a few more fast food job interviews. And what could be so bad about flipping burgers? A lot of people flip burgers for a living. Get really good at it, you'd probably get promoted. One day, maybe, I could be managing a crew of burger flippers. I don't know, might not be all that great. You'd have to train new burger flippers, and hassle with the public over technicalities like the meaning of *medium well*.

But fate had other things in mind. That's it, blame fate. Mine was, I was guest of a 'Tourist Bureau' existing largely in the mind of an exiled Hollywood hustler. Then there was the problem of the missing waitress, seen as not so much a problem because she was Mexican. And then the matter of her son, a victim of death by snooping. A less than auspicious introduction to the Eastern Shore.

All that and now a long and lonesome road into the boondocks, destination undoubtedly not the five star hotel I'd had in mind, the one with the Palm-rimmed pool and fun-filled bikinis.

And where was I now? There were stretches where the trees stood like soldiers in formation, testimony to human imposition of control, order, patterns: *human nature*. We discipline our lawns, parks and farms.

Signs advised *Tree Farm*.

But to a greater extent, anarchic forest prevailed in chaotic wild tangles of woods and brush. I had never seen such an abundance of misshapen foliage, crooked limbs of something between a bush and tree, not quite either, some green but many gray and, to my eyes, dead. I know, von Klonk had already given me an article title. But I wondered if he would mind changing it to *Eastern Shore: The Place Where God Went Gothic.*

Eastern *Shore.* Didn't that suggest vast stretches of water and sand? My inner child was getting uneasy: *Are we at the beach yet, Dad?*

Where the land stood cleared, awaiting a spring planting of corn or hay or soybeans, there were often elongated airplane hangars, up to a football field in length and usually windowless. As I soon learned, they were poultry houses; there might be just one, there might be a dozen or more. And from the road, not a clue that each was stuffed with thousands of chickens.

Once in a while a long lane disappeared through an arching canopy of trees. Did it lead to the hideaway estate of some guardian of old money, as the guidebook had led me to believe? From what I had seen thus far, I had my doubts. More likely, despite the guidebook hype, what lay hidden was a derelict plantation house or mildewed mansion, long since abandoned by owners fled to a distant tax haven.

Now and then the field and forest broke for a dwelling, a few cared-for and homey, others waiting for the earth to pull them in.

And there were lots vacant but for weeds, brush, and a few flowers. It was flowers that seemed the last testament to former habitation. There could be no other hint of an old homestead, but surely that was the meaning of a patch of daffodils or hydrangea holding forth along the road.

My mind wandered. What of this missing Mexican waitress? It wasn't his intention but Cole sure set me on edge with his dismissive attitude. As if to say, *a dead Mexican kid, a missing Mexican mom, no big deal.* Nothing gets me suited up in armor and mounted on the white horse quicker than hearing 'Who cares?' I know, it's wiser to look the other way, there's nothing but trouble to found in involvement in other people's troubles. But, once upon a time, at least in the fairy tales idealistic young reporters told each other, that was the business of the news business.

Don't despair, Dulcinea! Don Quixote to the rescue!

I tried to form a picture of this Serena Sanchez in my mind's eye. Probably a big mama of a woman in ruffled white blouse, flowing black skirt, a flower in her dark hair. Complexion naturally the bronze that Anglos suffer for as they bake in the sun or toast in the tanning salon. Yes. And speaking only a little English, just enough to get by: "How ees your pizza, senor?"

Her son. The kid who liked to play detective. Probably just curious about the world around him, maybe a cultural outsider trying to get a handle on local customs, trying to fit in. A stranger in an area where, no doubt, if they didn't know your grandpa, you did not belong.

Sure, that would explain why he was branded snoopy, he was just trying to learn how to get along. But that didn't explain why he would crawl into an abandoned refrigerator. What in the world got into him to pull a crazy stunt like that?

I'd been a kid once, a detective, checking out the neighborhood for villains. Was he a young kid or an old kid? "Kid" covers a lot of territory —- was he eight or nine, inventing stuff to detect, or fifteen or sixteen with real suspicions?

Well, enough of that. I needed to gather some atmosphere, local color and lore to pad out a story for *Here & There*. Typically, the reporting trick would be stop in at the local bar or tavern, interview the town drunks for some sappy quotes. I hadn't seen any sign of such an establishment, unless it was mobile. There were lots of empty beer cans along the roadside.

A welcoming committee of insects decorated my windshield. And it wasn't only bugs that paid a price for being in the path of an oncoming auto. A naturalist might have kept amused for a good while, guessing at the species of the plentiful carcasses, road-kill in various stages of decomposition.

Big, awkward black vultures picked at the remains. I might not mention vultures in my travel article; they were not the best evidence of a vacation playground suited to family frolic. Still, they were impressive, a combination of beast and beauty, staggering around like after-hours drunks until they took to the air, and, once aloft, soaring like proud eagles.

Why did vultures bring Barney Cole back to mind? What was his story? Coming here from LA, even if here was once home, had to be like swapping a Corvette for a golf cart, a real comedown. What wall had he hit? Well, Hollywood, what did that suggest? A wall of white powder? Or maybe, despite his practiced delicacy, he'd trod upon some mogul's toe? At any rate, if von Klonk thought Cole would be covering my expenses, I'd say he was greatly deluded. Hadn't my host stuck me with the bill for lunch? Dealing with Cole might require a bit of caution.

There was no traffic save for a forest-green pickup truck doing half the speed limit, weaving like a quarterback twisting through a mob of defenders.

Passing the truck I noted an official looking emblem on the side. The driver appeared to be in uniform. His face was a stubble-covered slab as he glanced my way and offered a tired index-finger wave.

Where in hell was ...

Welcome to East Westerly.

Not exactly a blink-and-you-missed-it little village, but two blinks would probably do the trick. Now, it really began to sink in how far I had come from Washington. Even in the pricier Washington suburbs where an attempt is made at architectural difference, there is sameness because the homes were built en masse. Here, one lot hosted a stately antique Victorian while the next featured a large modern box constructed on a factory assembly line, and then came a cottage, and next a practical farmhouse of two or three stories and an add-on or two at the rear, with a proper, white-spindled porch at the front.

And though you couldn't call it a ghost town, there seemed an abundance of *for sale* empty dwellings. Some were solid and inviting. There's so much talk about homeless people, who is standing up for people-less homes? Some were skeletal, with scatterings of fallen brick, blown roofing, broken glass. Several looked like the spooky old house in the horror movie, the one the heroine walks to when her car breaks down late at night on a lonely country road.

Yes, it was well along in spring, but some of the houses remained decorated for Christmas with strings of unlit lights and bedraggled storybook characters on the lawn.

Vacant lots indicated that homes now a distance from the next had once been part of a cluster of dwellings lining the main road, and a few of the buildings were undoubtedly designed for commercial enterprises, though now boarded up monuments to the good old days.

To the rear of many of the homes and outbuildings, hidden from view unless you looked hard, were junk piles. Heaps, some tidy and some unkempt, of old appliances, household furnishings, defunct autos and derelict boats, odds and ends of equipment.

Even at the little brick post office there were no signs of activity beyond the weak flutter of a flag, no cars in the lot, and only one out behind the building as evidence that someone might be on duty inside. My impression was of a sleepy little town content to continue its snooze.

Following directions, I turned on a side road and soon came to the pillared entryway of a drive where a small hand-painted plaque on one of the pillars announced: *Bay Breezes*. Had I not been on the alert for some indication, I would have breezed on by.

Once parked, I got a good look around, and it didn't look good. Looming before me was a huge old home in the grand plantation style, a two-story main house with one-story wings, but, like most plantations, its glory days were history. Shutters askew, a downspout hanging away from the side, and a greenish tint to the brick (was it moss or mold?).

I let myself into a long, wide screened front porch arrayed in weary wicker and rattan. When a polite tap failed to bring response, I resorted to the brass knocker.

"I'm looking for …"

"Sorry, we're not accepting guests at the moment." Brunhilde —- the name I would have given her —- took a guardian stance in the doorframe.

"That may be, but my stay was previously arranged by the Tourist Bureau. I'm from *Here & There* magazine."

"Oh, you're the writer. Well, the situation has changed. My help has disappeared and I can't provide lodging if I have no help. Sorry." But she didn't really seem at all sorry. She was just matter-of-factly letting me know I wasn't welcome.

"Just a minute, madam. You know, I'm doing an article and this place is to be featured. Do I say it's a ramshackle relic guarded by a rude battleaxe? You are making a big mistake."

"This isn't a debate, and if anyone is rude, it is you. Battleaxe! Print that and I'll sue for slander, and good day to you." The door slammed in my face.

Chapter Four

Wait a minute, think this thing through. No, the hell with thinking it through. I'll just beat this door to kindling. We all know what road rage is, but how about front door rage? It's probably as old as the first barriers at entranceways, but I don't know that modern psychology has yet added it to the list of mental disturbances. However, I created a potential case study at Bay Breezes. I may have knocked the hinges loose with my hammering.

From behind the door I heard a firm announcement. "We are closed, go away!"

There was obviously a failure to communicate, a serious misunderstanding. "Madam, I am not a tourist. I'm a professional journalist on assignment. I just need a place to stay while doing the story."

The door eased open a crack. "I'm armed!"

"Wonderful! My visit to Annie Oakley's Boarding House. You'll be famous."

"You must not have heard me."

"This is madness. May I at least come in and call Barney Cole?"

You would think I had asked the million-dollar question on a game show. She pondered. Finally: "I suppose so. Come in. But keep a civil tongue in your head or out you go."

It was a wise decision on her part. I mean, easy going I may be, but I've been known to, as they say, flip out. I could kick the place into toothpicks and claim insanity. Hers.

Miss Worple pointed to a telephone on a table down the hall. On a tabletop nearest her, I noticed a piece of artillery, which I took to be a .45 caliber revolver. Yes, revolver. It wasn't the squarish modern .45 with a clip; it was the Old West six-shooter of the type favored by Gen George Patton, the so-called Peacemaker. I'm not a gun nut, or a Patton nut, but somewhere in my research or reading I'd seen a little cannon like that before. It was the sort of instrument that could put a porthole in a man's chest, and it sure beat tranquillizers for calming a case of front door rage.

Cole, sputtering apologies, said he was certain there was some misunderstanding, and I agreed with that assessment. He asked to speak to Miss Worple.

I don't know if it was response to his tinsel town spiel or a bribe or threat, but her tone turned almost sugary.

"You are welcome to stay but you have to understand, I'm fairly helpless without my help. I'm busy enough with other things. I've just no time for looking after visitors."

Did I need looking after by the gun-slinging matron of a boondocks bed and breakfast? "No problem, I'll get by."

"You will be making your own bed and finding your own breakfast if Serena doesn't come in."

"How do you manage on her days off?"

"She doesn't take days off."

"Aren't there laws against that?"

"There's television in the parlor."

That was the least of my concerns. I rarely watch it. Sometimes for news, but I'd rather get my news from the weekly mags after it has settled down and become coherent and maybe even credible.

"First door on the left at the top of the stairs. Careful of the bannister. It's one of the things Sammy said should be fixed."

"Sammy?"

"Serena's son, the lad who got suffocated."

"I heard about that."

"He was always pointing out problems. I guess he was teasing, said he'd turn me in for operating a hazard. I told him I had a remedy for snitches."

"What's your remedy?"

"It's sitting on the tabletop in the hall."

I'd noticed. "He didn't risk it, I take it."

"Don't you dare even suggest such a thing. I'd never have harmed that foolish boy. Unless he turned snitch, then he'd be asking for it, wouldn't he? Just be careful on the stairs, all right?"

"All we need is a dark and stormy night."

"What was that?"

"I said I'm sure I'll be all right."

"You'd better be. I'm not running a clinic here. Wasn't long ago that silly lady from Wisconsin lost her grip and took a tumble there and we had to call the ambulance."

"And was she easily repaired?"

"Well, of course there is no local ambulance, it has to come from some distance. It was distressing. But she was only a little bruised up. She got over it. We had a good laugh before she left."

"For my part, I hope not to leave you in stitches."

"There are a few other problems. I wish Serena was here to give you all the warnings. I can't keep track."

"Sounds like Sammy might have been on to something."

" I suppose I shouldn't have opened to the public quite so soon. But it has been helpful having a few guests because they tend to discover and point out dangers to add to the list."

"Well, I suppose I should see about getting settled."

"Not until you've heard a bit about Bay Breezes." And I did hear a bit, quite a bit. Just as I was about to fake a medical emergency, she wound down.

I fetched my suitcase and Remington portable typewriter and trucked them to my assigned room, avoiding the banister.

The room belonged in a museum. All that was missing was the *George Washington Slept Here* plaque.

I really couldn't tell you whether a piece is Regency or Victorian or what; I recognize 'old' but that's about it. What I do know about antique furnishings is, things that survive to become antiques were sturdily built, and things that are sturdily built are not usually the most comfortable.

I tested the mattress on the canopied bedstead. It was made of some sort of feathery quicksand. I wondered if I might find any previous guests sunk down in it somewhere.

But at least I had a bed for the night. For a few moments there on the porch I had pictured myself camped out in the car at a highway rest stop.

Establishments of this sort have their public and private areas. Not finding Miss Worple in what seemed the public area, I assumed my nosy journalist personae and explored further. I tapped on a closed door leading off to one of the wings.

I wanted a key. I didn't know Miss Worple well, and with any luck never would, but I could tell she was the sort to keep the place under lock and key. I would need a key.

"Sorry to bother you, I have a question."

"Well, you have bothered me. I was in the shower. There's not often much hot water, so I wanted to get there before you used it all. What is your question?"

"I take it you don't leave the front door open, so would you be kind enough to let me have a key?"

Miss Worple opened the door, armored in a quilt-sized housecoat. I thought it might make a good scene for a Hitchcock film, right before discovery of the body. But I was quite willing to leave whatever went on behind her door, behind her door. "Of course you'll need a key. I'm not going to leave the house open without Serena here to see who comes and goes. Now, where would she keep the spares?"

We went on a tour, ending, as I could have predicted, at a pantry wall rack holding a variety of keys.

What was that smell? It was a harsh, danger-signal odor. "Is something burning?"

Miss Worple looked around with more curiosity than concern, as if I had asked whether she had a pen I could borrow. She sniffed the air. "I don't believe so."

"There's an acrid sort of odor."

She swept the floor with her eyes. "Oh, a while back there was a fire, nothing major, and I haven t quite got it aired out yet."

"Don't guests find that a bit disturbing?"

"I can't worry about every little thing people might complain about."

"It could be a big thing, don't you think? You know, some could find it difficult to sleep in a house that might be on fire."

"But it's just an odor." Was it nonchalance or obliviousness? "You get used to it, same as you get used to the ghosts." Well, she was no slacker when it came to changing the subject.

"The place is haunted?"

"And why wouldn't it be?"

"Oh, I don't know. If I was investing in a place for public accommodation, I would probably try to find one that didn't have potential for scaring the bejesus out of visitors."

Her look, askance with arms folded, might have been fitting if she was the teacher and I was the kid whose dog ate his homework. "This is the old home place, Mr. Holliday. These ghosts are family spirits. I suppose you think it's just pipes squeaking or rafters reacting to heat or cold, or wild animals killing each other out in the shrubs."

"It could be something like that."

"It's *nothing* like that." She led the way as far as the parlor, a sweep of an arm indicating that I might resume my role as guest and restrict myself to the appropriate territory.

The parlor might have been called the Burgundy Room; that was the dominant color, from window draperies hanging to the floor to fabric of an under-stuffed sofa constructed, I imagined, to enforce proper posture and ensure short visits. It even extended to the artificial flowers in a white porcelain vase on an end table.

Also on that end table I noticed an odd item; was it a miniature carved mask? It was a spooky looking thing, very out of place in this setting.

I asked about the strange object.

"Don't touch that, there's a curse on it. Some demonic Indian thing." She took a step backward, emphasizing her distaste.

"Cursed? Really?" It was about palm sized, a carved clamshell, not a natural shell color but a sort of scum green, perhaps due to being long buried. The face on it was incised, a crude nose that looked rather like a penis and beady little eyeholes punched clear through. Further decoration included thin lines like war paint extending from below the eyes to the jaw. Eerie indeed.

"Sammy left it here just before the accident. It came from down on the Point. I'm sure an Indian curse was set loose when it was dug up." Her eyes glazed as though she was entranced. "Don't you think, Mr Holliday, it's come to pass?"

"What's come to pass?"

"The curse. I just have a sense that things aren't going well here, in this house, in East Westerly, in this country … everywhere." She surveyed the room, particularly the ceiling, as if looking for confirming signs and omens.

"You left out the known universe, and the unknown."

"Mock me at your peril. There's something evil about that thing. I want Judge Wetherby to get it out of here."

I really wanted to pick up the little artifact, to have a closer look, but I restrained myself. I also wanted to avoid eviction. Play by the rules, Holliday.

"I'm afraid I don't know Judge Wetherby."

"The Judge is my good friend He comes by often. We're both active in the local Civil Defense unit. Co-captains, in fact. You'll no doubt meet him."

"Civil defense? You mean hiding from bombs, that kind of thing?"

Her eyebrows squeezed into a squint. "What bombs? Oh, it's your idea of a joke. It's no joke. Disaster preparedness, Mr Holliday. Hurricanes, cyclones, floods and such. We're on call for search and rescue. And it wasn't so long ago, was it, there were German submarines coming up the Bay? Might be the Cubans next time, who knows? We have to be on the alert."

"Cuban submarines. There's a threat the talk radio guys could have some fun with."

"Some say that's how dope gets delivered. We keep an eye out."

I said it sounded like a vigilance committee.

She didn't disagree. "If there's a problem and no law around, we do what needs to be done."

I backtracked to her earlier comment. "So, what's the story with Sammy?"

"Just as I told you. He's Serena's son. And he's dead. Probably the curse."

"A strange business. I'd like to know more about it."

"Why so? You don't believe in the curse. Anyway, I'm not a gossip."

"Surely not. But didn't your vigilance committee look into it?"

"It was an accident, brought on by foolishness. There's nothing to look into."

I was full of questions. "And about these Indians? It might be interesting to write about the Indians. And what's the Point?"

"Parkers Point, it's a section that juts out into the Bay, just down the road from here. No trespassing allowed. Didn't stop Sammy, though, did it? As for the Indians, Judge Wetherby knows something about them, or so he thinks. Actually, I wouldn't put too much stock in anything he says about that. Some of his ideas conflict with known facts."

"So where could I find this Judge Wetherby?"

"As I said, right here. Most days he drops by for morning coffee, though he'll have to bring his own with Serena gone, unless I can find some instant. And then most often we're off to a meeting." She studied the burgundy carpet, reflectively. "He's not a judge anymore. He's a power behind the scenes in local politics. But officially, retired."

"You say it as though he surrendered in battle."

"Some problems came up. He was bidding on tax lien properties and the do-gooders raised questions about it being unethical. Fact is, he was being helpful."

Well, it did sound a little dicey. "A judge is considered a public official. How was he being helpful?"

"Kept the newcomers from grabbing up the properties, kept the land local."

"There's a problem with newcomers buying property?"

I got a look as though I was about the most clueless character ever to have set foot in Bay Breezes. "Nothing is the same since the new people started coming in. All the old plantations are tumbled to ruin, fine old families scattered and gone. It's a sad state. Newcomers have ruined it."

"But you cater to tourists. Isn't that encouraging the newcomers?"

That brought a defiant retort. "The Eastern Shore has always been known for hospitality, Mr Holliday."

"Come visit, just don't wear out your welcome."

She was turning a shade closer to the room's dominant burgundy. She stood up. "I hope your room is to your liking." She was obviously turning something over in her mind. "I can't educate you overnight, but, you know, for three centuries, Mr Holliday – centuries! – this was a unique and special place. We fought nature and savages, built an empire of prosperous plantations, a world-renowned seafood industry, thriving little towns. Our economy was the equal of any. Wealth, the result of hard work and commercial genius, was almost taken for granted. And we had a proper society, everyone in their place, a culture where art, drama, music, learning and all the underpinnings of civilization handed down from the Greeks could be found in full flower."

Yes, and if you needed reliable help you could just buy an African or a deported criminal or kidnapped waif from the British Isles. I thought it, but kept the observation to myself. I wanted a roof over my head, at least for the night.

Miss Worple wasn't just lecturing me, she was lecturing the entire world and possibly the universe beyond that. I hoped to guide the tirade toward a conclusion. "And now?"

"And now?" It was as if to ask if didn't have eyes, that I couldn't see the current situation. "Debris, that's your answer, debris. Look around you, economic and natural debris, a model of achievement for mankind to admire, reduced to decay and ruin. And why? Barbarians, Mr Holliday. Barbarians from the north, barbarians from the west, pillagers disguised as investors; in truth nothing but robbers, schemers, shysters. They stripped us to the bones and then picked the bones, hauled the pickings off to their fancy antique shops and big city auctions. They left estates, plantations, entire towns to rot and vanish. And you don't believe in an Indian curse? Oh, it's real, all right. You'll see."

Well, what did I know? "Actually, from what I've seen on the main road, bilingual signs, bodegas and cantinas, it seems a lot of the newcomers you're blaming are Spanish-speakers."

"That's a whole different matter. The Eastern Shore is sliding into the Third World, as they call it. Those are field workers and laborers, they come for a season and then they just stay. They earn a little money, what do they do? Open a shop or a restaurant, settle in. And then they want rights, and if they don't get rights they protest and sue, and the government and the courts cater to them like royalty while we who have been here for generations get the tax bills and the cold shoulder."

"If they have shops I'm sure they must pay taxes."

She studied me like a medical student examining a first cadaver. I assumed she was wondering if she had wasted her speech on a fool. Indeed, it wasn't the sort of speech von Klonk would appreciate seeing quoted in the article. Although the Indian curse angle was tempting, if just to torment him a bit.

Miss Worple seemed to be gathering thoughts for another foray into education of the houseguest. What next? Hippies and communists, probably. In such situations I've found it best to dodge, try for a diversion. I said I'd noticed a lot of flashlights, seemed there was at least in every room.

"We often lose power in a storm."

"You get a lot of storms."

"I told you, Civil Defense is about hurricanes and such, we get vicious nor'easters as well. For that matter, your common every day storm around here can wreak havoc."

"Every day, you say? They happen often?"

"They come up without the least warning, though the watermen say they can smell them coming, monstrous storms, blinding lightning, deafening thunder, wind that can turn a sturdy boat into matchsticks."

I could be mistaken but doesn't that sound like good reasons for sensible people to stay the hell away? "And I'm to write an article enticing tourist visits? Might be of some appeal to those who would get a kick out of visiting, say, Transylvania."

Her fists dug into her hips. "Transylvania? You just let that sort show their faces around here. We know how to deal with that sort."

"I just thought the Dracula thing fit with ghosts, storms, all that." I hoped my best impression of an honest, open look conveyed – true or not – I didn't really mean any harm by the comment.

"I see what you're up to. Next thing, you'll have poor Sammy a victim of vampires."

"I'm not up to anything, Miss Worple, other than writing the story assigned to me."

"I hope that's the case. We have enough trouble around here without you strangers coming in, stirring things up. If you'll excuse me, I want to try again to ring up Serena."

Chapter Five

It was all too quiet on the screened porch; the stillness seemed a sound in its own right, imposing a meditational blank-screen of the mind.

Looking back, I recall how disconcerting it was at first to one used to city sounds. Noise is a constant at the big city's core, an audio soup of mechanical, electronic and human goings on. In the country, particularly at night, noise comes out of the stillness as individual sounds, a pinecone rattling down the branches to hit the ground with a distinct pat, the wind, sometimes building to a traffic sound, or – what was that? – now and then an unidentifiable outburst from the woods, a scream or a snarl, probably familiar to a local but disturbing and mysterious to the newcomer.

In the metropolis there is a war on against night, conducted by bright lights. There are lights in the country at night, as well, but they are called moon and stars. After so long in the city where the heavens are washed out by brightness, a cloudless star-filled sky can be overwhelming. Shapes and patterns appear, constellations that I either hadn't seen in years or knew only from pictures in books, if at all. And there, dominating the night sky, the moon, a huge orange lantern or perhaps a glowing portal.

Thoughts crossed my mind that never would have penetrated the filters of fast-paced city life. There on the dark porch in the eerie quiet of night I could accept that certain places might have their resident spirits. It seemed fairly plausible that not all ghost stories are the fabrications of nightmarish imagination. Possibly country people who claimed communication with phantoms and wraiths were telling a truth that the dizzy blur of city life blots out.

My brooding was interrupted by the sound of footsteps.

"I'm off to bed. Is there anything you need?"

"No luck reaching your helper?"

"She doesn't answer. Something must be wrong. I'm sure of that. But secrets aren't kept for long around here; I'll find out what's going on. You'll lock up when you come in?"

"Sure. First, I think I'll take a walk."

"Oh, that isn't done. You may have noticed, we're on a dark, dead-end country road."

Miss Worple was standing behind me. I was talking to her over my shoulder. "I'm on assignment. I've got to have a look at this place from various angles. I'll take a walk. Do I have to worry about bugs?"

She said the bugs probably wouldn't carry me off. This early in the season, they hadn't come out in force. "They joke about mosquitoes as big as turkeys. They're not that big. Greenheads, that's another matter."

"Oh, really? What's a greenhead?"

"A type of horsefly. They're quite large, and the female will get after anything with warm blood. That means you."

"Females. Of course it would be females."

"Just stating facts, Mr. Holliday."

"Well, I'll turn back if they're bad."

She came around to face me, making a bulldog face. "Really, you shouldn't be wandering around out there at this hour. It can be dangerous."

"Doesn't seem to be any traffic."

"Do you carry a gun?"

"Can't say as I do."

"Just about everyone around here carries a gun."

"You think there are problems out there that can only be solved with a gun?"

"Most likely. You never know what to expect of drunks and druggies, and what business do they have down this way in the middle of the night? All they'll find is a blockade at Parkers Point, and possibly Scrap Blevins and his shotgun."

I wanted to get on with my walk but now she'd got my attention. "Scrap?"

"That's what they call him. The property is his after you cross the rickety little bridge there at the gut. He rides around in an ATV collecting junk. Some he sells down at the scrapyard, some he makes into what he calls sculptures. It was Scrap who hauled the refrigerator where they found Sammy. He owns the Point and, as is his right, has it barricaded."

"Doesn't sound the most sociable person."

"They say he never really got back from Vietnam. Works on those ridiculous sculptures and they just sit there. I don't think he's shot anyone yet, just scares them off."

"It's lit up out there like day with that moon. Looks pretty safe to me, and if I see anyone waving a shotgun I'll turn tail on the double."

She studied the scene beyond the porch, lit by a yellowish lunar light. "It was a night like this Sammy disappeared, a bright moonlight night like this. Rode off and that was the last seen of him until they found him dead. You be careful."

"Why was he here?"

"Dropping off that awful artifact because he thought Judge Wetherby could make some sense of it. I wish the Judge would take it. Maybe I'll just toss it in the Bay."

"You were home that night when Sammy came by?"

"Of course I was home. I'm always home after dark unless there's a Civil Defense event."

I stood up, moving toward the screen door. Still, I kept the conversation going. "He would have gone back through the village?"

"Don't ask me which way he went. I don't spend my time peering out windows like some around here. He could have gone down to the Point. He was fascinated with the Point. You'd ask why, he'd just say he was 'checking it out.' He was often on mysterious missions of his own concoction, Mr Holliday. I wouldn't guess which way he went or why."

"And there was nothing unusual about that night, no traffic, no strange sounds?"

"Around here? If I took note of every strange sound ... Possibly a truck, not long after he left, but it could have been anything, distant thunder or a gunshot or Navy jets overhead; they're over the Bay all the time. What difference does it make, anyway?"

I couldn't say. I let myself out into the night.

By moonlight the road was easy to follow, but I made my way with some hesitation. After all, a country road at night is very different from a city street.

There was an odor I took to be that of the Bay and wetlands, a combination of the scents of brine, mud and decay.

I had a sense of being seen by many things I wasn't seeing.

Little unidentified flying objects whirred or buzzed as they passed near my head or collided with it. Bugs. Further overhead, darting shadows dove and swooped. I had to think for a moment before recognizing them. Bats.

I met no highwayman, riding, riding, but the sand road was indeed a ribbon of moonlight. I could translate shapes and shadows into branches and bushes, and I told myself they weren't spindly arms and fingers reaching out to touch or grab me, just the natural flora of forested marshland.

From what I'd seen of the countryside thus far, I knew that in broad daylight there would be nothing more eerie than a mad tangle of spindly trees, thick grasses, undisciplined shrubs, bougainvillea and other vines that could at times be lovely, but all the while they were strangling the life out of their hosts.

I should have brought a flashlight. Isn't it typical to think of things like that when well on your way?

Well, there was the moon. And there was nothing unnerving about the moon, was there? Beneficial. I thought of all that was good and wonderful about it. A full moon would be a boon at harvest time, and then there was the romantic side of it, a thing of great beauty, the lovers' moon. But that was for those who had romantic company on a night like this, not for the stranger in, yes, in a strange land.

My head was being sensible, telling me this wasn't really such a bright idea at all, but my feet kept moving forward, silently, along the sandy road. The rest of me reluctantly kept pace, like a child who has doubts about where the older brother is leading,

This older brother was leading me into aspects of the region rarely experienced by those in the outside world. The outsider wouldn't be likely to wander off down an unknown provincial lane in the dead of night. It was, though, the job of a reporter to be a scout, to report back to the home folks what lay beyond the edges of their known world. Wasn't it?

Not really, not in this day and age when reporters, hardly distinguishable from the celebrity crowd they reported on, clustered as a herd at the next press conference to ask facile questions of notorious liars. But I'd always imagined the reporter role to be that of explorer, at least in part. Explorer, detective, credentialed chameleon, empowered to poke into goings-on from the heights to the depths of the world around him. Or around her, of course, though when I joined up it was mostly a fraternity.

Why did I join? Well, there's curiosity. I can't understand people who have no curiosity. Surely it's a driving force of evolution. And then the hunt – despite the niceties of modern life, I do believe we're genetically engineered to kill something big. Which in my field translates to the scoop. Kill something big and reap the rewards, you can lie back for a while, feast, party, sleep through the alarm, bask in adulation. Hail, the Mighty Hunter.

Not so mighty anymore, not me. No sense kidding myself. I was not a writer for National Geographic or Conde Nast Traveler, searching out curiosities in exotic locales. I was writing for Here & There, which, so far as I could discern, was primarily devoted to showcasing the familiar in the faraway, the mall with slightly different shops, the fast food factory with a menu that wouldn't reduce little junior to homesick tears for his burger and fries, or the amusement park having a few rides different from the next one up the road.

As I walked, I mulled over the conversation with Barney Cole, earlier that afternoon.

"Tell me more about this place where I'll be staying, Bay Breezes."

His answer was to assume facial resemblance to a large fish. If you've ever tried to say anything with your lips pursed, you'll know right off that Cole didn't want to answer. I prepared to hear some fabricated public relations pap, valuable only because it might, between the lines, provide a genuine clue or two regarding my destination.

Cole shifted in his seat as though sitting on pebbles. "Well, you know, the truth is, I've been so busy with other projects that I haven't actually gotten out there to see Bay Breezes. What I know of it comes from phone conversations and local chatter. It's a work in progress, that's what it is. Miss Worple hasn't really advertised for guests just yet. Not quite at that stage. She's taken in a few visitors, trial run sort of thing. Just the spot for you, though, reflective of local character, and you wouldn't get that in a chain motel out here on the highway."

"Bay Breezes reflects local character?"

"You bet. From what I've heard, it's a charming old colonial home, or it will be soon, when the restoration's complete. Miss Worple is slowly bringing it back to its former glory."

"She's from around here?"

"She's local, recently retired. Actually, her family owned that place for what, centuries, I suppose. Then it had a few other owners, went downhill, until it came up at a tax sale. Miss Worple had a friend who swung the bidding her way, she got a good deal on it. Anyway, you probably won't see much of her. She's active in the community and leaves the place in the hands of her help, that being Serena."

"And the help has gone AWOL."

"We don't know, do we? Maybe she just had car trouble, like me. Serena lives out that way. She could probably walk the few miles to Bay Breezes but she'd need her car to get to work here at the restaurant."

After stiffing me for the bill, Cole walked me to the parking lot. "We'll meet again once you've settled in. I'll set up a few events and road trips. Weather permitting."

"You're expecting bad weather?"

He looked toward the sky. "There are beautiful days around here, Holliday, gorgeous days. But they come at a price. The price is, some days nature just goes nuts, cooks up storms you can't believe until you're caught in them."

"I wonder if I could get my assignment switched to someplace a little more my style, Cancun or Mazatlan, maybe?"

"Oh, you'll love it here – don't forget, Holliday, the nostalgia factor; lots of charm in these rustic old mansions. Why, I'm sure Bay Breezes would be a focal point of a house and garden tour, if we had one."

"You're the tourist guy. You could start one."

"There used to be a tour, very popular, but it's been called off since the last hurricane tore up the landscape. That might be a good angle for you, Holliday … a bed and breakfast with grounds just as God intended them to be, something like that. Play up the nature bit."

Nature bit. That should have set alarm bells ringing.

Chapter Six

And now here I was, miles from nowhere, plodding along a desolate dead-end road by the uncaring light of an indifferent moon. Or had the moon spotted me; was it cooking up some lunar surprise to highlight my welcome to this peculiar place?

I began thinking about how I could just disappear into the marsh that lurked back there through the thickets and brambles, I could wander until I stumbled into a bog or slough, become mummified for an archaeologist to unearth in a few hundred years: The Mystery of the East Westerly Bog Man. It could put me back on the front page of the newspaper, if such things were still around by then.

And who would be the wiser if I did disappear? My gnome-esis, the editor, probably wouldn't blink an eye, just hire the next fool to cross his threshold. Miss Worple could get some joy out of spreading the word: "I told him so."

Cole? He'd probably assume I'd been abducted by a band of vengeful deer. "Andy Holliday, you say? Oh, claimed to be a travel-writer, wandered off down there in the godforsaken swamps. There seems no next of kin to notify, can't find anything biographical about him, he's just Andy Who, missing and presumed forever lost. Maybe they'll find him tucked in an old refrigerator somewhere."

A chilling thought. There were other weird thoughts, brought on by being completely alone in an isolated backwater in the thick of night. If I intended to keep going I needed a boost in boldness. Whistle a brave tune? For my own benefit, not because there might be anyone around to convince of my bravado.

I've usually got some tune or other in my head, maybe just a melody, often snatches of lyric that replay until another comes along to replace it. There must be a thousand or more, lurking in the unconscious depths. I fished one out and began whistling, a bracing, marching, simple sort of tune, Yellow Submarine.

Well, of course, it was written for someone with the vocal range of a dog whistle, not much to it.

"Sheee-it. You scared him off."

I don't know if I actually jumped, but parts of me did.

The speaker was off just a little to my right at the edge of the woods, tall and cloaked in a trench coat, in one hand a device that might have been a cattle prod, held like a baton or wand, and some sort of briefcase hanging at his side. That's how it looked at first. "Damn it, you scared him off."

"Him? Who?"

"Screech owl, gone now. Way off there. Shut up and listen."

In moments came a maniacal whinny. It wasn't a screech, more like a panicky horse on mind-altering drugs. The call was repeated three times and then all was quiet again.

It wasn't as though the odd apparition I'd encountered was talking to me, he just said: "Death-bird."

Not the sort of remark I cared to respond to, so I stood as though listening for more sounds. The fellow kept glancing around, down the road or back over his shoulder, at the treetops and then the bushes.

At least he hadn't shot me or zapped me with a ray gun. I walked a few steps closer. "What sort of gadget is that?"

He came uncomfortably close and spoke as though sharing a confidence. "It's a shotgun mic, directional, feeds into this reel-to-reel recorder." He held up a rectangular box with two big tape reels on the side. "Who are you? What are you doing out here?"

"I'm visiting." I stepped back for breathing room. "And I guess you're right, I really should be on my way."

"You're up at the Worple place. Know much about her?"

"We just met."

"Woo-Woo Worple. That's what they call her. Always talking about ghosts. Used to be a prison guard. Did you know that?"

My head spun for a moment. "A prison guard? No joke?"

"At the prison for women in Jessup, that's a fact."

"I had no idea."

He was still too much in my space, leaning in as though passing along a sure-thing tip on a horse race. "Just letting you know. She's not exactly Miss Hospitality."

"I got that. I felt about as welcome as a Roman legionnaire in Pictland."

He stared at me for a long moment, and I can't say as I blamed him. "Yes, very good."

"Are you Scrap Blevins?"

"No."

And he was gone.

Blevins or not, he knew how to come and go in the woods at night.

I walked on as far as the rickety little bridge Miss Worple had mentioned. The breeze cranked up, not too strong but steady, in my face, urging me back the way I'd come. It wasn't a cold night but I was beginning to feel a chill, probably from being closer to the water – coupled with the aftershock of meeting the screech owl man.

There were no side rails to the little bridge. I decided to save a closer look for another time, in daylight.

Half asleep, I was in and out of a bizarre dream of a youngster trapped in a refrigerator. I could hear him struggling. But it wasn't all a dream, I could actually hear the sound of struggle. Past midnight I'd heard enough went to the window for a look. The sound was the spindly branch of a gnarled old tree, slapping at the glass. Well, I wasn't about to climb out and do battle with the offending limb.

It was a long, weird night in a strange place, quite the contrary to my idea of the easy-going, pampered life of a resort-hopping travel-writer.

But, in the relative safety of early morning light, the tapping of the tree limb was just one more thing to mention to Miss Worple, another chore to add to her lengthy list of needed fixes.

Then I thought of another. As I came more to my wakeful senses I remembered the lizards, or at least I thought it was lizards. Some scurrying creatures. I hadn't turned on the light to check, I just lay there at 3:00 am, listening to the pitterpat, pitterpat, imagining it was lizards.

I did welcome the light of morning. But hope of breakfast aromas was wishful thinking. There was only the sweat-sock smell of the old house, the odor of mold and mustiness.

I went to the kitchen in search of the makings of a cup of coffee. It wasn't a modern kitchen, though certainly a lot newer than the old colonial fire-pit in the wing. How much newer? I'd guess my grandmother would have felt right at home with the enamel-coated gas range, half-sized refrigerator and deep, boxy sink. What, circa 1930s or so?

There wasn't a hint of food or drink in evidence. If any existed it was tucked away in the stern off-white cabinets or cupboards, probably to keep things safe from ants, mice and other freeloaders. A big old silver-colored coffee percolator sat on the counter but there was no sign of beans or the ground stuff. Miss Worple must have heard me opening cupboards.

"How was your walk?"

"All right, I suppose. I met a fairly strange character down the road a ways."

"You must have dreamed it. There's no one out there at night but poachers – and if you'd run into them, I doubt we would be having this conversation."

"It was a fellow with a microphone and tape recorder."

"Oh, all right, you ran into McCobb. That explains it."

I thought she might, in turn, explain it to me, but she didn't. "Did you sleep well?"

I told her about the tapping branch. She said there would be a crew coming in to trim shrubs and trees. And I told her there had also been things, I don't know what kind of things, maybe lizards, scurrying around.

"Mice probably. Or, yes, possibly lizards. There are spiders as well, some big enough to shoot, but I haven't known them to make noise."

"And you're not afraid, living in house infested with pests?"

It was a you-can't-be-serious look; that of the karate master challenged by the street punk. "I'm certain it's the other way around."

"The bugs and the rest of the menagerie, they fear you?"

"Oh, I'm sure. They had made themselves quite at home while

the place was vacant, but I've let them know those days are over. They're trespassers now, and will be treated as such."

An image came to me of Miss Worple at 3:00 am, huge handgun at the ready, blasting away at lizards and whatever other creatures dared show themselves.

Through the back window I could see a congregation of birds visiting two empty hanging feeders. It was like a carnival, blue and red and yellow birds. Fascinating when you're used to city birds, brown sparrows and blue-gray pigeons. What had we here? Cardinals, bluebirds, canaries. But the country did have its version of pigeons; doves pecked almost robotically at whatever they found on the ground. And, perched on the outer reaches of a limb of a naked old tree – I guessed an apple tree, no longer fruitful – a squirrel staring in at me with the eyes of an accuser.

Miss Worple saw what I was looking at and shook her head. "Those wretched creatures."

"The wildlife?"

"Birds. God knows what diseases they spread. But Serena feeds them, so of course they're hanging around, pecking away at nothing, polluting with their droppings. And that ratty little squirrel, begging for a handout. Just look at him, trying to make me feel guilty."

And you should feel guilty, I thought to myself. And not just for neglecting the wildlife. What about me, your guest? How about cereal with fresh blueberries and maybe a couple of homemade scones, not those biscuity things from the supermarket but real scones, and, as long as I'm off in fantasy, could you provide a lemon curd spread? I mean, I know how a bed and breakfast should function.

"I'd get a cat but around here one cat somehow becomes a plague of cats. And Serena wouldn't have it, no cats. Well, it's not her place to tell me, is it? But I let her have her way, she was so adamant, no cats killing her little birdies."

"I suppose there are other ways to scare them off if that's what you want to do."

"Yes. I thought about hiring a gardener, some foreigner from a place where they eat that sort of thing. He could make a stew."

"A clever solution."

She fixed me with a stare perhaps intended to be hypnotic. "Go feed them, will you? They'll be nothing but a nuisance otherwise."

Right. I don't get fed, but I'm assigned to feed the birds and squirrels? I'm a guest, you could say a very special guest. You know, given the valuable publicity an article could generate, this isn't right. Yes, I was mounting my high horse again. "I guess it's an honor to be confused with St. Francis but, sorry, I'm here to write, not to cater to the appetites of local wildlife."

She cocked her head up like a robin eyeing a worm. "Oh, you're a far cry from any sort of saint, no doubt about that. But I mistook you for a gentleman, willing to lend a hand in a time of crisis. As it happens, I am allergic to birds."

"I don't believe it. I think you're allergic to doing what you can coerce someone else into doing for you." I slapped the countertop, emphasizing my fed-uppedness. But the damned squirrel was now sitting there, paws clasped in prayer. Little beggar. "I'll do it if you'll find some coffee for me. You said you might have a jar of instant for when the Judge came around."

"It's here somewhere. I'll see what I can find."

Of course, I had no idea what to feed the creatures or where to find it. "What kind of feed does Serena put out?"

"I think seeds and peanut butter – I don't know what all she keeps in the shed."

I found the supplies and got into the spirit of it, filling the feeders and dabbing peanut butter on a post that seemed designed for that purpose. If I didn't perform the chores as well as the absent Serena might have, at least I got the menagerie fed.

It wasn't any business of mine but it struck me that Miss Worple could profit by attracting wildlife to her window. Lord knows, she needed some positive points if she hoped to draw tourists.

I headed back to the kitchen in hopes of coffee.

Miss Worple stood at the range watching a kettle. On the kitchen table were a cup, spoon and a jar of instant. The contents of the jar had hardened into cement but I scraped loose a spoonful. "Do you have any pepper sauce?"

"I really don't think so. It's not part of a proper diet, you know."

"Si, senora, you don't like that we make it from the blood of the stupid gringos?"

"I hope your writing isn't as warped as your thinking, Mr Holliday."

The kettle whistled and she filled my cup. Meanwhile I'd spotted the cabinet holding condiments, and there was indeed a bottle of Tabasco. I was growing fond of the absent Serena Sanchez, assuming this was her secret stash.

I added a peppery splash to my coffee. Miss Worple watched, slowly shaking her head. That was the extent of her comment on the replacement I'd found for a morning shot of brandy in my coffee.

She went on: "Anyway, I'm seriously concerned about Serena. I would go and check on her but there's a man coming to see about the leaks. Some of the leaks, anyway."

I asked if Serena lived nearby.

"Off the main road, out toward the Bay, just a couple of miles. It's a sort of tumbledown trailer, housing for migrants, usually. There will be fog this early. You pass the old store where Sammy was found, then turn right at a little church on your left."

"Any chance of getting breakfast at the store?"

"It's abandoned, went out of business, the owners just walked away from it. They couldn't compete with Wal-Mart."

I should have had better sense but I was curious. "Well, I'm writing a travel article, I might as well have a look at the fog."

A finger went to her lips. "There's no need to mention the fog. You'll frighten off the tourists."

"I'd say the fog plays a fairly minor role in that regard."

Miss Worple's posture stiffened. "You should report that we are bathed in the beauteous glow of ever-present sunshine, dawn to dusk. I'm sure that's how it is done in travel magazines."

Come to think of it, based on a survey while awaiting a dentist or doctor appointment, she was fairly much on target. I couldn't recall travel features focusing on rotten or even challenging weather. A story like that might turn up in the alternative press but the mainstream did tend to accent the attractive.

And, hadn't I been told to skip any grim details, avoid controversy, paint a pretty picture? It wasn't my style, but what was I to do? I could just see von Klonk working over my manuscript, slashing out fog, rain, even clouds…

I had second thoughts about the proposed expedition. "Serena may not be in a mood to talk to a stranger. Shouldn't someone who knows her go out and check? She's probably depressed over loss of her son, she needs a familiar face to comfort her."

"I don't think Serena is depressed. She's angry, as if that does any good. There's nothing she can do about what happened."

The lady had a right to be angry, didn't she? She'd lost her son under grim circumstances. Miss Worple didn't seem very sympathetic toward her loss. I said so.

"Life can be unkind, Mr. Holliday. But that young man was almost destined to meet a bad end. You know how young people are, they go through strange phases, and Sammy was stranger than most, I'd say. He had an irritating way about him. He'd look at you suspiciously for saying 'good morning.' Do you know, he had the audacity to tell me I was descended from smugglers and pirates. The Worples! I could have wrung his neck."

"There wasn't any Swarthy Jack Worple, Scourge of the Chesapeake, I take it?"

"Certainly not. My ancestors were pillars of the church and community."

I thought but didn't say that there was often mischief behind the pillars. Meanwhile, I was getting more than a bit hungry. "Could I fix myself something? Eggs and toast, perhaps?"

"I did notice crackers in the cupboard and I believe there is cheese in the fridge. I had to throw some things out, they were getting that greenish tint to them. I'll have to go shopping."

"Well, if it's not too much trouble ..."

"After the plumber. The fog will have lifted by then. What shall I get? Serena always does the shopping."

"You know, I'd bet that a lot of people who take up the bed

and breakfast business make it a point to visit around first, see how the others do it. I mean, just to get an idea of what's involved. The breakfast part, for example. How complicated is it? Cereals, eggs, sausages, biscuits … breakfast food."

"I'm not a cook. I go to town for meals if Serena isn't cooking."

"So, in her absence I guess you should just shorten the name of the place, call it Bay Breezes Bed?"

She ignored my clever suggestion. "Don't just sit around like a mugwump, Mr Holliday."

"Did you say 'mugwump'?"

"I most certainly did."

Chapter Seven

Why was I on this treacherous road, blundering through the murky mist in unfamiliar country? It was hardly my role as a guest to go hunting down the hired help. So what was my game? Call it the curse of a curious nature; I wanted to know what had become of Serena Sanchez.

Or in keeping with von Klonk's rude but probably accurate suggestion that I was a modern don Quixote, maybe I'd read too many tales of knighthood and chivalry as a youngster, maybe they got under my skin and stuck there like one of those diseases that you can never quite shake. The rescue impulse, a sort of malaria of the psyche.

True enough, in my former incarnation I would not have spent much time on a hunt for an AWOL waitress, unless of course she had also been the missing mistress of a prominent politician. But back then it was a different story, wasn't it? I had been a prince of the city, a force to reckon with, a power player on one of the world's most important fields, Washington DC. Politicians and bureaucrats cursed or shuddered at mention of my name, my phone calls prompted spilled coffee at the least and head-for-the-hills panic as often as not.

It may sound grandiose but it was simple truth. More than a few among the herd of Washington journalists fed off my reports, big names in the investigative reporting and insider gossip trades offered partnerships. There were days when I set the agenda in Washington with just a few explosive paragraphs.

Then, wham, in what seemed the blink of an eye, it was all over. Well, not exactly all over. Surveying the bombed-out aftermath I found I still had bills, and basic needs – food, shelter, transportation.

And didn't this new life, if you could call it a life, take some getting used to? What had only yesterday been a tip left after a steakhouse dinner was today's lunch money. Thanks to a very clever job of bushwhacking by enemies unknown, I now had to adjust to an abrupt and depressing lifestyle change, make the best of adversity … in short, survive.

So, here I was trying to find my way along a narrow country road, fogbound, trying to solve the mystery of where to make my turn.

Pulling over to wait for a clearer view might mean an encounter with one of the drainage ditches that frame the back roads in the tidewater lowlands. You don't always see the deep trenches for the reeds and scrub, but steer too far to one side of the road and you'll find one, and likely you'll be a long way from help.

Speaking of help, what looked like someone struggling to get out of the roadside ditch caught my eye, a weak wave of an arm. I was going slowly but I slowed further. Up closer the thing turned into a large black plastic trash bag, flapping in the breeze. That it appeared to be a live, crawling, clawing creature was just an ominous misperception.

Seeing things in the fog that aren't there is one thing. The trick, of course, is to see the things that are there. I passed the abandoned store. You could tell it had been a store by the advertising signs, blurred in the fog. And then came a church, a landmark Miss Worple had mentioned, a long white ranch-style box with no steeple or fancy windows. No telling what the sign out front said, not in this mess. Something about sin, something about salvation.

So, make a right at the church onto a dead end road. I'd know it was the correct turn if I passed a run-down old house, barn and sheds on the left, probably with a small refrigerated box truck parked in front, Miss Worple had said. The emblem on the truck would be *Better Days Seafood Company*, though the markings probably wouldn't be visible given the weather.

There it was. I could barely make out a man standing at the far end of the drive near the barn and sheds. Off to one side of the drive loomed the great ghost of a house, from what I could see, weathered to gray-brown wood. An artist with a camera might have felt compelled to stop and capture the eerie scene. I felt compelled to stop and ask directions.

I backed up and pulled in. The resident made no welcoming move, just continued wiping moisture off the windows of the cab of the old gray box truck. The task was a stretch for him. He was small and round, his bib overalls filled like a denim balloon and a black captain's hat topping a moon-like mug.

I got out and walked back to where he stood, watching my approach like a guard at a top-secret installation.

"I don't have any crabs for sale." He looked at me like a hunter deciding if I was worth the shot.

"I wasn't asking about crabs. I wondered if you could tell me if I'm on the right road to Serena Sanchez's place?"

"Don't go out much anyhow, anyhow, I don't. Getting into the charter business, had enough commercial fishing. What is it you're looking for?"

"I'm looking for Serena Sanchez. I was told she lives in a trailer out this way."

"Sanchez? Might be. Is she in some kind of trouble? I've heard about that; trouble, the immigration people …"

I waved the trouble aside. "No trouble that I know. I just came to check up. I'm staying at Bay Breezes and she hasn't shown up for work."

He spit off to one side, almost as though spitting was part of his next sentence. "There's people don't show up for work all the time. It's no crime. Might be drunk, or dead."

"You think that's likely?"

"I worked hard all my life, I did. Never missed a day. Not many, anyway."

"So you're not drunk or dead."

He did a good imitation of suffering a toothache. "Another joker. Ever-body's a joker these days, some kind of disease going around." He stamped a foot, killing the virus. "Fell on hard times, that's all."

"Sorry to hear that. Well, do you know if Ms Sanchez lives down this way?"

"I reckon. Usually see her going in and out. Not these last couple days, though. Lives in a trailer, like you said. That trailer past where old Smoot has a wishing well in the front yard. Good luck to him, living on wishes."

At least I was on the right road. "I'll find it. Thanks."

"I'm Lucky Brevard. Hate that, being called Lucky; they're making fun of me, calling me that. But they do." He shook his head, bewildered by jokers.

"I'll call you by your right name. What is it?"

"Doesn't matter. Lucky it is, their idea of a joke, something you might call a one-eyed, three-legged dog."

I sensed that was a stock introductory line with him, pity-bait. I didn't bite. "Okay, then it's Mr Brevard. I'm Andy Holliday, here to write an article promoting tourism." We shook hands. My hands have had the luxury of no work harder than banging on a typewriter. His hand felt like tree bark.

At close quarters I got a good whiff of yesterday's seafood catch.

"It'd be Captain Brevard. I do have a boat, not the one I want though. You're a tourist? Well, not much to see, particularly with this fog, but not much anyways. You wouldn't be a treasure hunter by any chance?"

"Not my line. And I'm not exactly a tourist, either. I'm a travel-writer."

"Treasure. I'm making it my line. Used to be pirates around here. Where there's pirates, there's treasure. It's how I'm going to finance a brand new charter boat. Bank just laughs in my face."

"I don't think I ever met a laughing banker."

He clenched a fist. "Ain't that the truth? They get all righteous and sull up. I'll be the one laughing, I get my boat."

"Good luck to you, Capt Brevard."

"Lucky. Call me Capt Lucky, everybody else does. Like it's some big joke. Fact is, all I want to do is make Ingrid proud of me."

"Ingrid?"

"Yep. Love of my life. She's a movie star."

"As in Bergman?"

A big smile creased the moon face. "That's her all right."

"You were close? You and Ingrid Bergman?"

"Seen all her pictures. Some a bunch of times. Love of my life, that's her."

The words "I really should be going" were careening around in my head, but for some reason I stood courteously still. "Anywhere hereabouts I can get a good cup of coffee?"

"Used to be, over there at the store. Been shut for some time. Couldn't compete with the Wal-Mart. Folks go to town. These days, you've got to go into town for whatever, even a cup of coffee."

The mist was clearing. In the yard behind him I could make out a stack of large cages. They looked to be about four feet by four feet, made of heavy mesh. I had to ask. "What do you use those for?"

"I don't use them for anything anymore. Damn regulations make an outlaw of a man trying to earn a living. They're called bank traps. Best way to catch peelers, soft-shells, set 'em close to shore. Now, you're looking at me like I'm speaking in tongues. Surely you know soft-shell crabs." It was a statement, not a question.

"It's just, I thought crab pots were smaller. Those look big enough to catch a shark, or maybe a man."

"Crab pots *are* smaller, those are bank traps, like I said. What few regular pots I've got are set out. Not catching much right now though."

"So bank traps are illegal?"

"Sure are. Damn game warden, Biggers, came in here and grabbed a couple, said they're evidence. Plundered around through everything, he did, even searched my truck. What can you do?"

"If they were just sitting around, harmless, I'd guess you could complain."

He pushed the idea aside with a flick of his hand. "Sure you could. And have Biggers seize everything you got. Boat, truck, traps and all. They got the power, those guys in the uniforms, not us working people."

It sounded like something to dig into further, if I was a local reporter. I wasn't. "Well, thanks for your help. I better get on down the road."

I had a feeling that if I didn't get moving I'd soon be hearing his life story. I nodded and walked back toward my car.

Lucky let me get halfway and then shouted. "Turn around if you hit sand. And mind the ditches if you turn around." He seemed in his element talking loud across a distance, which made sense for a waterman used to hollering from one boat to the next.

"I'm warned. Thanks." I waved, unsure if he'd heard me. I was attuned to talking across a desk, not yelling from one boat to another.

It was a fair warning, to turn around if you hit sand. With the Atlantic on the east side and the Chesapeake Bay on the west, there's hardly a side road on the Eastern Shore where you won't come to water and have to turn around. That or sprout wings, or get drowned.

Or get drowned and then sprout wings, if you were worthy of salvation. I figured it was in my best interests to turn around if I hit sand.

Chapter Eight

The morning sun began to find its way through the fog, turning the day a muted shade of orange. Images became solid, shapes more distinct. A gray heron rose up like a ghost from the roadside ditch and escorted me for a few hundred yards before turning off over the tall marsh grasses.

Following directions, I came to a mobile home, so-called, though the only mobility in this one's future would be a trip to the scrap yard. Strips of the siding buckled out from the frame and a blue tarp covered a section of roof. The lot appeared well kept, spring flowers – I only knew tulip but there were many – bloomed in well-tended beds.

I pulled in and parked next to a small hatchback that had served, I would say, above and beyond the expectations of the maker. From the front seat a large dog – or was it a domesticated wolf? – studied me without comment and then turned his attention back to the front door. The big fellow's worried look struck a sympathetic chord. Like children, dogs are dependent for care and kindness, and it's not always there. Not by a long shot.

A woman dressed in jeans and denim shirt came out of the trailer and stood on the porch. That had to be the elusive Serena Sanchez. She wasn't at all what I'd expected. She was tall, as slender as a serious runner, with dark hair and darker eyes. She had nothing to say as I walked toward her. By the set of her jaw and taut creases to the sides of thin lips, she viewed my approach as a sign of trouble.

"I'm staying at Miss Worple's. She asked me to come and check on you. She's worried because you're not answering the phone."

She looked to the sky. "I'm not answering anything, I'm clearing out, that's all. Florida, I am going to Florida, the devil take the Eastern Shore."

I wanted to keep the talk small while I gathered a sense of what was going on. "Your dog doesn't look too happy."

Quick shrug. "It's like he's waiting for Sammy to come back. I wish he'd run off, find himself a good home." Her voice was soft, and not just from the exhaustion and pain that showed in her eyes, the softness was her style.

"A stray doesn't have much chance of finding a home."

"He was Sammy's dog. Can you take him?"

"I'm traveling, sorry."

"He wanted to be in the car."

"Dogs are like that. He knows something's going on. Afraid of being left behind."

"I don't know what to do with him."

She didn't exactly invite me in but she was holding the door open and I walked past her. She watched me with indifference, not even questioning.

There was some order to the disarray. Clothing, bedding, towels and curtains made up one pile. Across the room was a small collection of pots, pans, storage jars and other containers, silverware and cutlery, the items that make up a kitchen. Another corner held a cluster of lamps, knickknacks, tabletop stuff.

Prominent on a counter was a framed portrait of a square-jawed, handsome young Latino, his smile one of confidence rather than humor or warmth. He appeared to be in his mid-teens.

"Whoever broke in, I wish they'd taken more."

"You had a break-in ... with that big dog?"

"I went to the park beside the river, had to get out of here for a while. I took Baron along, that's when they broke in. It was mostly Sammy's room they went through, not much there. Mad, whoever it was." She led the way to one of the bedrooms, which I took to be Sammy's.

Someone had scribbled on the wall with a black marker: *Death to Spanish!*

"Whoever broke in did that?"

"Yes. I don't get my kicks writing crazy stuff on the walls."

"They're either dumb or playing dumb. You called the police?"

It was a look you might get if you stopped at a gas station to ask directions to the nearest gas station. "It would just be more trouble. I'm leaving. What do I care? Let the mad people have this place."

We walked back to the front room.

"I can't take much with me." She wandered among what auctioneers or the courts might call her estate, picking up the odd thing and then putting it back down. "Help yourself to anything you want. All this stuff, I'm leaving here."

"Like I said, I'm traveling, I don't need anything. But thanks, anyway. How come you're leaving?"

"Zinker says immigration is coming for me. He got a tip. Besides, someone killed my son and no one gives a damn. Just another dead Mexican kid. Who cares? I can't stand it around here anymore."

Zinker. "Who is Zinker?"

"The local cop. But he isn't a cop, just someone hired by the rich people. He's creepy, doesn't have any business bothering me, but he comes by."

"Well, I don't know that much about immigration law but it sounds a little fishy unless you're in trouble. I take it you're not here legally?"

"And why else would they be after me? But it's been many years, this country is my home."

The same was true of millions of others. "You said someone killed Sammy. I thought it was an accident."

"My son wasn't stupid. And he hated being closed in. He wouldn't have gotten in that damn thing by himself. He was killed."

How far could I probe without hitting a wall? "Were there any indications, wounds or injuries?"

"The coroner said he got banged up when they moved the fridge. It was heaved on a truck with other junk, crashed around some on the truck. Then it was pulled off the truck at the salvage yard, that's when they opened it."

I could picture the way scrap dealers handled junk. They handled it like what it was, junk. I voiced my thought: "It went through some rough treatment."

"He might have been bruised by that but not banged up like he was. But they settled for what they wanted to see, called it an accident."

"As next of kin, couldn't you request a more thorough autopsy?"

"I'm here without any papers, don't you see? I couldn't stir things up without attracting attention to my status."

The thought that struck me was that someone was responsible for the death trap. "Who owns the place where he was found, the abandoned store?"

"I have no idea. They're long gone, whoever it was."

My mental searchlight went on. Questions were coming to mind. "Was Sammy working anywhere? Is there someone who might know more about what he was doing that night?"

Her shrug was disturbing.

"You're asking questions, I don't have answers. I only have more questions. Like, where is his bicycle? They shrug it off. Somebody saw it lying there, took it for abandoned. Is that an investigation?"

In the good old days of journalism, if you had a question, you worked the phones or went physically into the environment where the answer might be found, you went after a story like a cop going after a case. They called it *legwork*. There were hang-ups, dodges, doors slammed, but every now and then someone would be intrigued with the idea of talking to a reporter, and you could – possibly – get somewhere. At least you might get a lead, even if just the name of the next person to ask.

These days, it seemed, reporters would make a perfunctory phone call, enough to satisfy an editor that they had made some effort, but otherwise they waited for the official word, for the spokesperson to speak or the issuance of a carefully-worded statement.

"He worked now and then for the local watermen, a deckhand. But I don't know who or where. Sometimes that guy up the road, Lucky. But he says he doesn't know anything."

"I met him. He didn't mention knowing Sammy, but I didn't ask."

"Sammy worked on his boat some, and ran errands on his bike, delivering crabs to local customers, that kind of thing. He said Lucky called him 'FedMex.' Some joke. Sammy was born here in the US."

"So you're just going to clear out rather than try to get answers?"

A toss of her head dismissed the challenge. "If I wait for INS, they'll deport me to Mexico. Oh, Zinker says he'll protect me, come with him. No thank you, I'm going to Florida."

"You have relatives in Florida, friends?"

She looked away, perhaps toward that distant state. "Not really. There was a guy through here, nice guy, not a slobbering Zinker, said he has a fishing shack down there I can rent cheap. Some town on the Gulf. I have it written down. I'll find a job. You can always find work if you work for peanuts."

I asked when she was leaving.

"As soon as I'm done. I have a few things to do; close the bank account, empty as it is, see if I can get some refunds on utilities, pick up my last check at the restaurant. But I can't just leave the dog. Don't you know someone who can take him?"

"I can ask Miss Worple if she has some ideas."

She looked at me like I'd revealed myself as a visiting space alien. "Miss Worple? She thinks the only good animal is the one you can eat."

"I don't know what to suggest. I'm a stranger here. I don't know anyone."

"Well, if you did it wouldn't matter. Just like I said, nobody gives a damn."

"Miss Worple's concerned."

"About me? No, about Bay Breezes. Heaven forbid she would have to spend time there looking after business. But she'll find other cheap help."

"You're leaving today?"

"Probably tomorrow. Like I said, a few things yet to do."

I left, but not with any peace of mind.

The dog watched me, impassive but very alert, as though trying to figure out my role in whatever was going on. Normally I have something to say to dogs, just a couple of words to encourage friendliness. I couldn't find any words. I suppose it sounds a little crazy, but I didn't want to give him false hope.

I had a dog when I was a kid, Rufus. It's hard to explain but to me he was just another kid, a real pal. I used to share dog biscuits with him. One day he grabbed a chunk of meat off the kitchen counter. My father got boiling mad, dragged Rufus out behind the house and shot him.

I never forgave that. I guess partly because of love but also fear. If my father could shoot my best friend, what were chances I'd be next?

Chapter Nine

With the fog lifted, my parting view of the home Serena was leaving included a gang of dark and monkish vultures, keeping vigil in the upper branches of the tall pines behind the trailer.

Another half-dozen scavengers soared and swooped in circles in the sky above. They apparently weren't finding anything to their liking, disappointed shoppers at a ghost town garage sale.

Vultures. Some people compare reporters to vultures, particularly when it is they who are being circled. And isn't that so? Behind masks like 'the public's right to know' and all that, aren't journalists vultures of a sort, focused on the doomed in hopes of a morsel? Well, no, not always. Maybe only ninety percent of the time. Or ninety-five.

It must have been true, as Serena said, others didn't know or didn't care what had actually happened to her son. She knew in her heart, but not in real-world certainty. Was she right? Was this a case of murder overlooked by those who couldn't be bothered?

Unanswered questions take root in my psyche and become fixtures until I've worked them through. Most often, the only way to get an answer is to roll up my sleeves and get busy with a reporter's shovel – dig, dig and dig.

First rule, make sure you're asking the right question. And that would be? The classic question is, who done it? If Sammy was murdered, who had it in for him in the worst possible way? That was the trunk of the question tree, branching off into puzzlers like, how was I, an outsider, going to get answers from the insiders?

I really don't think, at least this once, it was the vulture asking questions. It wasn't right that Serena was getting no help whatsoever. But where could she turn? Officialdom, as I understood it, had already declared the death an accident, case closed. Legal and investigative help was expensive and it was easy to see, Serena didn't have money. So she was left with a heart-wrenching question, one that could torment her day after day, night after night, for a long, long time. Maybe a lifetime. On the chance that she was right, who killed Sammy Sanchez?

And I needed to have a good talk with myself about this growing concern and curiosity.

But I knew I wouldn't listen.

No, wait, I had to make myself listen. Really, it didn't matter if Sammy was zapped by space aliens or throttled by the Chessie sea monster, it was no business of mine. Getting involved was a ticket to trouble, and I really didn't need to go there.

So I went back to Bay Breezes. That didn't make a whole lot of sense either, since I should have been out on the road scouting for touristy things to write about. But then, of course, I should first sit on the porch for a while and strategize, map out my expedition. I mean, it's reasonable to be cautious in unknown territory, right?

Miss Worple hadn't returned from what I hoped was her shopping trip. How spoiled we get in the city with our food choices, a bar serving sandwiches, a little café, a fast food outlet or two or three, almost on every block. Here? You might as well be a caveman, get to know your roots and berries.

I decided to have a daylight look at the road where I'd turned back after meeting the strange guy with the shotgun microphone. This time I drove.

It was a blue-sky day, nearly cloudless. In fact, I'd seen nothing so far of the harsh weather that seemed to haunt local minds, the storms or wild winds or surging tides. Maybe the tourism gods had decided to display only the sunny side of the Eastern Shore for the length of my visit. Maybe ... maybe if I stopped and bought a lottery ticket I'd win a million dollars and could tell von Klonk what to do with his ridiculous article ... maybe ...

Not far beyond Bay Breezes I was back on a narrow corridor of packed sand meandering through a forest of crowded, stunted pines, scattered cedars and wiry scrub brush. It must have been an old farm road, following property lines instead of taking the straight path of most flatland roads. I suppose it benefited from occasional maintenance, it wasn't overgrown or seriously rutted. There were no houses, not even the tumbled remains of one, though little patches of daffodil here and there hinted at former occupation.

Getting closer to the water, the bordering woods gave way to a wall of tall marsh grass. It looked like bug paradise. I'd armed myself with spray repellent, courtesy of Miss Worple. She said it was the strongest stuff on the market.

I left the car at a clearing where other vehicles had parked or turned around and followed the road on foot to the bridge, or what there was of a bridge. The rickety plank structure supported by pilings, stretching only about twelve feet across a stream, was more on the order of a pier than a serious bridge.

Obviously it wasn't called upon to support much traffic, the whole thing looked ready to tumble into the water below. The bridge crossed a stream that appeared out of the tall grasses on one side and wandered on toward a cove or inlet on the other. On the inlet a dozen or so fussing ducks sped skyward, commenting harshly on the intrusion.

Just beyond the far side of the bridge stood a barricade, a barbed wire fence with a bent and battered cattle gate that no longer met the post meant to hold it shut. The gate was decorated with a hand-lettered *No Trespassing* sign likely legible from low flying aircraft.

I was tempted to explore further but Miss Worple's warning about Scrap Blevins held me in check. So I just stood there, having a look around, trying to get past my first impressions and into a real sense of the place. It struck me that the guidebooks and brochures never mention how much of nature is dead, decaying, dying. It was quiet and beautiful, but the vibrant greenery rose from hidden rot.

The sound of a vehicle coming from the marsh put me on alert. It was an ATV. The driver, in mottled camouflage, had snake-like beady eyes and a thin smirk somewhere between dangerous and mischievous. Even if he wasn't a giant of a man there was still the impression of half-man, half-alligator; a real swamp creature. The man shape I was looking at didn't have gator jaws but there was a greater threat. His left hand was on the vehicle's wheel, the right apparently holding something concealed on the passenger side floor. My intuitive radar flashed g-u-n.

As I stood there, I'd become a magnet for a huge bug that I took to be a greenhead. It seemed attracted to the repellent Miss Worple had so kindly provided.

"You need to pull yourself off a cedar switch, mister. You can't fight greenheads with your fists."

"I've never seen a fly that big.'

"You'll see plenty here, long as you got blood in your veins. Lost? Or do you have some business here?"

"No business, just a tourist."

"Sure. Well, this is a historic event, because the last tourist through here was Capt John Smith in sixteen-oh-eight. I bet you're part of that Baltimore mob, even if you don't look like Sonny Liston or dress like Malcolm X."

"I'm not part of any mob. I'm a writer, staying at Bay Breezes."

I can't imagine there was anything amusing in what I'd said so I guess the widening smirk, the faux smile, was of the I-don't-believe-a-word-you're-saying sort. My guess proved correct.

"Sure. I know your type. Dollars to donuts you're in cahoots with that shyster Indian son of a bitch. That it? Slick big city lawyer come to terrify me. That it? Good luck. I'm as broke as the last time I had to run you bastards off."

I was getting a little fed up with being framed as someone I wasn't and my impulse was to tell him so. But that might just delight him, since he, so I suspected, had the gun. "I'm not in cahoots with anyone; I'm a writer working on a travel story. I heard there was a historic light down this way."

"Well, write something about the piss-ant vermin that trashed that historic light, tore it up, wrote all kinds of crap on the walls … damn near wrecked it, what was left of it." The faux smile shrank back into the little reptilian smirk. "It was pretty much a shambles anyway."

"Sorry you've had trouble. Can I get a look at the light?"

"It's back there in the grass and merkle bushes but you ain't going back there, nobody goes back there. Private property." He raised an ugly shotgun from behind the seat. I'd never seen anything quite like it, a big tube with handgrips and a cylinder, like the old tommy gun but bulkier.

Was this guy at all stable? Was my life in danger? I didn't see any pile of dead bodies. I hoped the artillery display was just for impression.

"No problem, whatever you say. My name's Andy Holliday, and I take it you are Scrap Blevins?"

"Look, this ain't an interview, Mr Writer. Just clear off."

"That's exactly what I had in mind. But could you put the weapon aside for just a minute and help me with one small question? I'm curious about what happened to Sammy Sanchez. You're the one that found him, right?"

"You some kind of investigator? Look, I just hauled the fridge to the salvage yard, they found him when they opened it there. It's too bad, even if he was an aggravating little son of a gun."

"How was he aggravating?"

"Little Mister Check-It-Out, I called him. Down here day or night, snooping. Ask what he was up to, he'd say *just checking it out*."

"Checking out what?"

"Darned if I know. He'd get on me about how I didn't really own the land because it was Indian land. In cahoots with that fake Indian there at Chincoteague. At least he was until he found out — what a surprise — the guy's as phony as a street-corner shell game."

"But you gave Sammy a relic found down here?"

Much to my relief, he put the weapon behind the seat. "Well, aren't you a regular Sherlock. He was a pest, coming on my land to poke around, bad enough in daytime, what did he want down here at night? Came near to shooting him a time or two, snoopy twerp. I gave him that relic, nice piece, thought that might shut him up."

"And did it?"

"Not really. He was going to make some big issue of preserving the Point as a historical site."

"How did he figure this is Indian land?"

"Talked about broken treaties. Hell, I didn't make any treaties. It's my land."

I turned to go but decided to take one more stab at getting answers. "One other thing. Who owns the store where Sammy was found? I know it's abandoned but I suppose someone hired you to clean up around it?"

"You don't know when to fold 'em, do you? I told you this ain't no interview. Don't push your luck." He reached back and patted the beastly looking gun behind the seat, in a casual way but serious enough to send the message that our chat was concluded.

"Well, I'll be on my way." Maybe it wasn't an interview but that didn't mean I couldn't try for a quote or two for the article. No guts, no glory, right? "There is one last thing. I can just quote you as a local outdoorsman –- since you won't say who you are. What is it you like most about this area?"

He considered for a moment. "Bugs."

"You're kidding. You're not going to lure many tourists down this way saying the greatest thing is bugs."

"Right. You about done? You've overstayed your welcome by a good while now."

"I'm on my way. But there is something. What is a merkle bush?"

He fixed me with a hard stare. He shook his head in a way that said "hopeless." "Mister, you got too many last questions. Keep it up, one of them's really gonna be."

He started the ATV and roared back into the marsh.

I wondered what would become of anyone who got on the wrong side of – he didn't acknowledge it, but this had to be – Scrap Blevins.

An answer of sorts was quick in coming. I ducked at the explosive sound of the first round but he wasn't firing at me, just letting the world know who was boss of this particular patch. Four more minor explosions followed. And then it was quiet.

On the walk back to the spot where I'd left my car, I thought about how this wasn't the big city. In the city, I could shout the journalistic equivalent of 'Hey, Rube!' and a hundred reporters and editors would come running – if for no other reason than to watch me bleed.

I looked back a time or two, just in case Blevins decided he hadn't put enough *war* in his warning.

Chapter Ten

I was met by brewed coffee, biscuits and strawberry jam. Maybe the coffee was thick as motor oil, but a splash of hot water cut it down to tolerable. Life was good. Nonetheless, I felt like complaining. "There's some damned little bug keeps nipping at me. I can't see it but I sure feel the bite."

Miss Worple presented a patient smile, a saint dealing with the mentally impaired. "No doubt where they get their name, no-see-ums. Biting midges, tiny little flies. They attract to new blood. When you've been here a while, they get bored and leave you alone. Now, what did you find out about Serena?"

I told her Serena seemed to be having some kind of a breakdown and had a wild idea about taking off for Florida with the vaguest plan in mind, talked about renting a fishing shack. My spiritual side uplifted by biscuits and jam, I said I thought a good dose of human kindness might be in order. Maybe Serena would reconsider.

"Are you going to help her?" It wasn't a question or plea, more like a slightly accusatory command. Miss Worple had a Queen of Sheba attitude, and the rest of us were loyal Shebites, or whatever they were called. Shebians? Whatever, I wasn't one.

"I'm here on assignment. I've already gone out of my way to check on her for you. I have work to do."

"What kind of writer are you, anyway?"

I let the question hang in the air for a few moments as an indication of annoyance. "Meaning what? There are all kinds of writers. I'm a travel-writer."

"I thought writers took up causes. You're nothing but a glorified tourist."

If I'd been all that glorified I probably would have taken my business elsewhere at that point, but I was indeed on assignment and I'd been sent to Bay Breezes. I could hear von Klonk's response if I were to tell him I'd moved to a motel and expected him to cover the expense. "I just can't get involved. I've got to get on with my assignment. It seems to me a desperate situation where you could be of some help."

"What do you mean, desperate situation?"

"Serena's situation, her need to find out what happened to Sammy."

The disdainful look said my assessment wasn't worthy of consideration. "What happened to Sammy was, he poked his nose where he shouldn't have and paid the price. She has to come to terms with what happened."

"I'm not sure that's true about Sammy. There wasn't much of an investigation into the so-called accident or, from what I know, even a serious autopsy. Doesn't it seem at all strange to you that he left here in the evening, never got home, and was later found in an abandoned refrigerator?"

"Just like a writer, I suppose, go promoting some crackpot theory. I was simply asking if you'd help Serena. I meant, counsel her, get her to forget Florida and come back to work. You brought up the accident."

We were getting nowhere. I felt compelled to make one last pitch. "And what I'm saying is, the help she needs is finding what happened to Sammy, an answer to put her mind at rest. You have connections around here. It's far more the sort of thing you could initiate, asking local authorities to take another look at what happened."

She mulled. "I'm not going to stir up any fuss. But I'll go out and have a word with her. I'll take Judge Wetherby along. Maybe he can talk some sense into her head."

That seemed a good place to let it drop.

"By the way, I was looking something up in my guidebook and couldn't find it. I ran into Scrap Blevins and can't make heads or tails of one thing he said. What is a merkle bush?"

Another saintly smile bestowed on the ignorant. "You won't be writing much of a story if you don't pick up on how the locals talk. You have to listen closely. Miracle bush, Mr Holliday, miracle bush."

"Miracle bush."

Back to my guidebook.

Turns out the miracle bush is a common wild shrub in these parts, like a laurel in looks but actually a wax myrtle. People treat it as trash. In the old days it was medicine; the colonists made a cure-all tea from it. They learned that from the Indians. It was also an insect repellant, and, you can boil wax out of it for candles.

A pretty interesting bush. But probably not for inclusion in my article. I could hear von Klonk. "When I need a botany lesson, Holliday, I'll go to the Arboretum. Forget the damn merkle bush and go find the money tree."

Taps on the front door interrupted my study of local flora. Miss Worple went to answer and returned in the company of a gentleman in a white linen suit, sporting a smart panama hat. "Judge Wetherby, Andy Holliday. Mr Holliday is among us to do a travel article."

Wetherby's smile said there was much about the world that amused him. It was somewhere between a mischievous schoolboy smirk and a good old boy aw-shucks grin. His long, lined face had seen a lot of sun and wind. You could call it a horse face but of the noble sort, in the league of Man o' War or Secretariat. His eyes had the deceptively sleepy look that I guessed didn't miss a trick.

Miss Worple parked us in the parlor and disappeared into the kitchen.

I gave the judge a moment but he didn't seem inclined to start a conversation. So I pulled one of my usual tricks and went provocative. "Life moves awfully slow, out here in the provinces."

Wetherby went studious on me. After a few moments he said: "You're right, there's not a lot of hurry here. But there's a certain sanity to country life that seems greatly lacking in the cities."

A philosopher. Somehow I doubted von Klonk would be looking for philosophy in the article I was supposed to write, any more than botany, so I tried another tactic. I asked how Scrap Blevins got his name.

"You might meet someone called 'Redtop,' that's the way he marks his crab pot floats, a dab of red paint at the top, and everyone knows just who you mean. Sometimes there are very interesting stories about how nicknames came to be, a few of them fairly racy. Often as not, they're used behind the person's back." Carried on a deep voice, his words flowed languidly, like verbal molasses.

"But Scrap, in particular?"

"He runs the back roads with his ATV, looking for cast off metal. There're others collect it, but that is to sell. He sells some but he also makes things out of it, sculptures. Very strange constructions. He's all right, though, keeps to himself and expects the same of others."

"Interesting about nicknames. Maybe I can work it into the article I'm doing."

Wetherby's hand went to his chin. He seemed to be reflecting on an intriguing thought. "Glad to help. Now, I'll tell you what's interesting to me. A travel-writer named Holliday. That's probably not just a curious coincidence, is it? What is your real name?"

He had me cornered. Fortunately, Miss Worple returned with cups of coffee on a tray. The oil slicks at the top of the cups told me this was going to be another encounter with her gelatinous brew. I thought the judge deserved a word of warning and so complimented the hostess on the espresso. She answered in a puzzled stare, first at me and then at my coffee cup.

Miss Worple opted not to comment on the coffee. She told the judge what I'd found in visiting Serena. "I'll put her up here for a while if she'll come. Better than being out there all alone. She can store her things in a rental bin. But no dogs – I won't have the dog."

The judge said he had a kennel. "We'll get her straightened out. She's been through a rough spell. You've got to get her back, Mardela. If you keep making coffee like this, you can change the name of this place to Killer Caffeine Bed & Breakfast."

I left them to a little spat and made for the kitchen and the bottle of hot sauce I'd found there. When I returned, Miss Worple was telling the judge about my idea, that things wouldn't be right for Serena until she found out what happened to Sammy. "Mr Holliday seems to think the young man was murdered."

"Murdered?" He turned to me. "Oh, I don't know about that. Wherever did you get the idea he was murdered?"

I was on the spot again, fishing for a substantial answer. "I don't really know enough about the case to say more. The thing is, Serena thinks he was killed. And you would have to admit that it's strange, he left here in the evening on his bike and didn't make it home. It doesn't seem likely that he left here, rode to that store and, on whim, crawled into a refrigerator."

The judge pondered. "Well, you didn't know Sammy, he was unpredictable. And there was no sign of shooting or stabbing. As I understand it, any breakage or bruising was attributed to rough handling of the refrigerator before he was found."

Attributed? That could mean it was nothing more than a guess. "Suppose he was beaten to death before being dumped there?"

"I won't deny the possibility, however unlikely."

There was no point in pursuing it. I had no facts. "By the way, Scrap wanted to know if I was part of a Baltimore mob. What's that all about?"

Wetherby was slow to answer. It wasn't particularly annoying, just his style. I could imagine a five-minute story taking ten minutes or more. "Well, I'm not one to tell tales, but I suppose he asked for it, saying that to you. There's some foolishness in him, that's for sure. He got in over his head with gambling debts up in Baltimore, owes money to a rough crowd."

"That can be an unhealthy situation."

The judge nodded agreement. "He's handled it, so far. Any of those Baltimore boys that went down to Parkers Point after him probably took early retirement when they came out, if they came out. It's not just that Scrap was raised around here and knows the marsh upside and down, he spent three years' ground combat in Vietnam. They may make them tough in Baltimore, but not back-country tough."

"Scrap was sporting a weapon that looks like a tommy gun."

Wetherby explained that the artillery piece in question was called a Streetsweeper, an automatic shotgun capable of dispensing twelve rapid-fire rounds. "Fairly unreliable weapon, so I've heard. Known to jam up. They're trying to make them illegal. Might be a reasonable idea; they're a bit much for normal hunting and they would play hell as home protection."

"What's to protect down at the Point? It looks like swamp."

"They call it marsh."

"There's a difference?"

Another thoughtful pause. "Well – pardon me if you already know this, I'm just trying to help – for one thing there are more trees and shrubs to a swamp. A marsh is mostly grasses. But about what's to protect; there's no telling what Scrap's accumulated by the law of finders-keepers, if you can call that a law. Another thing is, those sculptures that seem weird to me may be guard-with-your-life treasures to him."

I asked if his protectiveness might be connected to the idea that there had been an Indian village on the site. "I mean, maybe there are other artifacts like the clamshell he gave Sammy. I'm no expert but I know those old relics can be valuable."

"It's possible," Wetherby said. "Long ago there was an Indian village in the area. The textbook story is that a hurricane destroyed it and the Indians left. Not just left, as in moved next door, but actually emigrated, vamoosed. With all the Anglo settlement, there wasn't anywhere for them to go around here, so they went north or west, far away. At least that's how the textbook story goes." He paused for a moment. "Just as an aside, it may not have been a hurricane that destroyed the village. Local legend says wreckers ran them off."

"You've got me on that one. Wreckers?"

"It's shallow water down there at the Point. Before the light was put in, there were shipwrecks. That means there were goods to scavenge. All sorts of treasures might wash ashore or could be had by wading out a ways."

"And the wreckers didn't want competition from the original inhabitants, is that it?"

"That's a reasonable assumption, human nature being what it is."

"So Scrap, with his finding and scavenging, is carrying on a proud tradition."

"You could say that. Certainly you could say that. Of course, his harvest is mostly for that strange artwork. Hardly the same as being a pirate."

"Artwork he doesn't show anyone."

"For your purposes, Scrap may not be the local artist to feature. We have some showy artists that would welcome the attention, mostly woodcarvers. No one carves decoys for hunting anymore. They carve them for the art festival. For hunting you buy factory-made decoys at the sporting goods shop."

I asked about Parkers Point, wondering if it was named for some historical figure.

Wetherby chuckled. "Not really. There are Parkers around, sure, but that name is the work of locals repenting the sins of their fathers. You see, it used to be Pirates Point. I guess they chose Parker because it wasn't too much of change. But the new name has some truth to it, or did until Scrap put up his barricade. Couples used to go down there to watch the moon. Parking and sparking."

The judge went quiet again. I turned over what he'd said in my mind, looking for points of interest. "That's intriguing about the Indian village. Some way I could learn more about it?" Like Sammy's death, the subject wasn't likely to be grist for the kind of story *Here & There* wanted, but I was curious.

Miss Worple recommended a book by Professor Morton Zogby.

Wetherby snorted. "That book's a pile of horse crap."

Miss Worple tilted her head in the judge's direction, sighting in on him with furrowed brow. "The Judge doesn't agree with Zogby about the departure of Indians from our region. The way the Judge sees it, they are still around, their spirits, I suppose, prowling like cats in the night. More ghosts to worry about."

"Not their spirits, Mardela. They are here, in our schools, in our churches, in our shops and neighborhoods. They are among us."

I asked Wetherby what he meant, exactly.

He drew himself up and seemed to be talking more to Miss Worple than to me. "According to Zogby's poppycock, all the indigenous peoples of the Delmarva region high-tailed for the north and the west, and some went over to the Virginia mainland. And no one questions that because it's the esteemed expert Zogby. Well, there are those who question, but they aren't very popular."

"You are among them?"

"What I am saying is, many of those people didn't go anywhere at all, they remained and blended into colonial society as best they could."

Miss Worple stood up. "Come along, Judge, we'll go see if we can get Serena calmed down. For reasons that elude me at the moment, she thinks you're a sensible person."

The judge looked at me, his amused smile in place. "Mardela and I go back a ways, back before she went off on her career path. We were both young once, weren't we?"

I wouldn't have imagined anyone could make Miss Worple blush but he succeeded.

As if to apologize for bringing on the blush, he added: "These days, we mostly work together on Civil Defense projects."

"Projects?"

The smile disappeared. "Staying prepared in case of trouble, natural disaster, nuclear attack, revolution, terrorism from wacky people like that bunch in Iran that had the hostages. Might happen some criminal needs attention, we're a long ways from the authorities."

"But you've got that fellow Zinker."

The judge frowned. "Zinker isn't our man. He's just for the rich out of towners that own so much property hereabouts. You'll find this neck of the woods divided into two camps, Holliday. There are those of us who've lived here all along or at least call this home, such as Mardela and me. We don't mind beneficial progress but we don't want to see the locals and the land run over roughshod by outsiders. I don't mean all the come-here people but there are those who just buy cheap from locals in distress, figuring on future gain."

"No offense, Judge, but where are indications there'll be any gain in the future around here?"

He rose to join Mardela, who had wrapped her shoulders in the fur of some beautiful wild beast and crowned herself with a sequined turban. If you'd wanted an image to go with *eccentric*, you couldn't have asked for better.

Judge Wetherby turned at the door. "Probably seems unlikely as you look around but there are schemes in the works hereabouts; that is a fact."

Chapter Eleven

Yes, I should have been out and about, gathering material for the article. But the porch had become a comfortable place to be. True, I wasn't being paid to *be*, I was being paid to do. But I wasn't being paid very much and so I didn't feel like doing very much.

I took stock of my situation. It was hard not to drift into resentment over happenings of the recent past. I'd been framed, and I couldn't figure out how to escape the frame and get back into the big picture. Looking at the here and now, what leverage did I have?

There was a possibility right under my nose.

Maybe one of my old pals at a slick national magazine would buy into this Indian burial ground story. I knew it could be a grabber; there was a lot of public interest in Native American culture. Payment for a major magazine piece would beat months of slaving for *Here & There*, plus it would be a big step along the comeback trail, a gateway to more good assignments.

What were chances? My old pals had been fairly distant since my reputation hit the skids. But we were brothers and sisters under the same banner, right? Fellow journalists. One for all and all for one. (Had Miss Worple laced that coffee with psilocybin? I was definitely delusional).

I made some calls. Three were all that were needed to take the wind from my sails. My old pals were all booked up with great stories, thanks anyway. When I pushed, two said they would have a look if I wrote it on spec, but no promises. When I said I was hoping for a bit of an advance before going ahead, I got the fog button. The accounting department had tightened the screws, blah blah blah.

Bummer.

I owed von Klonk a call. My gut said forget it but my head presented various arguments such as overworked credit cards, unpaid bills, even an image of a man in a tattered overcoat huddled under a bridge, hiding from the world's slings and arrows.

Hopefully the exalted editor would be out, poisoning pigeons in the park or however he spent his time away from the office.

No such luck.

"So, how's it going?"

"Fine, I suppose. I've been checking out the wildlife and sunsets. All nice color for the article."

"Birds and sunsets don't buy ads, Holliday. Quit messing around. I want you to get with that fellow Cole and stir up some business. We want the chic shops, the hopping nightclubs, the ritzy resorts, the five star restaurants."

Fortunately he couldn't see the rolling of my eyes. "Have you ever visited this part of the country?" It seemed as though I should add an intimacy, 'boss' or 'pal' or even 'sir', but I couldn't come out with it.

Once upon a time – back before I put a plug in the jug – I spent too many evenings in a hideaway bar where the bartender referred to me as *Your Lordship*. It was as cornball as could be, but he delivered it with a straight face, and for a brief while propelled me into a countryside English pub where I was the local squire. Ridiculous, but after a few ounces of Laphroaig unblended, I took the little fantasy trip. And paid for it with a generous tip.

But even if I put myself in the place of the bartender and tried to imagine von Klonk as a big tipper, I couldn't muster a friendly sobriquet.

"I'm the editor, remember? If, and I say *if*, I needed birds and sunsets, I would hire a poet to get me some, you know what I mean? But that's not what I need. I need smiling faces in the advertising department, singing my praises to a greedy, money-grubbing publisher. That requires kissy-kissy mentions of potential advertisers. Am I by any chance getting through to you?"

Through, yes, right under the skin. "I'm trying to tell you, venerable sahib, that this is not Ocean City. If you buried Ocean City in the sand and went away for a hundred years maybe this is what you would come back to. It's mostly wilderness and marsh. The people eat muskrats."

"Muskrats?"

"It's a cross between a rat and a beaver. And there's more. They also eat turtles."

"Sure they do."

"Turtle soup; it's a delicacy."

"I'm wondering if you're in the right country, Holliday. Maybe you made a wrong turn somewhere? What next, snakes?"

"I think that's further south."

"I know damn well there's got to be places that serve regular food. Isn't that area known for seafood?"

"You're right, of course. Crabs are big. Oysters. But I'd say the really big thing is fried chicken."

"OK, there must be some primo spot famous for fried chicken, find it. Play it up big and we'll do a special fried chicken section."

"There's fried chicken everywhere. Most every place sells it.

But the best, they say, comes from a gas station."

"This is more of your jive, right? A gas station?"

"Regal Gas and Go, everyone says that's the place for fried chicken."

"Well, chicken, at least that's the kind of thing civilized *Here & There* readers want to hear about. Get some good chicken quotes. Forget the damn muskrats, forget turtles. But don't forget to write the damn article. I-want-to-see-a-story, soon. Just get on with it."

"Absolutely. I'm just heading out to have a look around."

"Do we have a bad connection? You'll be looking around the want-ads if you don't get me what I ask for, and pronto, Holliday." There was a pause. For all I knew, he'd signed off. But then he spoke again. "You know what I like about how you're handling this job?"

"No, what's that?"

"I'm looking for suggestions."

"I hear you, noble prince of the publishing world. The story is as good as on your desk … just a few little odds and ends to pull together."

"Get pulling, then. Don't forget, our deal is probationary, thirty days, pal, tick, tick, tick. And can the honorifics." He hung up. Well, I was warned off. But he called me pal, maybe that would be acceptable? In the old noir movies it's kind of noncommittal, like bud or mac or chum.

Amigo. How about that? I could call him Amigo. But with a name like von Klonk? OK, how about Mein Fuehrer? Probably wisest to do as he said, can it.

Yes, I was spinning my wheels. I needed to move, to get going on the article. But instead I sat on the porch and brooded, not about fried chickens but about questions that needed answering.

What had happened to Sammy that night? What would become of Serena? What was becoming of me, when I should be at the top of my game, adored, feared, raking in the loot, courted by the high and mighty …

All collapsed like a ton of …

Well, for some reason the genes preached survival. So, I would have to buck up and pump out a few pages of fanciful fluff to please *Here & There* advertisers. Here, chicken, here, chick-chick-chick.

Where to start? Might as well just follow instructions, go see Barney Cole.

A loud mouth blue jay urged me on.

But was he really urging me on? Or was that raucous squawk a warning: Don't let what's left of your spirit or soul rot away like this, chuck it, chuck it all, walk away from the whole damn mess, hit the beach and walk until you reach tomorrow.

I know, an unrealistic flight of fancy, get back to the real world. But what the hell was the real world showing me that would make it at all attractive? And who's to say, could be a long walk down a lonesome stretch of beach might refresh my spirit. I could get some business cards printed: *Wandering Beach Bum At Your Service*. And, I wouldn't have to worry about not having a permanent address. Beach bums just hang out wherever they happen to be, right?

But, what the heck, I got in the car and headed for town. "Live as you ought and obey orders." Someone said that. I think it was one of those old Taoist guys. I wonder exactly what was meant?

They were tricksters, those old Taoist guys, you have to look around and under what they say. Like, whose orders are you supposed to obey? Think about it: You could say the call of the wild is orders. Well, you *could*.

Cole may have retreated from a posh office on the West Coast to a sparsely furnished cubbyhole on the East, but he still wore the man-about-town costume. Dark blue British-style blazer, club tie, gray trousers. An interesting contrast to local garb, which ran more to bib overalls and a work-shirt with most of the color washed out of it, topped with a baseball cap.

"Where have you been so far?"

I told him I had seen a bit of Parkers Point.

"Parkers Point? What's to see out there? Just muck and marsh." He tapped out what may have been a little distress signal with the fancy fingernails of his right hand. "Come to think of it, there's a great little event tonight, just what the doctor ordered. I was supposed to go with Red Mulroney, he's a state senator. Something's come up, so you'll be my stand-in."

He made a brief phone call and then told me I would be attending a firehouse crab feast that evening with Senator Mulroney as my host. "He's a progressive, a man of vision. He'll attest to that himself. That's what this region needs, vision. Too many people dozing off in dreams of yesterday."

"So he's a politician, I get it. Any other interests?"

"I don't know, probably teaches Sunday School, sponsors a mile of litter cleanup along Route 13, public service things."

"Sounds like fascinating company."

"That attitude won't get you anywhere, Holliday. Mulroney's a mover and shaker, a man of substance. Why else would anyone spend a fortune campaigning for a job that pays less than fifty grand a year? Good man to know, he can be a big help with your story."

I expressed my insincere gratitude for the pending connection with the state senator and then, of course, put my foot in it again. "I've been learning a bit more about that situation you were telling me about, the death of Sammy Sanchez. It seems the authorities didn't really show much interest."

"Why should they? Can you imagine how many cops we'd need if they had to monitor every stupid move by every bonkers kid?"

"I don't think getting murdered can be fairly described as a stupid move. It's not like the victim has a choice."

"Murdered? Where'd you get that? It was an accident."

Had everyone around here been inoculated against curiosity and skepticism? "He was heading home in the evening on his bike. He never got there. It sounds fishy to me."

"Serena worked nights. Sammy probably got used to amusing himself with no supervision, playing dumb detective games."

"There's other peculiarities that make it interesting."

"Really? Name one."

"Miss Worple has this weird little carved clamshell that Sammy left behind. She says it's cursed, some kind of Indian curse."

"Oh, man. Tell me you're not going off on some hoodoo voodoo trip. Sammy Sanchez, victim of voodoo." He shook his head, giving me a pained look. "Holliday, you need a holiday."

Maybe I could get through to him in a language he understood. "Let's think Hollywood for a minute, Barney."

"Yeah, right. OK, go for it."

"Well, let's see. We open in the twilight shadows of a country road, a young man on a bike, looking intent, he's on some sort of mission, we see him make a turn, we follow him around the turn, and – he's not there, poof, gone."

"Uh-huh." He was studying the ceiling. "Then what?"

I was having fun, killing time that would otherwise be spent productively. "Next comes the strange lady who lives in the creepy mansion nearby, carrying on about an Indian curse and how the fellow on the bike was digging into things better left alone, on land guarded by a psycho gun nut."

Cole's look suggested medical concern. "This is your article?"

"No, not at all. I'm just telling what interests me. Throw in a gang of hoods from Baltimore and land claims by a fake Indian …"

"I'm going to tell Miss Worple to have the water checked out there."

He didn't say it with a smile. He seemed genuinely concerned that I was going to go off the deep end. I reassured him. "Don't worry, you'll get your publicity piece. It's just that, being a Hollywood type, I thought you might see the story that could be, the real possibilities."

"Dead kid, a few oddball characters? Maybe, if you pile on some gory bloodbaths and orgiastic sex. I wouldn't waste my time. You shouldn't either. It's not really much of a story."

"Why do you say that?"

"Sammy's Mexican. Mexicans come to bad ends all the time. It's like a cultural pastime."

Do we really need another war with Mexico? That kind of talk could stir one up. "Sammy was born here. But don't you think that anyone, anywhere deserves justice? Sweeping a suspicious death under the carpet is corrupt."

"A journalist with principles. They should put you in a glass case."

"I told you before, I may not have principles but by damn, I have limits. Looking the other way in a murder situation exceeds my limits."

"Sure it does. Calm down. Anyway, aren't you here to do a travel story? What else is on your mind?"

What else? Personal stuff. Try Visa, MasterCard, maybe some unprincipled activity like robbing a bank or any other nefarious skullduggery that would support swift relocation to Belize and a new life …

Thoughts best kept to myself. So I went with an appropriate reply: "My editor has got it in his head that there are tourist attractions on the Lower Shore. As I've mentioned, Chincoteague and Assateague are off limits. What does that leave?"

"Hmmm. Well. Let's see. There's … you know, each little village has its charm. You've got the brochure, haven't you? Restored mansions, a few museums, marinas, parks, fishing villages, fairs and festivals now and then. Some interesting cemeteries …"

"Right. The thing is, the editor wants revenue generators, amusement parks, shopping malls, fine restaurants, boardwalks, that sort of thing."

"Then he'll just have to come and build them."

"That's not the answer that will please him."

"Look, the story about what's here is about what's not here, you know? Noise, traffic, pollution, crowds, mile upon mile of tract housing. Turn the negatives into positives, promote the history, the slow pace, life on the water."

"So how do you operate the Tourist Bureau when there aren't any commercial attractions?"

"Make the best of it, what else? I get out on Route 13 and visit what businesses there are. That's all I know to tell you."

"Well, I guess I'll get on with it."

"You're going to drop the Sammy craziness?"

"I don't think so. Why?"

"No reason. Just wondered."

Chapter Twelve

The fire department often seems to be the most prosperous enterprise in a small town. The bank may have needed a facelift ten years back, town hall might be a construction site trailer, the school looks like a gray prison barracks, but the big, handsome firehouse stands like a proud fortress, all spiffed up for inspection.

Dinner at the firehouse is an everybody-knows-everybody event, so it came as no surprise when State Senator Red Mulroney spotted me, the stranger, coming through the door. I was probably the lone unknown.

He was young, maybe thirty, adding some maturity with a beard as well trimmed as the fairway of a world-class golf course.

I met the chief and then the assistant chief and ultimately several captains before we were allowed to sit, our table perched on a raised platform with a commanding view of all the others.

The senator being a special guest, we were served platters rather than having to go through a line. Platters? Well, our food arrived on tray-like box tops from big shipping boxes, lined with paper towels, the down-home version of platters. The deliveries came through swinging doors that revealed a gleaming kitchen suited to a fair-sized restaurant.

The buffet tables bore heaps of corn on the cob, mounds of coleslaw, piles of hushpuppies. Steamed crabs were spread on one long table as they came from the kitchen. There were rolls of paper towels. Crabs are steamed whole in spices that give them a sticky, messy coating.

With a shell like thin porcelain, crabs are not the most cooperative of foodstuffs. But I was among experts, working over their meals with a fairly quiet crack and crunch. Unlike vacationers at a first-time crab feast, no one felt compelled to beat the creatures into shattered submission.

Iced tea both sweet and unsweetened, bottled water, sodas and beer flowed from a stand near our table.

Like Cole, Mulroney was a talker. He went on about virtues of region, and on, and on … it was a great locale for a vacation home, wonderful place to retire, paradise for the hobby farmer, and you could hunt, fish, cruise the Bay and the ocean. He could have been the poster boy for von Klonk's dictum that travel isn't reality, it's fantasy. "You're not taking notes?"

"I have a good memory."

"Just so you remember to put me right up at the front of your story, the rising star of the Eastern Shore political scene, a man of vision, destined for greatness." Did Barney Cole write his lines? It was said with a smile but his eyes let me know he was serious.

"Oh, I've got it all right."

First impression? Mulroney was the sort who would feel right at home in Washington or any environment where they play hardball in the fast lane. By that I mean the political or corporate world where you wake up thinking, 'What can I get today, and how fast can I get it?'

Not to say such people don't now and then do the right thing. They look at a troubling situation, count their own guns, count the guns pointed at them. If the prospective outcome looks unfavorable, 'I have reconsidered my position.'

And now Mulroney was off on local prospects for generating power by harnessing offshore winds. "The profit potential is huge, all that's needed is investment and visionaries like myself in office to keep regulation under control."

I tried to appear interested while I struggled with the crustacean on my plate.

"How do you eat these things?'

"I don't. Bottom feeders. Leave 'em to the tourists, that's my policy. When this wraps up we'll head over to Ray's Shanty for a good hearty prime rib. How about that?"

"I've got to try crabs for the sake of the story."

"Your choice." He squeezed his face into a look that said it was the wrong choice. "Holliday, this area has a future but the locals want to live in the past. They think progress means becoming better oyster-shuckers and chicken-pluckers; hardheaded, that's what they are."

"These are the people who vote for you, you're talking about?"

"I tell 'em what they want to hear. God, motherhood, apple pie. But someone – and it might as well be me – someone has to drag them kicking and screaming into a new era."

I'd managed to crack a claw and dig out a wafer of white meat. "What new era?"

"The future is technology. That's the future."

"Looks to me like the future around here is in manufacturing *For Sale* signs."

That remark merited a look that had previously been reserved for the bottom-feeder crab. Fortunately, someone whom the senator had to make feel important came up to chat. An envelope changed hands and disappeared into the senator's inside coat pocket. I'd seen such maneuvers often enough in Washington to recognize an unreported campaign contribution. But, hey, *Here & There, the Magazine of Family Travel*, definitely wasn't interested in political shenanigans.

"You need some help?" The question came from the diner to my right, a beefy, ruddy fellow with a mustache that traveled down his chin as though trying to be a goatee.

"I haven't got the knack of getting at the meat of these things."

He turned the crab I was working on onto its back. "Well, you seem to have it down as far as cracking the claws. That centerpiece is called the apron. Pry that up. Take the little monster in both hands and separate the bottom shell from the top. Break the bottom part in half. Get to work with your fingers and the knife, eat what looks good and toss what doesn't ... the yellow stuff is called 'mustard,' that's fat, some eat it some don't, but it's tasty. That's about all there is to it."

As I made moderate progress with the crabs, my neighbor polished off a small mountain of them. He introduced himself as Warren Pierce. "I'm up here with you because I'm a big contributor to this outfit. I've got a dozen chicken houses down the road, so I keep on good terms with the fire department in case of trouble."

"A dozen? I haven't seen more than three or four on a farm."

"There are a few really big operations around, I'm in the middle. A lot of these fellows, they have other jobs; it's them and the wife taking care of a few houses in their spare time."

I got a serious briefing on the travesties inflicted by regulators at various levels of government and the airy-fairy notions of environmental crusaders in general. Turnabout being fair play, I told Pierce about my assignment and where I was staying. "There is something you might help me on. I'm looking for interesting aspects of local history. Readers seem to enjoy that kind of thing."

Pierce chewed that over with another big lump of crabmeat. "I came here from Pennsylvania, so I'm an outsider and not the best source. All I can think of offhand is how, out where you're staying, law and order has fairly much been handled since early days by vigilance committees. Something happens they don't like, they'd call a stomp."

"Now you've lost me. A stomp?"

"I shouldn't be telling you this. Forget it. I shouldn't have opened my fat yap."

"Mr Pierce, I assure you, I've faced jail a time or three rather than reveal a source. I walk out of here tonight, I don't even remember your name."

Pierce studied his pile of picked shells. "Well, the way it goes is that if somebody crossed those folks or got out of line – violated one of the commandments in the Bible, say, something like that – they'd corral whoever it was, and they just march, chase the bad one right into the Bay."

"Seriously? Kind of like pirates making someone walk the plank."

Pierce emptied a big cup of cola in a couple of long swallows. "Fact of the matter is, if something like that ever was, it was probably long, long ago. Way long ago."

"Did you ever hear of any specific incidents?"

"Say, good talking to you, but I've got to get up early, look after them chickens. Just don't forget, far as what I told you, forget where you heard it." He offered a ham fist which I pumped, country-style. I'd noticed the difference between local handshakes and the more delicate twitch practiced in the big city.

"No problem. One last thing, though, what becomes of the victim, the one who gets stomped?"

"Well, I wouldn't know, but I guess them that didn't swim out a ways and drown … what would become of them is the stompers would just stomp 'em, into the ground."

Mulroney and I hadn't parted on the best of terms, or any terms at all for that matter. After the chicken farmer left, I turned back to where the senator had been sitting. The seat was empty.

Looking out over the crowd, there was Mulroney holding forth in the middle of it all, shaking hands and patting backs.

It seemed to me a good time to get some fresh air, and after I got a little I decided to get a lot more. I should have said some thank-yous and goodbyes but I'd had my fill of socializing for the evening. Particularly socializing with a politician. If I ever found myself in a down to earth or heart to heart conversation with a politician, I'd believe what the mystics say about life as a dream. With a few remarkable exceptions, it wasn't something that might occur in the world I was inclined to take for reality.

I'd captured a bit of feature material, the assembling of locals to devour a mountain of crabs, and I'd gathered tips on the proper way to dismantle said crustacean, something to pass along to big city readers used to dealing only with shredded meat and filler on pasty buns.

But, being me, instead of getting down to writing all that up as a highlight of my article, my thoughts were drawn to Pierce's weird story about the vigilante ritual, the stomping party.

That night I had a mob of stompers marauding through my realistic dreams, gray-cloaked shapes carrying sticks or staffs, some muttering, some shouting, all marching with an exaggerated step – in my direction.

Mulling it over in the morning I wondered if it was really me in the dreams, or had I taken on the role of Sammy? Suppose he was as annoyingly nosey as I'd been told. Maybe he'd poked that nose into the wrong situation, somehow riled a whole community against him. If so, no wonder so many were willing to go along with the accident verdict. What might turn up if there was a local investigation?

Later, when Judge Wetherby appeared, I took the first opportunity to ask about Warren Pierce's anecdote. "Judge, you mentioned being a student of history. Have you ever heard such a thing as this …?" And I went on with the tale of the stomp, without mentioning my source.

Wetherby waved the idea off with a chuckle. "My goodness, the yarns people spin. A mad and murderous ritual! Your informant must have been smoking those funny cigarettes, Holliday."

"Nothing to it, then?"

"There were plenty of vigilance committees in the past; that much is true. It was common enough for citizens to take the law into their own hands, particularly in colonial times when official assistance was hard to come by. But the sort of thing you're talking about sounds more Dark Ages, maybe medieval England. You know how fantasies grow from a kernel of truth, perhaps it's an exaggeration that grew out of a true story. I mean, there's the truth of beating the bushes for animals and birds, and then some yarn-spinner puts a man in place of the wildlife."

"So nothing of the sort ever happened around here?"

That brought a hard look. "You wouldn't have gotten it into your head that Sammy was a victim of vigilantes? I trust you're not going to go spreading wild tales." There was challenge and warning in his tone. "You'll have them thinking we're some sort of KKK. We can't have that."

"Right. I go on these tangents of curiosity, Judge. Often they lead nowhere."

He mellowed both his tone and the hard look. "I understand; it's your line of work to question everything. And I can see where an outsider might – might, if he was of a suspicious nature – get an idea that vigilance committees still exist. You take for example our civil defense unit, just a neighborly bunch, getting together to do good deeds, say a few prayers and tell a few jokes, all decent and wholesome sorts of activities. And, I suppose, if outsiders aren't invited to join then they might make up wild tales in retaliation."

"Never taking the law into your own hands, of course."

"The word *never* covers a lot of ground. We're some ways from the sheriff and state police, we would certainly respond to an emergency situation. But only to subdue and restrain a miscreant until the authorities arrive. We're not a lynch mob, Holliday."

At that point Miss Worple appeared. "Serena would be here but she has to take her things to storage. Is there a chance you could help, Mr Holliday? The Judge and I have a meeting we must attend or we'd lend a hand."

"I'd be glad to, of course, but I am, as I may have mentioned, here on assignment. I've got an article to research. Surely she has friends who'll help?"

I should have left it at a statement and not added the question. Miss Worple said Serena was without friends, alone and unaided, and the project wouldn't take much time at all, it only involved a quick trip to town, and I'd have all afternoon for my article. "And then she'll be here. That would be a blessing. You'd have clean sheets and a nice breakfast in the morning. And we're only talking a few minutes of your time."

A few minutes. What about that fellow Zinker? Well, from what Serena had said, he wasn't one to be called a friend.

Chapter Thirteen

A police car pulled away from in front of Serena's trailer. As it passed in the opposite direction I noticed that it wasn't really a police car, though it had a little blue light on the roof. On the side door was written: *Zinker Security Services* and a phone number.

I didn't get a good look at the man behind the wheel. He was big and wore a khaki shirt. I didn't see any insignia. I'd say his expression was grim. He glanced my way as his car gave a jerk of quick acceleration.

Serena met me at the door, looking only slightly less melancholy than when I had last seen her. "It was Zinker, the one who tells me immigration is after me and only he can save me. He's not welcome but he keeps coming around."

"He didn't look happy."

"I had to set him straight in terms I am sure he would understand." She stared in the direction of Zinker's departure, as if a mean look would further his understanding.

"Can't you report him?"

"Report him? He is as much as there is of local police. He is it."

"I mean, to the sheriff or the state police."

"And say there is a guy, a gringo rent-a-cop, trying to make time with Mexican me, an illegal from the land that, in their minds, is whorehouses, dope smugglers, mass murders? I don't think so."

"I'm sure not everyone thinks that way."

She squinted, as though looking to see if I was serious. "You're sure? Where did you get your sure from? Want to trade skins?"

"If he's out to scare you into doing what he wants, maybe he's the one who put that graffiti in the back room."

"It wouldn't surprise me. But who's going to investigate that? Dismissed as a childish prank, you can bet." She waved me into the disarray. "I rented a storage place. I don't really know what I'm doing next, but if you, Mardela and the Judge say don't go, I'll stay. At least for a while."

"I'm glad to hear that. But I do understand how tempting it can be; the idea of running away."

"It's good of you to take some time for my troubles, Mr Holliday." She said it as though talking to a four year old who wasn't taking her seriously. "Don't worry, though, I can handle this. There's not much to take to storage."

"I'm Andy, OK? And to tell the truth, I wanted to talk to you. I've been thinking about what happened to Sammy. I wake up in the night wondering if you could be right. You know what I mean?"

"Of course I know what you mean, Andy. Look, I hope you don't mind, when we are around Miss Worple, you remain Mr Holliday. She is ... what would you say, *proper*?"

As good a word as any, I guess. Proper. Mule-headed, I might have said, and a relic. Not even a real relic but one out of old novels. "I understand." But there was a lot I didn't understand. "I was wondering, have you ever thought of going home to Mexico?"

"Home? That isn't home anymore. I come from a good family. They still have a big ranch in Sonora, far as I know, but they disowned me. They have no use for a crazy girl who ran off to the USA with a hired hand."

"You've tried to set things right?"

"My people don't forget and they sure don't forgive. Besides, the Mexico of my childhood is not the Mexico of today. I can never go back." There was a look in her eyes of pain beyond the reach of anything I could say.

She turned away. She was crying. I didn't mean to, I just impulsively opened my arms and she was there, held in a hug.

It was a genuine act of comfort, but, being a man with feelings, I was feeling Serena's womanly warmth.

I eased gently out of the embrace. She stood there, arms at her sides, biting her lip. My sense was that I had given her something to think about that she didn't want to think about. Same here.

I parked that thought and tried another. "So you came to the US. How did that go?"

"I came here with Miguel. Life was more difficult than either of us had imagined. We got in with a harvest crew on a bus, and the bus stopped here. Miguel thought the money grew on trees in this country, but the reality is that what grows on trees is fruit for Mexicans to pick. There were only nothing jobs, so he started chasing the fast money. I don't know exactly what happened but I know drugs are smuggled through here. Things didn't go his way, and one day he was gone. It was just me and Sammy."

"He doesn't send anything to help with finances?"

She shrugged. "I haven't heard from him. He may be in prison; he may be back in Mexico. He's been gone a long, long time. We had nothing, so he left nothing behind. Well, probably by accident there was a silver belt buckle, a pretty thing with coral and turquoise inlay. Sammy wears it all the time."

"You got a divorce?"

She frowned and looked down, as though there was an old scrapbook on the floor. "It wasn't needed, Andy. We planned to marry once we got settled. Or so I thought, anyway."

We were standing close, each talking quietly. "You've had a hard life."

"Some people don't even get that chance. It could have been worse. Seems it's getting worse."

There was one point that wasn't quite clear; I asked why the police hadn't looked further into Sammy's death.

"They looked, but it was just a passing glance. The coroner said Sammy suffocated. He was badly banged up but they said it was due to rough treatment of the refrigerator, loading and unloading before it was opened. I don't believe that, but for a real examination they have to send the body to a state lab. They said there was no need, it was accidental, the lab is overworked with people killed in Baltimore, end of discussion."

"Do you have any idea what he was up to, out on the road that night?"

Her expression turned to one of frustration or perplexity. "I worked most nights, you know? Had to. He would go out. He just said he was looking for information, checking things out. He didn't explain. I wish you had known him, he was so curious about everything, he might have told you what he was doing. All I remember is, he said something about knowing the little fish and wanting to find the big fish, but I have no idea what he meant."

I didn't say it but that might explain Sammy's death, if Serena was right about it not being an accident. If he got too curious about the wrong big fish …

Suppose the fish was a shark. Suppose it was a whole committee of sharks.

They might have posed for Eastern Shore Gothic if an artist were inspired to create such a work: Judge Wetherby in his white linen suit and Panama hat, Miss Worple in fur wrap and a little sequined turban. I was fairly sure I was awake but they looked like characters in a dream.

I was sitting on the porch, drifting between brooding and daydreaming, when they arrived. I asked about the civic meeting.

Miss Worple said it went well, and her tone indicated I'd heard all I would about that. She left Wetherby and I to amuse ourselves as we saw fit. We saw fit to sit in wicker rockers and converse.

I mentioned my continuing interest in the case of Sammy Sanchez. "It doesn't seem to me his death was very thoroughly investigated. It could be he didn't die there at the old store."

"But you have no proof."

"No, just speculating. You know of anyone who might have been out and about at night and seen something?"

He gave that some thought, not being one to blurt an answer. "Around here those who prowl at night aren't the sorts who would come forward. Well, there is Nathan McCobb. He claims to be producing a recording of some kind: *Night Sounds of the Chesapeake*. He's a strange character. I doubt he'd say much even if he knew."

"I may have met him." I recounted the incident along the sand road on my first evening there.

"Yes, that would be McCobb. Another possibility would be Clem Biggers, the game warden. Or the poachers, but of course they're not going to tell you anything; and you wouldn't even want to suggest to anyone that they might be a poacher."

"Biggers, would it be worth talking to him?"

Another lengthy pause as thoughts were composed. "Not likely, but if you catch him right you might get some sense out of him."

"I don't quite follow. He's a public servant … he must be fairly sane and sober."

We both had a laugh. "There was a time, no doubt, when he was somewhat stable. He couldn't have gotten the job in the condition he's in now. He was never exactly a straight arrow but these last few years he's getting worse. I suppose you'd find him fairly coherent in the rare event he's not drinking."

"And if he is?"

Again, Wetherby was in no hurry to answer. "You'd almost say a brain problem, undoubtedly induced by the alcohol. The Environmental Services Police would have sacked him long ago but they're overly cautious about that sort of thing these days."

"Why is that?"

He explained that there had been court cases lately where the person fired came away rich, at least on paper, because the courts allowed a personal suit against the administrator responsible for the firing. With that threat hanging over them, no one wanted to make a decision that might result in a lawsuit. "Doesn't mean Biggers would win a challenge, not by a long shot, but they won't go after him until they've got a rock solid case."

I said Biggers sounded like an unreliable source.

"And a damn shame. Game wardens, marine police, they don't get much respect around here, it's always been so. It's in the interests of those fellows to be above reproach. They're unpopular to begin with and they don't need problems added on."

"I suppose the primary problem is that they enforce the laws."

"Yes, and so you get the independent waterman versus the authority of the state, or the hunter putting food on the table in hard times versus the enforcers of regulations. There is an ... animosity ... that is not totally unjustified."

Before I could ask another question, a weird racket interrupted the tranquility of the evening. It sounded to me like the screech of a huge gear that had never known oil. "Tree frog," said Wetherby. "Cute little thing, hard to believe it can make so much noise. Bit of rain this afternoon, he thinks it's something to sing about."

My nerves settled back down. "Well, Biggers aside, is there anyone else who might have seen Sammy out there that night?"

"There is that bunch that comes out here now and then from Chincoteague. A troublesome crew. Their appearance depends on the moon or voices heard by their leader or who knows what odd motive. They hold rituals."

I asked if he meant witches.

"No, they follow a fellow, says he's an Indian. Claims Parkers Point is sacred land, they say they are eco-warriors. There's been vandalism and destruction, a few wildfires started when they come through, but nothing proven."

"Was Sammy associated with them?"

"You know, I had my suspicions. I asked Serena about it. She said Sammy got in with them because he thought they might be dealing drugs. He fancied himself some sort of secret agent, I believe."

"She didn't mention that. What came of it?"

"He wore out his welcome in a big way, accused their leader of being a phony, said they preached preservation but all they really wanted was to tear things down. The situation almost got out of hand. They ganged up and were going to cleanse him, so they said, with smoke. Can't say I like the implications of that. Nutty varmints might be cannibals, for all I know. Or maybe they are into human sacrifice. But he got away."

Oh, great. Cannibals. Sacrifices. Hey, von Klonk, have I ever got a story for you … "And was he right about the leader? Calling him a phony?"

"The fellow who leads them goes by the name Thundercloud. I don't know his heritage but if he's full-blood Native American I'll eat his feathered bonnet. There's a lot of mystical mumbo-jumbo involved. As for destruction, they've threatened to burn us out because we're trespassers on sacred land."

"I don't imagine that goes over well with the locals. I'm thinking it's the bunch Scrap Blevins accused me of being in with. Fake Indians, he said."

There was no answer and I looked at Wetherby for an indication that he'd heard me. He didn't seem inclined to answer, so I continued: "Why do they come here if they're headquartered at Chincoteague? They have the whole Assateague Island for their antics."

"They got kicked out of the park, harassing tourists and disrupting the pony roundup."

"Is it a commune? How do they support themselves?"

Another pause, to ponder. "I'd call it a cult, I suppose. Most are young people who come down from the cities when Thundercloud sends out the call. And he's got an eye for the women, mostly going through some crisis, trying to find meaning in their lives. That's what I've heard, anyway."

"What is his pitch? Is it a particular philosophy?"

"Thundercloud plays to what I call the Hollywood mentality, the folks who watched too many Disney films. From what I hear, he treats his followers like they are little children in kindergarten."

One of the first questions that comes to mind when an investigative reporter looks at a case is, *cui bono?*, Latin for *who profits?* "And there's profit in all that?"

"Oh, sure. He tells the young people, get some money from your parents and bring it to me. The women, if they haven't got it in their own right, he says take it from your husband, you need to make a contribution."

"So it's just made up that this area was sacred to the Indians?"

Wetherby searched the dark distance for an answer. "Might have been sacred for all I know. The Indians didn't leave any history in the documentary sense, so we don't know what those living here believed or didn't believe."

We sat quietly for some time, each lost, I suppose, in thoughts, or perhaps the judge was simply listening to the sounds of the night.

"Calm and peaceful, isn't it," he said at last.

"I'm suffocating in green and brown. And it all just sits there, there's nothing happening."

"Like I said before, you're looking for the city in the country, Holliday. It might take a while but the country will get you. You'll wonder what you ever saw in those madhouse cities. And I do believe you've found a few interests here."

It was foolhardy, considering my assignment, to be digging into the cult of would-be Indians, wondering what sort of rituals they practiced by the light of the full moon or whether their ecowarrior tactics, if they were more than local rumor, extended to violence.

But it was far more interesting than cruising the highway looking for tourist attractions or whatever it was I should be doing.

What was up with these pseudo-Native Americans, anyway? Were they a harmless lot of misguided fools or was there something sinister, some menace in the way they viewed critics as treasonous enemies? If they had gone after Sammy once, when he got away, what's to say they didn't go after him another time?

The questions went into the notebook of my mind for future reference.

I went back to the big question of the moment. "So far, the prospects of finding someone who might have seen Sammy that night seem slim. Anyone else who might have been out there?"

"The Point is more or less the edge of the earth as far as most folks are concerned. Just supposing Scrap put out the welcome mat, it's still not particularly inviting even to the hunter or fisherman when there are so many places easier accessed. The chances are that anyone with business there at night doesn't have any business being there." He invested a moment in further thought. "There's Red Mulroney. I can't think of any reason he'd be out to the Point at night but I know he'd like to get his hands on that property."

"The state senator. I've had the pleasure. Why would he want that tract if it's the edge the earth? Must be plenty of far more attractive properties easily had?"

"Ask *him*. I'm not one of his confidantes; we're not on the same page politically. He'd probably tell you something along the lines of how he wants it for a bird sanctuary."

"You don't seem so sure about that."

I heard a quiet chuckle. "Red's idea of a bird sanctuary would likely be a big chicken farm. He's the black sheep of an old and influential family hereabouts. At one time they owned vast acreage and held high offices. He gets elected on his daddy's name but he's nothing like his daddy; he's always angling to get in with the big money boys, this scheme and that."

"There's a scheme?"

"I have to live around here, Holliday. I've got to exercise some discretion. I've probably said too much already."

"Well, let me take a wild guess. I get the impression that Mulroney sees some profit potential in the Point and Blevins won't sell."

"Oh, Scrap has to sell and, like I said, to most people it's just a worthless patch of marsh, so it's sort of a Red or dead situation."

"What do you mean, he's got to sell?"

"Scrap is basically a good fellow despite what people say, but he got hooked on gambling in a big way. Perhaps you know how that goes for some. They lose and then they gamble to try to pay the losses. Maybe they're kiting checks to cover the losses and then they're bouncing checks and finally they're at the mercy of people who don't have any mercy."

"Sounds like a ticket to jail time. So he has to deal with Mulroney."

"Others, myself included, have tried to help. Scrap is stubborn, he wouldn't take help from friends, had to go elsewhere. Now, I think I've piled it high enough on your plate for one night, probably a lot more than a travel-writer needs to chew on."

He got up from the rocker and was heading inside to where Mardela was watching television. "There's one more person I can think of, though I seriously doubt he'd have been cruising at night. Come nighttime he's usually at some watering hole telling lies."

"And that would be?"

"The security cop, Chub Zinker. He's not really an officer of the law at all – he was hired by some of the big out-of-town landowners to watch their property – but he comes on like he's a genuine cop. Tries to throw his weight around."

"I've heard a bit about him. I didn't like what I heard."

"No need for you to worry. Once you explain why you're here he'll be all sweetness and sunshine, hoping for a favorable mention in your article."

And he left me there listening to the sounds of the night. Of which there were few, an odd thump, a distant bark, somewhere a motor. But I was more at home with the night sounds than when I first arrived.

I kept my own company for a long time.

For a while I dwelt on the way Wetherby had stopped short in his comments about Red Mulroney and the property at the Point.

What in the world could an ambitious politician find of interest in a desolate, isolated marshland like Parkers Point?

And, if there was something being kept hush-hush, had Sammy got wind of it?

In a strange way I felt related to Sammy. Not related exactly but kindred … a kid full of curiosity, adventurous, maybe a bit of a troublemaker, full of grand ideas, seen as a bother by most of the adults around him … I knew a kid like that … long, long ago.

Chapter Fourteen

You might think I'd have had sense enough to get an earlier start, but I was still in mulling mode. At the center of my meditation was a vision of Sammy searching for something. I didn't know what. Sammy the junior investigator, the trouble-making snoop with a knack for crossing people.

Maybe if I had a year to spare I could get a grip on the various parts of the puzzle.

The more I learned about the situation, the more it was becoming a question of who wasn't upset with Sammy for one reason or another. But angry enough to kill?

If he'd been shot, there would be plenty of suspects. I'd bet most everyone around here had a gun, some had dozens. I know, doesn't make them homicidal maniacs. I could see where, around here, a gun is a tool. It puts meat on the table, and protects against the rabid fox.

Bring the subject up and the locals would be quick to tell you, the founding fathers weren't talking about sport when they stipulated a right to bear arms. You can counter that times have changed. And they'll tell you, with law enforcement few and far between, knowing most people are armed is the best way to discourage prowlers.

If you get out of theory and look at how guns are used, there's country practicality versus city mayhem. But I doubted von Klonk would go for an essay, however brilliant and insightful, on the difference between city guns and country guns.

An unfortunate consequence of sitting around thinking deep thoughts was that I was there when von Klonk called. "Where is my story, Holliday?"

Good question. What could I do but bluff? "It's down to crossing *T*s and dotting *I*s, darn near on the fax machine."

"I'm on to you, hotshot. You haven't written the first *I* or *T*. Sit your ass down at a typewriter and get me that story, now."

The situation called for a diversion. Was he at all human? I mean, maybe this Gestapo commandant routine was just a front, his way of keeping the world at bay. And even if he was a member of some subspecies, the last stand of an evolutionary dead end, maybe he might yet be endowed with some human qualities. Mightn't he? I mean, humans lived side by side with Neanderthals, so I've read. There was probably cross-breeding.

The demons that occasionally offer such bad advice or goad me in an unhealthy direction dared me to go on. "You know, editor sir, there is a genuine story here, one that could no doubt expand your readership. I believe it's a real murder mystery with quite a few fascinating angles." In my temporary fit of madness I thought somehow the word 'fascinating' would have a mesmerizing effect, and I had to resist a temptation to use it over and over again.

Von Klonk didn't react. Could he actually be considering the idea? But no, it became quickly evident that the silence was only the time it took to draw the deep breath necessary to fuel an eruption.

"Have you lost the few remaining functional shards of your so-called mind, Holliday? *Here & There* is not a sensational rag. No scandal, no crime, no murders. Your job is to decorate around the ads, pretty words to go with pretty pictures. That's it. I may have made a mistake taking you on, but it is easily corrected, there's always some hungry hack out there waiting for my call."

Hungry hack? Von Klonk was becoming private enemy number one. I looked through the window to the surrounding woods. I could just drop the phone and wander off; to where I don't know, just leave this crazy life behind.

Whatever became of that travel-writer fellow? Oh, one fine spring day the beauty of the marsh just reached and grabbed him, got hold and wouldn't let go, pulled like a mystical magnet and that was the last seen of him ...

"Well, sir, how about sea monsters?"

"You've got sea monsters down there?"

"One in particular. So they say. Chessie."

"You're putting me on."

"There are lots of locals who will testify to Chessie's existence."

"What, after they empty the whiskey jug? Forget it, forget sea monsters. We're not a tabloid, Holliday. Focus on food. The food industry spends big bucks attracting customers. Do you think you might be able to focus on food? It's not asking a whole lot."

"Food. Sure. How about if I just put a spin on what I've already got? No doubt my hostess has a recipe for that local delicacy, sea monster stew."

"You're aberrant, you know that? You have a serious case of flake. Get on with it, Holliday. We're a monthly not an annual. And may I remind you that your position is very temporary unless you miraculously prove to be of some slight value to this organization. Thirty days. Tick, tick, tick."

Unless, in my alleged flakiness, I was into talking to myself, the conversation ended abruptly.

The geography of the Chesapeake Bay's eastern shore is simple to master. It's a peninsula stretching from southern Delaware, down through Maryland, and then on to Cape Charles in Virginia and the seventeen-mile long bridge-tunnel to Norfolk.

That's about two hundred miles, north to south. But most tourists follow Route 50, located about midway on the peninsula, the east-west artery through the Maryland portion, leading to Ocean City and other vacationland beaches to the north.

The focus of my article was supposed to be what is called the Lower Shore, a region of few commercial tourist attractions. The big draw is the town of Chincoteague, Virginia, and adjacent Assateague, a sandy barrier island famous for its herds of wild horses. Assateague is part national and part state park. Nearby is Wallops Island, a rocket launch site not quite the Cape Canaveral of the mid-Atlantic, but with aspirations.

But von Klonk had warned me off of Chincoteague and so I had to look elsewhere.

Most of the guidebook entries on the Lower Shore are what you might call drive-bys, historic homes and other structures in private hands, or sites of various notable incidents in the past, identified by historical markers but otherwise not in evidence. There are many references to what could have been seen a hundred and more years ago, back to colonial times.

Among several exceptions to the drive-by rule is Onancock, Virginia, three hundred years old and an important port from colonial times on into the recent past.

Onancock welcomes tourists, but without so much grandstanding as the resorts. It has treasure-filled antique shops as well as boutiques, galleries and restaurants, but there remains strong evidence of traditional life on the Eastern Shore – genuine local food markets, hardware stores, boutiques and galleries, a bakery. There's a population that traces back generations, mixed with a good many newcomer retirees and others from far afield who've found a place they want to call home. And as for homes, there are many grand old residences in the style that elsewhere are likely converted into funeral homes or apartments.

It's still an industrious seafood town. The harbors at the far end of Market Street host as many workboats as pleasure craft. It seemed to me Onancock might be the hook to hang my story on.

"But, truth is, it's a lot easier just to go to the store and buy a can of Old Bay, same kind of flavor, just as good. Not saying I'd dream of doing such a thing."

And what was that all about? Well, choosing among Onancock's cafes, bistros and pubs was no easy task but I'd opted for a side-street mom-and-pop-style little restaurant that the guidebook listed as specializing in soul food.

The interior was as sunny as a fine spring day, the warm yellow walls with white trim mirroring the colors of the checked tablecloths.

I was a bit early for lunch, the lone customer. From the kitchen came an invitation, "Sit on down, hon. Be with you in a minute."

I took a seat. I mean, didn't I need a good dose of nourishment for the soul? It was there, just for the listening, in the form of a sort of bluesy rendition of Amazing Grace coming from an overhead speaker. But somehow, sitting at one of several little tables, glancing over the simple, hearty menu, I just couldn't find an appetite for fried this or fried that, chicken to fish to venison, or for black eyed peas, collard greens, cornbread. Another day, most assuredly, but for this visit I settled on the shrimp boil.

The lady who was with me in a minute was, as they say, ample of figure though she must have needed a stepladder to reach the higher kitchen shelves. She took my order and introduced herself as Cordelia. "I'm the owner. And waitress, cook and cashier. Something to drink with that?"

I asked for unsweetened iced tea.

The meal was a flavorful treat, a pile of tender shrimp with potatoes, carrots, onions, corn fresh off the cob and thin rounds of spicy Andouille sausage.

"Compliments to the chef."

"That's me. I'm all there is, if it needs doing, it's up to me." There was nothing frantic about how she covered the various responsibilities; it was more of a flow from role to role.

I asked what sort of spices went into the boil. She mentioned pinches of paprika, ginger, cayenne, black pepper, nutmeg, ground bay leaf … there was more, but she saw that I was a bit out of my culinary league and added the comment about Old Bay.

Dessert? I ordered coffee and the Smith Island Cake. I've got to tell you, Smith Island cake is unreal. It comes from an old colony located on an island about twelve miles out in the Chesapeake, long isolated, lately getting attention for a cake concoction of eight to sixteen layers, each layer separated by a thin spreading of fudge, and all topped with a peanut butter cup sprinkle. The menu proudly announced it as the official dessert of Maryland. Stand up and salute, if you can stand with a belly full of Smith Island cake.

There was hot sauce on the table and I was tempted to dose up my coffee, but somehow the thought of pepper chasing around after that sugary desert didn't sit well.

When the check came I asked about muskrat.

"I don't serve it. Some do because it's popular at certain times, you'll see church suppers and fire-hall dinners made of it. I don't serve possum, I don't serve muskrat, none of that. Tourists don't get it, they'd think I was cooking the zoo, see what I mean?"

"You could give it some fancy name, make them think it's a delicacy ..."

She mocked a frown and shook her head. "Some folks hereabouts call it marsh rabbit, but it ain't no rabbit."

Von Klonk having warned me off of any mention in the article, I asked, just out of curiosity, how it was prepared.

"Simple enough. Skin and gut it, then you let it sit overnight in salt water, then parboil it. Roll it in flour that's got Old Bay type seasonings. Put it in a pan with a quarter cup of vinegar and a quarter cup of water, lay some bacon slices over it. Bake it 'til it's done. Pull it from the oven and call the dogs."

"You make it sound almost tempting. But you don't serve it. Still, I guess most of what you serve is produced locally?"

"Sure, as much as possible."

"Your venison steaks, for instance?"

Her smile faded and she folded her arms. "Mine comes from the game farm, of course. But it isn't too damn smart to ask or to tell about such things."

I was forgetting for the moment that I wasn't in the investigative racket anymore. "Such as, menu items governed by fish and wildlife laws?"

"Such as, whatever you're fishing for won't be found in these waters, mister. You can pay now." She marched to the register, obviously ready to see me out the door.

I'd really put my foot in it. Her jaw was set, her look cold and distant.

My hostess followed me outside. She looked up and down the street. "Mister, you're not from around here so I'm going to tell you something: You don't talk poaching. There's people in jail, people lost cars, trucks, boats, guns. There's poor people got fines that put a real hurtin' on them. You just don't talk about it."

"Thanks, Cordelia. Sorry for being careless."

"The man gets the wrong idea, he'll have me staked out. I won't get no business at all." She grimaced, nodded a goodbye and turned back to her business. And, yes, I should have minded my own.

I visited a few shops and had a look at the historic Ker mansion. Onancock deserved an article all its own. Maybe I would tip a few of my travel-writer buddies to my find. Or maybe I'd keep it to myself. After all, I was now a travel-writer, wasn't I? I could get some business cards and letterheads printed up. If I ever had a permanent address again.

Chapter Fifteen

I toured a few side roads looking at places that used to be, tumbled chimneys and boarded up doors and windows, not really paying much attention. Driving time can be thinking time, if you don't numb your brain with music or the rantings of a talk show motor-mouth.

It was beginning to dawn on me that the Sammy question was becoming my therapy, not hardly a happy pill, but somehow the medicine I needed to keep from plummeting into a depressive abyss.

Sure, I'd found a way, at least for the moment, to pay the basics, a room in a motel if I needed it, probably some no-stars crash pad where drug deal arguments woke you up in the middle of the night, and I could handle the credit card minimums, car insurance premiums, all the nibbles and bites involved in living this side of the homeless shelter. But I sure didn't have my heart in scribbling sweet nothings for *Here & There*.

So I guess I was fortunate that the Sammy problem was big enough to crowd the bleak and depressing thoughts out of my head. It provided a shot at recovering some self-respect, a chance to be someone's hero. Even if I couldn't deliver good news to Serena, I might at least bring her some peace of mind, some relief from the torment of not knowing.

Finding what became of Sammy didn't have to sidetrack the job at hand, if I used uncharacteristic good judgment, if I struck a balance between the two projects. After all, the *Here & There* article was something I could write in my sleep, wasn't it? But if so, why hadn't I done it? Maybe I was up against some kind of writer's block?

I was hashing all this out with myself as I headed back to Bay Breezes when I noticed a car with a little blue light flashing on the roof. I'd seen that car before, pulling away from Serena's trailer.

In the city it could be any sort of lunatic or mugger impersonating a police officer. I wouldn't have stopped until I saw a regular squad car. But out here I wasn't likely to locate a squad car anywhere nearby, so I took the risk and pulled over.

Whoever was tailing me pulled in behind and a uniform got out and walked toward me.

The rearview mirror told me there was too much of whoever he was for the uniform, particularly where the tailored shirt hugged a big middle like the plastic wrap on a bulging supermarket roast.

Closer, his mug brought to mind a folk-art face jug, the features purposely disproportionate. Squinty little eyes belonged on another face, one with smaller ears and a less prominent nose.

I sat, hands on the steering wheel in a display of innocence, wondering how I was going to squeeze a speeding ticket into a very low budget expense account.

"Welcome to East Westerly, sir. You know, you were doing thirty-nine in a thirty zone?"

"Sorry about that, officer. Thing is, you round that curve and the speed drops before you can fully adjust."

"Oh, it is a bother to newcomers, that's for sure. If you don't mind my asking, what's your business around here?"

"Happens to be the beach I washed up on."

"I asked a reasonable question."

"For what reason? Okay, I'm a travel-writer, here by invitation of leaders in government and industry. I'm supposed to write it up as a welcoming and wonderful place to visit." If this guy was acting in any official capacity, why wasn't he asking for my driving license and registration?

By now I'd noticed that his industrial blue uniform was sparse on insignia. A logo on his blue baseball cap was repeated over one shirt pocket and there were patches at the shoulder on each arm, but nothing in the way of rank and insignia.

He surveyed the empty roadway behind us and up ahead. "Not many visitors out this way."

"I guess they're trying to fix that. Look, I'm new to the area; I didn't see the sign until it was too late."

I'd seen that smile before. I think it was in a documentary about crocodiles.

"Don't worry about it, sir. I'm Chub Zinker, in the private employ of the property owners' association here, not authorized to issue tickets, see, so this here is a warning only, and I'm sure you won't make the same mistake again."

"You're not a cop? What's with the uniform and flashing light?"

He looked down at his belly and then at his car, as if noticing for the first time that he was wearing a uniform and had a blue flashing light on his car roof. Being as bemused as I was, he let my question pass. "Now, as a travel-writer, no doubt you want to make the acquaintance of the real high-rollers and celebrities around here, like the ones I work for, right? I'm the man to make the introductions, that's me."

"Well, that certainly makes you a good person to know. Maybe you could just gather up some autographs for me. I could do the interviews later."

Zinker didn't seem at all sure how to take that. He decided to play it as it lay. "I'll see what I can do for you."

"I'm staying at Bay Breezes, Miss Worple's place. Is she a member of the outfit that employs you?"

"No, not hardly. It's mostly out of town millionaires that have vacation homes or hunting lodges, important people from up Washington, Baltimore, Philly. Here's my card, call any time." He didn't wear a badge but his card did.

"I might do that. I'll probably see you around. I'll be here for a few days."

"Great. That's really great. But, look, just a helpful hint, don't poke around too much. People don't like it."

"Who's poking around?"

"Well, take for instance, you were seen calling on that Sanchez woman. How does she fit in to a travel story? I mean, if you'll pardon my curiosity."

Given that he wasn't a cop, my inclination was to mention that it wasn't any of his damn business what I was doing. But I figured that at least for the moment it was best to play along, so I tried to keep it civil. Fairly civil, anyway. No doubt I sounded annoyed. "I went to see her at the request of Miss Worple, she was concerned that Ms Sanchez hadn't shown up for work. And, as a matter of my own curiosity, where's the crime in that?"

"Troubles she's had, you know … I take a special interest in her safety, that kind of thing."

"Well, I did hear that you scared her real good with some story about INS being after her."

"Oh, I've got my sources. I've got connections, don't you worry about that."

My bullshit detector flashed. Maybe it was time to talk about something else. "What's with the roll of duct tape tied to your belt?"

"Oh, that? It's like this: Say I've got to restrain a perpetrator trespassing on a property under my supervision. I could use handcuffs and cause serious embarrassment, see, among their friends and neighbors. But I just use duct tape. It keeps it kind of, you know, friendly. I try to keep things friendly."

"No joke? And instead of mace you use WD-40?"

He clenched his fists but the smile stayed in place. "That's a good one, mister. I'll have to remember that. You got any more cute ideas?"

"No thanks necessary, officer, just being friendly."

"You just call me Chub. How's that for friendly?" A bully's taunt would have sounded friendlier.

A big black Cadillac with tinted windows blazed past us doing about seventy. "Shouldn't you go after that one?"

"Not really. It's the preachers from Baltimore, nice bunch of guys. I stopped them once, got a hundred dollar tip out of it. No need to push my luck."

I heard a hundred dollar hint. "So speed limits disappear for the right price?"

"They know how to be friendly. Offered to take me down to the creek and baptize me. I figured word would get around, me being baptized by a bunch of black preachers. What if somebody took pictures? But I didn't say nothing, just *thanks anyway*."

"I don't have a spare hundred, I work for Scrooge."

"Maybe you should find another line of work."

"So I could afford protection against this kind of hassle, is that what you mean?"

He looked at me like an entomologist examining a previously unknown bug. He patted the pistol at his side as if to say, "I'm not an entomologist, I'm an exterminator." But what he actually said was: "You have a nice day now."

Back at Bay Breezes there was a message to call Barney Cole. He asked how the crab feast had gone and I assured him a good time was had by all.

"You're getting around okay, finding what you need?"

"Doing all right so far."

"And the Sammy stuff? You seemed kind of intrigued there for a while, anything new on that front?"

"It's as much a mystery as ever, Barney. Didn't think you were interested."

"No, not really."

"You have a peculiar way of showing it."

"Anyway, give me a call if I can help with anything. Talk to you later."

Weird? Weird. Unless my instincts were leading me astray, the point of his call was to see if I'd done any digging on Sammy's death. And, if my recall was functioning, hadn't he fairly much blown that off as an unimportant matter?

Cole didn't strike me as a good sounding board, someone you could share ideas with in the hope the exchange might bring some clarity. If I had him pegged right, he was a taker, giving as little as necessary in the process. That was just the way he struck me.

I escorted my wayward thoughts to the front porch.

Judge Wetherby was sitting there when I stepped out. He was smoking a cigar. "Mardela hates these things. You care for one?"

"I'm easily persuaded, thank you."

"I know where she hides a jug of bourbon if you're in the mood for a chaser."

Sore subject. "I've chased and been chased about enough for one lifetime, Judge. You go ahead, I'll pass."

He made no move. "Well, how goes the article?" When Wetherby said 'well', he said it all the way to the bottom of the well.

"Slow. I got interested in what happened to Sammy and it's throwing me off course."

"How so?"

"Oh, I've been asking around a bit. Seems like most everyone I've talked to has some grudge against young Mister Sanchez."

His questions were noncommittal, simply urging me on. "Who have you talked to?"

"Blevins, Cole, Mulroney. And I met your local constable, if you can call him that, but I didn't get into the Sammy thing with him."

"Zinker. As I told you, he's just a security guard with delusions of grandeur. The bunch that employs him should be called the Outsider Land Grabber Association, there's nobody local involved. In fact I'd say the locals resent their attitude, insinuating that they need protection against thieves."

"I'm not sure I follow."

"You don't get a lot of strangers out this way, so who is Zinker hired to protect property from, exactly?"

It was a question that didn't need answering. I countered with my own, which, it seemed to me, did need answering. "Why is he even necessary? What about the regular police or sheriff's department?"

"This isn't a rich county by a long shot. So the population centers get the attention. There have to be priorities. You'd wait half an hour or more for a proper cop to get out here."

"Zinker stopped me, gave me a warning for being just over the speed limit. Nothing on paper, just verbal."

"Locals would kick his butt if he tried to pull that traffic stop stuff on them. They know he has no authority. So he targets lost tourists who're caught by the shift down to thirty miles an hour from fifty when they make that curve coming into the village. I suppose more than a few slip him a gratuity, thinking they've avoided a ticket."

"He seemed concerned that I'd visited Serena. Is he investigating Sammy's death?"

It wasn't so dark that I couldn't see the smoke ring the Judge blew, a big floating zero that evaporated into mist. "Not really his function. I think it's just he's taken a shine to Serena."

"And is that shine reflected?"

"Not in the slightest, as far as I can see."

If anything, it seemed to me, Serena wanted Zinker to quit pestering her. "That was the impression I got, as well. But I was wondering, as much as Zinker must prowl around out here, do you think he knows more than he's told about what happened to Sammy?"

"Couldn't say. He and I aren't conversant like that. We keep an eye on him, though. One of these days he'll overplay his hand. He's up to mischief of some sort."

"Meaning something other than petty graft, or whatever you'd call this game with the tourists?"

"Maybe." He didn't seem inclined to go further.

I let it drop. I'd been thinking about Serena. I'd seen her at, I suppose, her worst, but my mind's eye put her at her best. The problem with feelings of attraction is that, like the other emotional currents that run through us, they want to do something, to bust out into some kind of expression.

The psychologists say it's possible, depending on one's talents and interests, to write the feelings out, paint them out, run or yoga them out. But in my experience it's damned difficult to force the focus in a direction other than where those feelings want to go.

Maybe it's a character defect, a failure in self-discipline. I could fill a book with the trouble it's led to, when you just let 'er rip and take that wacky ride.

I shook off what were becoming worrisome thoughts and listened to a sound in the dark distance. It wasn't the screech owl, it was the more common one, the *who-who* owl.

Chapter Sixteen

What was the story with the microphone man I met out in the woods on my first night in town? He seemed a likely candidate for having spotted Sammy on the fateful night. From what Wetherby had told me, his name was McCobb. I couldn't find anyone by that name in the local directory but Wetherby gave me a number after I'd sworn never to reveal how I came by it.

"How did you get this number?"

"I think it was an owl told me."

"Right. An owl named Wetherby. I knew he couldn't be trusted."

"Who?"

"Cut the crap. What's on your mind?"

"I'm a travel-writer, like I told you. I'd like to know more about your project, collecting night sounds."

"Sure you would. OK, I'll meet you, but not around here. You know the lighthouse at Assateague?"

"If I recall, the guidebook said it's about a hundred and fifty feet tall and painted with red and white stripes. I feel fairly confident about spotting it."

"Can you be there in an hour?"

"Sure thing. I guess you'll be the guy in the dark glasses and trench-coat?"

He hung up. I was on my way out the door when Miss Worple said I had a call. Of course it was von Klonk, looking for leads on potential advertisers, demanding names and phone numbers.

"Coming right up. I'd really like to tell you all the great stuff I've pulled together, but I've got an appointment."

"If this is more of your bullshit I hope that's an appointment for a job interview. Maybe you'll get lucky, find your lifework down there, herding chickens, something suited to your talents." Click.

On the way to Assateague I had a good talk with myself. It was time to at least cruise the main highway and pick up some business cards, time to feed the advertising sharks.

And I would do that, just as soon as I'd met with McCobb.

It was hard to believe but there it was, *it* being a fellow in a trench coat, Bogart fedora and dark glasses. "So, Holliday, how are you liking the Eastern Shore so far?"

"I should have come later in the season when there are more tourists around and more shops and restaurants open."

"Later is hotter. And there's traffic, you wouldn't believe the traffic. A million or so visitors here at Assateague each year. And you get hurricanes."

"Hurricanes are a regular thing?"

"Sure. The wind tries to tear the place apart. You wouldn't want to be here. Nowhere to hide. But then come maybe four beautiful months of autumn, something like the Mediterranean, the best time around here. You wanted to talk to me for some reason."

"Well, I was generally curious about what's out there at night in places like the one where we met."

He was into that earlier tactic, moving in too close, like there was a need for confidentiality. "Night birds, of course, that's what I'm after, mostly. Screech owl and the great horned owl and so on. Bob White and Chuck Will's Widow, a few more. It's when the deer move around, much safer for them in the dark. And there are foxes, possums and raccoons. Trees creak, the wind moans. Sometimes you hear sounds you can't identify, strange sounds, shrieks and cries. Hunter and hunted, death and dying."

Was it the sea breeze? Listening to him, I felt a chill. "It doesn't sound very commercial. Wouldn't the market be for sweet and pretty bird sounds, nature's music?"

"Depends on the purpose. Imagine putting someone in solitary and playing the chatter of a thousand starlings for three days and nights. They'd tell you anything. I blend the weirdness I collect into something sounds like a riot in a locny bin, it's what my clients want."

I was curious, of course, but thought it best not ask about his clients. "In regard to what's out there at night, you haven't mentioned people."

"People? Lovers who can't risk or afford a motel room. Drunks hiding out from the do-gooders and nags. There are people out there, most of them making trouble of some sort for themselves or others. Sometimes you hear a powerboat out on the Bay. Sometimes you see strange lights."

McCobb matched every step I took backward or to the side. He didn't actually take steps. He slid. It was a weird dance.

"The Judge mentioned poachers."

"I don't bother with them except to collect the sounds of gunshots. It's no concern of mine."

I told him I'd worked up some curiosity over the death of Sammy Sanchez and asked if he had any ideas about it.

"I know who you mean. I'd noticed him, prowling around at night, thought he might be a lookout for drug smugglers. He wouldn't be the first to come to a bad end in Bay Country, that's certain. I haven't looked into it."

"It's not really my thing either, McCobb. But I've met his mother, and she's convinced he was murdered. I'm trying to help her."

"That's noble. If I run across anything pertinent, and if I happen to be feeling noble at the time, I'll be in touch."

"I'd appreciate that. But you're sure you don't recall anything unusual about the night Sammy died?"

"Seems to me it was that night I heard a vehicle hit a deer. Happens all the time, none of my business. I was hoping for collectible noise, a squeal of brakes, but there was nothing, just the thump."

"I'm wondering what exactly is your business."

"Wait here a minute, I'll be right back."

An old man and, I presumed, his daughter showed up to marvel at the lighthouse. "I'll tell you one thing for sure," the old man said to the young girl, "if you owed a fellow a lighthouse, I'm darn certain he'd take that one and consider the debt well paid."

The girl, college age, blond, a candidate for Miss Assateague, looked over at me and smiled. I wish they wouldn't do that, it was catching. I waited some while but McCobb didn't come back.

I spent some time driving Rt 13 collecting business cards and brochures, mostly from tobacco outlets that thrive due to low Virginia taxes. The same shops usually offer a clutter of souvenirs: caps, cups, tee shirts, wall plaques. With relative ease I resisted any urge to own a coffee cup celebrating Big Assawoman Bay, an inlet near Ocean City. According to the guidebook, the meaning of its Native American name is unknown. I gathered further plunder from the racks at the visitor information centers located at the Maryland-Virginia border.

What are chances I'd ever have a real job again? I felt like I had about as much connection to the news business as a kid with a paper route. In short order I was disgusted with the project and, without really thinking about what I was doing, found myself headed back to Bay Breezes.

You can run but you can't hide; isn't that what they say?

Von Klonk again. Didn't the guy take a day off? It's one thing to work straight through when you're on assignment, but wouldn't you think someone with a cushy editor job would knock off once in a while?

Not von Klonk. "I need that list for advertising, Holliday. Now."

"It's coming at you, soon as I get into town and a fax machine."

"There's no fax where you're staying? Are you holed up in a cave?"

"Primitive is a fair assessment. They message by jungle drum out here."

"Jokes, jokes, forget the jokes and get me that list. By the way, I hear there's one of the biggest marinas on the East Coast down there, let me find the note. Oh, yeah, Somers Cove at Crisfield, Maryland. Big marina, must be a hopping place, Holliday. There'll be restaurants, hotels, all kinds of stuff. Go have a look."

"Last time we talked I got the impression I should wrap it up and head back so you could fire me."

His initial reply was to himself, a muffled but devious chuckle. And then: "Fire you? Holliday, you're the ace, you're our star. Perish the thought."

"Rest of the staff quit to look for real jobs?"

Click.

I'd put together a list that should bear a resemblance to what von Klonk wanted. I stopped at Cole's office to use the fax. Being a tourist outfit, he was open on Saturday.

Cole didn't bother shifting from his leaned back, feet on the desk pose. He didn't even invite me to take a seat, but I did. "I should boot you out of here, Holliday. What kind of crap did you pull with Mulroney? He says you're a crazy radical, ought to be fed to the sharks."

I feigned surprise. "That's kind of extreme. I mean, surely he knows a reporter is supposed to be adversarial, ask the tough questions."

"Then he took it back, said he didn't want to get busted for shark abuse. I don't know if I'll ever get another favor out of him. A state senator, for God's sake. I need him."

"Sounds serious."

"You're damn right. He wheels and deals with the kind of people who pay top price for public relations. He could steer me into some lucrative contracts. Which, at this point in time, would be most helpful."

"Don't sweat it. He'll be tickled when he sees the article. I'll testify that he makes the lame to walk, feeds the masses turning cow patties into crab cakes."

Cole rubbed his temples. "Don't they have a sane, normal writer they could send down?"

"Nope. Just talked to editor and I'm it. Everybody else quit."

"Your publication is doomed."

"Have a little faith, Cole. By the way, the editor also said he wants something on Crisfield. Anything worth writing about in Crisfield? He mentioned a big marina."

"Crisfield, well, it's in a bit of a slump right now, not a whole heck of a lot going on except for the festivals. I mean, sweet little town, lots of great people, but there's not a lot to lure the tourist right at the moment, good many places closed. You ought to come back for the crab races, that's a pretty big deal there."

Crab races. "The boss wants Crisfield. There must be some angle. What's the photo op situation?"

"Well, the best shot is from offshore. You're a photographer too?"

"No, but I get points if I provide some ideas."

He made a little box shape with his fingers and peered through it. "Coming in off the Bay, it looks like a happening place. Tell you what, I'll get you out on a work boat, take a look at Crisfield from the water, maybe you'll get an angle out of that."

"I'm not real big on boat trips."

"You'll love it. Honey of a craft this one, weathered many a storm. They don't make them like that anymore. Old wooden boat. Everything's fiberglass these days. Hang on, maybe I can set it up for this afternoon, might as well take advantage of a decent day. You never know around here."

Cole sat upright and made a phone call. He rolled his eyes toward the ceiling a couple of times in the course of the conversation, repeating something he'd just said. He assured whoever was on the other end of the line that he would pay for gas.

"Captain Lucky Brevard, he'll take you out, that's what they call him, Lucky."

"We met. Somehow I don't find it very reassuring that they call him Lucky."

"Oh, it's just a joke. He's had some hard knocks so that's what they call him. He's a bit, I don't know, eccentric. But he must be a good captain. He's old; bad captains don't get old."

"Well, good of you to cover the gas. I don't think my editor would go for an expense like that."

"I was about to ask for your credit card number."

"Forget it. Account's frozen."

"I'll take it up with your editor."

"Good luck. What's in it for the captain?"

"Lucky wants me to steer charter business his way, so he doesn't mind volunteering for a little promotional work."

Where was the catch, what trap was I being baited into? "You mentioned a work boat. Isn't that different from a charter boat?"

"Yes. He hasn't got the charter boat yet. But, to hear him talk, he'll have it any day now. You'll want to change into casual clothes. Those old wooden boats, sometimes there's chinks out and you get a lot of water coming in."

Cole was being helpful but I wasn't at all sure I wanted that kind of help. "The thing is, these *are* casual clothes, as casual as I ever get. And another thing, I don't think I care to go out on a boat that takes in a lot of water. Just doesn't sound like a pleasure cruise."

"Nothing to worry about, Holliday. Brevard's got pumps, and he hasn't sunk in fifty years. Of course, maybe that's why they call him Lucky."

I still didn't like the idea. "I don't have a lot of boating experience. Friends have told me about spending half a trip leaning over the side."

Cole's smile was like that of a used car salesman who just talked you into the most catastrophic wreck on the lot. "Brevard's tub isn't some racing boat, it's an easy ride and I'm sure you'll feel energized by the salt air and cradle-rock over the little waves. It's a real get-away, nothing but calm water and clear sky, serenading gulls and leaping fish."

"I read a spiel like that in your plagiarized brochure." Looking through material from the visitor center, I'd seen several word-for-word instances.

"Plagiarized? You sound like Sammy, he was fussing about that. My researchers let me down, gave me notes without attribution."

My bet was, he had as many researchers as I did, which could be counted on an amputated finger. "All right, so I'm going boating. Any survival advice?"

"Stop by Wal-Mart. Some khakis and a sport shirt, sneakers or boat shoes, that won't set you back much. And a hat. Get a hat with a brim, not a cap."

"What's with the hat?"

You'd think he had notes inscribed on his glossy fingernails, the way he looked at them instead of the listener. "There's watermen around here haven't got as many ears as they're supposed to have because they wear baseball caps, the sun bakes their ears, they get skin cancer."

On defensive impulse, I massaged an ear. "Hat with a brim, check. I need all the ears I've got."

It was a rare occasion; Cole actually made solid eye contact. "Glad to see you've put that Sammy stuff aside. Locals don't like outsiders poking into their affairs, you know what I mean?"

"I might. I'm hearing it often enough. What I don't get is why you care."

He looked studious, concerned. "Suppose people get the

wrong impression, decide you're here to stir up trouble. It'd be guilt by association because I brought you here. I'm in business, Holliday. Can't afford that."

I wasn't buying it. Cole was just a little too interested in knowing what I was interested in. But I hadn't figured a way to make him show his hand.

I got myself an outfit. I hadn't worn tennis shoes since childhood, but they were on sale. None of it was my style, though maybe I needed to get over being hung up on style. If I blew this job and had to live out of my car, I might be outfitting from the bargain rack at Goodwill stores.

Chapter Seventeen

My instructions were to meet Captain Lucky and his boat at the public dock at Crisfield. I'd know his boat because the name *Better Days* was written on the side.

"Be careful on the finger pier. It's a little shaky."

A little? A finger pier is an elevated wooden footpath out over the water and about as stable as a mudslide. I felt like a hula dancer and was fairly sure I'd tumble in and drown. I got on board but I wasn't at all certain I could stay upright. My legs were a lot happier on solid ground. I sat down without ceremony on a built-in storage bin.

"You'll get used to it."

"Sorry, I flunked Navy in school. How come there are so many boats in the harbor, not a good day to go out?"

"Sunday. Recreational fishing only. No commercial fishing on Sunday."

"Why is that?"

"Most around here go to church, and it's a mandatory day off."

"Mandatory?"

"It's the rules; give the fish a rest."

"Whose rules?"

My barrage of questions was met with a tired, 'don't you know anything?' look. "State bunch, Mother Nature's police."

Lucky slipped loose the ropes that held us to the dock and disappeared into the pilot's cabin, a small shed at the front of the boat. Momentarily the engine fired up and we were off.

The engine rumbled and grumbled as we pulled out of the slip and then it kicked up to a nerve-rattling roar once we hit open water. I had it in my head that boats sort of glide across the water but Brevard's seemed to be muscling its way through like a swimmer fighting a riptide. Sport boats zipped past us.

There wasn't much point trying to talk over the sound of the engine and the rush of the wind. Well, no point for me to try to talk, being used to a quieter environment. Lucky, on the other hand, was right at home. "Diesels run a little rough, that's typical. Fairly typical. Haven't been keeping her up like I should, just didn't have the money. Time for a new boat, soon as I find treasure."

He slowed the boat. The sound level was down to nerve-rattling grumble. "It's safe, though?"

"Should be. Can you swim?"

"Across a pool. Not across a bay."

"Well, that beats what I could do. Anyway, the radio seems to be working today, and that's a blessing. We'll hear if there's any advisories. "

"Advising about what?"

"Storms, mostly. You don't want to be out here in five and six foot seas. Gets dicey."

The racket coming from the radio was in a language that sounded almost foreign, I could make out a word now and then but had no idea what was being said. "What are they talking about?"

"Weather. That's what a waterman cares about, weather and the price of the catch."

"They're talking English? I'd heard they've got a language all their own."

"The fellow on there now is from Tangier Island, I guess you'd call it the King's English. Though I never heard a king talk. Watch your footing, it gets slippery, it does."

The reason it got slippery was that water was spurting in through chinks in the sides of the boat. We hadn't gone far from the marina when Capt Lucky cut the engine and came out of the little cabin. "There's your view of Crisfield, that's what Cole said to show you. Pretty as a picture, ain't it?"

From where we sat the town had all the characteristics of a thriving waterfront community – commercial wharves, packing and canning factories, a huge ice plant, streets lined with shops and homes, church steeples, a big brick institution that turned out to be a hospital, a railroad bed, and of course the marina. The trouble being most of it was in neglect, not really doing what it was it meant to do. It wasn't exactly a ghost town but it was headed in a spooky direction.

I turned my attention back to the boat. "What kind of a boat is this? I think Cole called it a work boat."

"That, but it's rightly called a dead-rise, that's the real name because it's built for getting into the oyster beds where the water's shallow. So you've got a vee bottom instead of rounded. That's the way they built the old skipjacks. You won't find 'em anywhere but around here. If you find 'em. You don't see many skipjacks anymore."

"Seems kind of like the whole way of life here is headed into the museums."

"It's a hard life making a living on the water. The government would just as soon be rid of us, the government would. We're just in the way of their science projects. I don't blame the young people for moving away."

"Young people aren't taking up the work?"

"You don't walk in off the street into commercial fishing any more than you do farming, and that's a fact. Family thing, you learn it young."

I played the dumb card, asking what the big deal was, all you have to do is go out in your boat and catch fish.

As expected, Lucky looked at me like I had a serious case of stupid. "Just go out and catch fish. Some go out a hundred miles and more over in the ocean, some dredge, some use haul nets, some like me set maybe a hundred pots. There's ones that do it all, depending on the season and how the catch is going. It ain't just fish, or crabs, or oysters either, there's lobster and conch right here on the ocean side. Down on the James, down in that area, there's a lot go after eels, sell them to Europe. And then there's the huge trawlers in fleets. Why, they grab up millions of tons of menhaden, spot the schools from the sky, from airplanes."

I remembered reading about how there used to be wars between the fishermen of Virginia and Maryland. They were of such intensity that the states set up patrols to keep the peace. I asked about the wars.

"Lasted about a hundred years, and that's a fact. But those days are long gone. All that's left is stories. You might have disagreements now and then but nothing like what used to be, not a lot of shooting, that sort of thing. If there's any wars, it's between the fishermen and the government. And, to be honest, even that's not really war anymore, just folks trying not to get caught."

"Caught at what?"

Eyebrows that could have nested small birds shot up. "Maybe going out at night, that's not legal, or they'll go into the sanctuaries, places that are off limits."

"Poachers."

"Just taking what God provides, as I see it."

"Smugglers?"

Lucky scanned the Bay and spat.

I tried again. "Smugglers?"

"That was the old days. Doubt there's much going on today."

"Must be some. Young Sammy's mother thinks he was practicing to be a DEA agent, might have been looking for drug runners."

"That's ridiculous. You think Sammy was chasing drug pushers? Ridiculous. Good way not to get old, messing with that kind of thing."

"He didn't get old, did he? He was last seen near Parkers Point. Is that anywhere close by? There's an old lighthouse I wanted to see but the guy that owns it wouldn't let me in."

"Scrap Blevins, that would be. Loose cannon, that one. It's some ways to Parkers, but we can go have a look. Cole's footing the bill."

I thought about telling him my experience with Cole at the restaurant, how he might want to get his money up front in the future. But he was still talking. "Keep an eye peeled for crab pot floats, we could get tangled up in a line and foul the prop, that's a fact." And then he went back into the wheelhouse and the engine roared. We were done talking for a while.

I didn't try to prove myself a seasoned mariner. I held onto the side and the wheelhouse, watching for the floats that would indicate pots. But Brevard knew something about piloting; we wove between floats now and then but never got close. I peeked into the cabin to watch him at work. Beside him on the console was a picture of his fantasied love, Ingrid Bergman.

After a while he slowed to a crawl.

"There's your Parkers Point, and that thing looks like a crashed flying saucer, that's the old lighthouse, what's left of it. It's high tide but I'm not going any closer in. It's dangerous close to shore."

"I thought lighthouses were tall, like at Assateague."

"Some. That's a screw-pile."

"Right. Meaning what?"

He turned the boat to make a second pass by the Point. "Well, it's the screw-pile style, nothing else I know to call it, there used to be a big light to it, and a fog bell in the middle with the keeper's house built around it. Nothing but a ruin now, though, anything of use has been stripped off."

"Okay, but what is screw-pile style?"

"Has to do with how they anchored the lighthouse, it was screwed into bottom. That's about it."

"But it's on land, not in the water."

"Was in the water, hurricanes and storms shuffled the land and water around. Happens."

Screw-pile. An odd term, I doubted von Klonk would allow it in his family-oriented magazine. "I heard this was once called Pirates' Point."

"I suppose it was. Back then, no motors, anyone could get blown in here in bad weather, smash up real good. That would bring out the wreckers, that's how the original name came about."

"Someone else mentioned wreckers. Local folks, pirates of a sort."

"Just people salvaging what was left of any ship caught in the shallows. As I say, making the best of what God provides. But I suppose if it was your ship, you'd probably say pirates."

We'd headed back toward Crisfield when the engine went silent. I thought maybe there was something of interest Brevard wanted me to see. He stepped out of the cabin shaking his head.

"The prop's not turning. Must be a line wrapped around it, loose from a crab pot."

I sure didn't like the sound of that. "Now what do we do?"

"There's nobody close by I can signal to, and I don't want to use the radio. If the Coast Guard hears me and comes to get us, they'll charge five hundred dollars for a tow. I haven't got it, have you?"

"No way. So we just sit here, maybe all night?"

"We'll drift. We're not anchored."

"Should we be?"

"I don't use it, too heavy for me these days, hauling that thing up. I just let her idle. Anyway, drifting, we might get somewhere."

"South America?"

"This ain't funny, not a bit. The other thing is, the electrics are a little tricky, so with no lights we might get rammed at night."

"This boat should be in the junkyard."

Brevard had nothing to say to that, he just studied the empty distances. After a time, he said: "Somebody has to go over the side and cut that rope away from the prop. I got a heart condition. You said you could swim."

"I can swim, but I'm not a Navy Seal. This is ridiculous."

"That's as may be. We can just sit here, hope there's no storms or no saltwater cowboys in cigarette boats ramming us. I'd say you could clear the prop in five minutes, likely survive fifteen minutes in the water this time of year. Maybe longer."

"Give me a knife." He went into the cabin, came out and handed me an antique butcher knife.

I felt the edge of the knife. "This thing's dull as a rock. Give me a sharp knife."

"There isn't any other. All I've got is a pocketknife. It was my grandpa's, it's an heirloom."

"Give me the knife."

"I will not."

I pointed the dull butcher knife at his chest and took a deep I'm-coming-for-you breath. "Give it to me, or ..."

"What?"

Killing the old bastard would be hard to explain. I threw the dull knife over the side and took a step closer. "Just give it to me."

"Mutiny!" Shaking his head sadly he handed me the knife. It had a good edge.

"Where's the prop, exactly?"

"It's just below the stern, same damn place it's always been."

I was about to go over the side, possibly for my last swim ever, when I spotted a skiff headed across our path. I waved my newly acquired hat like I was cheerleading a high school football team. The skiff veered our way.

As it pulled alongside I could see the man at the motor was Scrap Blevins.

"What you got yourself into now?"

I explained the predicament.

"And you're standing around with your finger in your ear because ...?"

"I don't know a thing about boats."

"Figures. Okay, might as well go down and have a look." He

stripped to shorts, strapped a hurting knife to his side and dove. He came up. "Tough cord. It's crab pot line all right, wrapped tighter than granny's girdle."

He dove again. The third time, he surfaced, rolled into his boat, pulled on his trousers, stood and said: "You're good to go."

I thanked him and revised my opinion, he was an all right guy.

Brevard had sequestered himself in the cabin after I'd mutinied. He didn't come out. "I'm sure the captain thanks you too but he's in a mood. I guess I should apologize if I want to get back to Crisfield. I was a little rough. "

"Hey you old buzzard," Scrap bellowed, "start your goddamn engine and get this gent back to Crisfield. Or do you need some help with that too?"

Brevard stuck his head out of the little cabin. "Mutineers! Pirates!" He turned back to the controls and cranked the engine. Scrap grinned, shook his head, started his motor and took off.

I left Brevard to his captaining chores. The future didn't look bright for continuing friendly relations.

At the dock I waited while Brevard secured the lines. I don't know the knots beyond square and granny. He was better off without my help. Not that I felt particularly helpful at that point.

He'd tied up. He marched to where I was standing on the dock. "You owe me a pocket knife and an apology."

"Is that a fact?" I handed him the knife. "You know, if you're going to run a charter boat you're going to have to learn diplomacy."

"Diplomacy be damned. I'm the captain, do you know what that means? It means I run things. Everyone on the boat listens to me, and I'm responsible for the security of the vessel. And it's my duty to report criminal activity by hijackers and terrorists."

"You know, that boat's a major safety hazard, if you want to talk about reporting things. You'd be up against a fist-full of citations."

"Clear off, mister. You got your tour." He turned his back.

I walked away. I could hear him, back by his boat, muttering comments. Should I have been kinder, gentler? Usually I am. Sometimes, anyway.

I'd been a while without a meal. The good old boy announcer on the country radio station was carrying on about free chicken at a bank on Main Street.

Free chicken. Why pass up a free meal? Von Klonk would certainly approve of my initiative.

I pulled into the lot.

There wasn't any crowd, the way you'd think it would be for an offer of free chicken. A banner over the entryway explained it all.

"Free Checking."

Well, that was one for the collection. It would fit right in with the merkle bush.

Chapter Eighteen

I slept in, worn out from my adventure with Capt Lucky, had a bit of breakfast courtesy of Serena. She said Miss Worple was off on one of her missions.

"I'm glad you came back, Serena."

"Maybe I will be, too. I don't know."

There was a loud commotion overhead.

"Geese," she said. "Headed north."

"In Washington I often heard of people coming to the Eastern Shore to hunt them. It made for big talk at the bar, like it was some kind of exotic expedition."

She wrinkled her nose as though at a sharp odor. "City people. They dress for war and hide in little bunkers. The geese come to a baited field, boom-boom. Great sport. Around here, geese are practically tame. You could kill them with a big stick."

"But it's money in local pockets, those people pay to hunt. And it's meat on the table."

Serena gave that a moment's thought. "I understand all that. And yet ... they are so beautiful in flight, sometimes fifty or a hundred spread out in formation across the sky. Then, after the hunting, there are stragglers, calling for friends long gone."

I guess you'd call my smile rueful. "I should steal that for my article, I'll have the tourists in tears."

Apparently my smile hadn't come across to her as I meant it. "My feelings aren't a joke." She turned her back and strode away.

I went for a late morning walk.

Coming toward me down the side of the road was Sammy's dog Baron, the big fellow Wetherby had offered to look after. He stopped at some distance, probably twenty feet, and sat, watching.

I wasn't sure quite what to do. He'd been friendly enough when I'd first visited Serena's trailer but I couldn't be certain of his present mood. I called to him but he just sat, staring. I figured the best thing would be go back to Bay Breezes and alert Serena that he was loose.

I'd turned to head back when a forest green pickup pulled up and stopped. A man in a rumpled, dirty green uniform, his hair wild as a bramble patch, stepped out.

It was Biggers, the game warden. He was unsteady on his feet and looked as though he had slept the night face down in a puddle. "What's going on here?"

"Just looking to see if that's a dog belongs to a friend of mine."

Baron was up now, in a crouch, no sound or show of teeth but intent on Biggers.

Biggers unholstered his pistol.

I couldn't believe my eyes. "What the hell are you doing?"

"I'll handle this, Buster. I'm an official officer of the law, protecting the public." He said 'pertecting'.

"The dog is lost. I know where it belongs."

Biggers fired three shots at the dog.

Baron just fell on his side.

He struggled, kicked, but just for a moment. His eyes were open, staring at nothing.

He lay there.

A lightning bolt of adrenalin surged though me.

Gun or no gun, I charged Biggers like an enraged bull at red cape, slapped the pistol out of his hand. I slammed him against the side of his truck and, as he crumpled, uppercut him in the jaw with all the force my fury could muster.

A car pulled up. It was Zinker. He was out of the car in a flash, barreling toward me like a runaway train. "What in blazes is going on?"

I was still almost too mad for words but I got it out. "He shot the dog for no reason. Son of a bitch, he's drunk on his ass."

Zinker studied Biggers where he lay on the ground by his truck. "I saw you hit him."

"He was drunk. I was afraid he'd turn the gun on me."

"Well, I should detain you. Beating the shit out of a game warden is a serious violation. But I guess hauling you in might get Serena upset, wouldn't want that."

"I don't care who's upset. I could kill the bastard, no regrets."

"You better clear out. Knowing Biggers, he won't remember what happened. I'll handle him, get going."

"Somebody should bury the dog."

"Later, man. Show you got a little sense. You best not be around when this crazy sack of shit shakes it off. Get gone."

Two men were working like demons on the tangled landscape surrounding Bay Breezes, bringing it somewhat in conformity with civilized ideas of a yard. I took them for Mexicans and greeted them in my rudimentary Spanish. They both glanced my way for only a second before returning to their task.

I told Serena about the shooting. The look on her face was tiger-fierce. "Baron was just trying to find Sammy. I'm going to get a gun and finish the job on that Biggers."

"Hold on, Serena. Think. You'll never find what happened to Sammy if you're locked up. Give this some time. There'll come a way to settle with Biggers."

"You can believe that. I prefer to settle it now!"

"We can go to the sheriff. I can't believe Biggers has authority to kill domestic dogs for no reason."

"They don't do anything about Sammy and you think they are going to do something about Baron? A dog? You are dreaming. All that would happen is you get arrested for assault."

I suggested that maybe the two men working in the yard could bury Baron. He deserved a decent burial and not to be left by the side of the road. "I spoke to them in Spanish but they ignored me."

"That's because they don't speak Spanish. They are Mixtec."

"What's that?"

"You think Mexico means Spanish language but it is many, many languages, changing sometimes from village to village. I will talk to them, they have a little English. I'm sure they will handle it. Possibly for a small donation they would handle Biggers, too."

"Not now. It would be too easy to connect events."

"Do I care? You Americans have no pride. Wrongs should be avenged."

"Many Americans have what you call pride. And many of those are dead or in jail, Serena. I don't want that to happen to you. Biggers will pay, all in good time."

"Good time? That is a stupid thing to call it." She left to talk to the workers outside.

I sat on the porch. I knew very well it would be best to get into action, to go somewhere even if that was nowhere, just to keep from dwelling on settling things with Biggers.

But I sat, brooding. Serena brought sandwiches and iced tea.

"Won't you join me?"

"Can't. Not my place."

"Who would notice?"

She thought for a moment. "Work has to be a particular way of acting."

"How does that go?"

"It's the American thing about lazy Mexicans. So you show them it is a lie, you prove yourself every moment. Then maybe you keep your job."

"It doesn't sound easy."

"It isn't easy, it's work. Do you read books?"

"Of course I read books."

"Sammy had some books. I don't know what to do with them."

"Can I take a look?"

"Sure. The box is in my room."

It was a big box, the kind that holds reams of paper. Popular archaeology, forensics, history; an interesting collection. There was also a binder-style notebook. I began leafing through it.

"Take what you want to your room, Mr Holliday, you can't be found here."

It wasn't as though we were busting the bedsprings. "I'm just looking at books."

"No visitors in my room."

"Ah yes, the Worple standard, established by pillars of the church and community."

Her shrug said 'whatever.' She said: "Keep what you want. The rest will go somewhere, the library or a nursing home."

"You don't want the notebook, either?"

"I don't know, maybe so. Take it for now. You may make some sense of it."

Chapter Nineteen

I took the box of Sammy's books and the notebook to my room. Didn't I have things to do, an article to write? I could feel von Klonk peering over my shoulder. I would just spend a few minutes with the notebook.

A few hours later I was still looking through a collection of newspaper clippings, questions and observations under various headings. For the most part it appeared Sammy would have made a good reporter for one of the sensational tabloids. There were stories on UFOs, buried treasures, quirks of history, daring crimes. There was one about Thundercloud, the alleged Indian.

Noted beside the clip: 'Fake, con artist.'

And another note: 'Called Prof Zogby. He's all wrong.' Zogby, I recalled, was the history expert Miss Worple had mentioned, the one who wrote about Native American emigration from the region.

I'd seen similar notebooks, years ago. In what move, or what split-up, or what job change had they been left behind or stored away, never to be seen again, or thrown in a bin because I was momentarily fed up with research, thinking, writing?

By mid-afternoon I had skimmed through the notebook, and then I searched the box again for a copy of Professor Morton Zogby's book. No luck.

There was a handout advertising a lecture by the great one, with a picture. He was balding, with a puffy face as though constantly blowing up a balloon. As royalty he might have been known as Zogby the Smug. There followed a few paragraphs laced with references and a lot of *etc*, indicating that a complete accounting of his accomplishments would require the efforts of a team of biographers.

The switchboard at the university put me through to Zogby's extension, answered by someone who said the professor was *far* too busy to take calls. I could leave a message. I argued that I was a reporter on deadline and really needed a couple of quick quotes from his exalted grand self. "Our demographics are the cultural elite. He won't want to miss this opportunity."

That worked, as evidenced by short pause and then a "Yes?" from Zogby. "And which magazine was this?" His voice was meant to sound cultured, a tone heard in high society films of the 1930s.

I mumbled something like *Vomity Flare*.

"Sorry, I just don't have the time." That might have done for a turndown, but he was just warming up. "My schedule is arranged months in advance. I leave now for New York for the Dr Feelfree show. Then there's the *Digger of the Year* awards ceremony, of course. You know, I can't just dawdle around chatting with reporters. I have consulting and speaking engagements, and, as you might suspect, certain obligations to the academy which employs me."

Talk about a bloviater. I played the deadline card again. He trumped it.

"You may pull what you need from my published material. My assistant can provide copies of the many articles that have featured me ... and, of course, you've read my book."

"Oh, yurumhum."

"What was that?"

Aware that he might ring off at any moment, I figured I might as well lob the grenade. "Actually, I wanted to ask you about

Sammy Sanchez. He had some questions regarding the credibility of your work. Isn't that so?"

"San-Chez?"

"Youngster. He seems to have been interested in Parkers Point."

"I have nothing to say about that ignorant little nincompoop. He was toying with my reputation." His reputation stretched out to the fullness of its syllables, as though a key word in a royal proclamation.

"But were his questions valid or not?"

"He shouldn't have even seen the report. It was confidential."

"Report, right. And that was the report on ...?"

Call it intuition. I knew I had seconds before I would hear a call-ending click. I charged ahead. "Professor, Sammy was found dead. You may be able to help find out what happened to him."

"As an improbability, that ranks in the top tier. Good riddance, I say. Goodbye."

Class dismissed.

Report. Report. There was nothing in Sammy's notes about a report. My best guess was that he'd found something to seriously counter Zogby's version of history.

And what might that have been? I needed Zogby's book. From what I'd gathered so far, Zogby's basic argument was that the Native Americans of the region had departed after having sold their lands, fair and square, to the newcomers.

Was it possible Sammy had found something proving the contrary or at least seriously challenging Zogby; a treaty or evidence of a treaty assuring the land rights of the original inhabitants? Maybe they were guaranteed a reservation or some other arrangement that would turn the professor's account on its head.

If there was any sort of dispute involving Native American claims, I'd been in contact not so long ago with an expert who should know the details. Benjamin St Pierre headed a Native American rights group headquartered in Washington. The group had successfully lobbied Congress for resolution of several claims beneficial to various tribes, and had supplied legal expertise in cases that went on to court. He'd been a good, candid source. I called him.

"Zogby? Heaven help us. Sure, I know his pitch, how Native American land claims are invalid due to gifts, sales, treaties. Are we talking for publication?"

"I'm trying to find the truth behind the death of young man down here on the Eastern Shore. It's a long story. No, I'm not quoting you."

"How can I help?"

"Are there any claims still in contention on the Delmarva peninsula?"

"There are several in the region. I'd have to look them up. We don't have much chance down there though. I mean, Zogby's right, generally the land was sold – sold by people who had no concept of real estate."

Sort of shoots down that theory. "How about the claim that all the original inhabitants left the area once the land was sold?"

"Horseshit. Native Americans disappeared from the census because the category disappeared. The law was revised so you had to be black or white. There were no other categories. And a Native American had no standing in court, so it would have been impossible to dispute whatever the power structure dictated."

"So the Indians never actually left?"

"Many of them did. They moved over to the Virginia mainland where there were reservations or went north, Delaware, then New York, then Canada. Others went west to Oklahoma. Some were enslaved and sold as far away as Barbados."

So what was he saying? They left, one way or the other. "Then Zogby was right?"

"Well, he's not all right. There are today many in the region descended from the first people. Proving it might be another matter. These days if you're of mixed blood, you call yourself what you want to call yourself. But officially, there's still some reliance on blood quantum; some tribes and the feds, they use it."

"Blood quantum?"

"Goes back to the times you're talking about. Basically, to be a legitimate person you had to be seven-eighths European, otherwise you couldn't vote, you had no standing in court, you were about on par with livestock. Back then, if it had to do with the courts or government, you had to swear an oath on a Bible, right? Who would trust a heathen non-European savage to swear an oath on a Bible? So you weren't allowed your day in court."

I went fishing. "I guess it's a long shot, but say Sammy, the young fellow I mentioned, found something, maybe a document, a valid claim on certain land?"

St Pierre paused. I'd found in the past that, for an attorney, he was fairly willing to frame his answers in down-to-earth terms. That proved to still be the case. "In that rare event, I sure wouldn't want to be him. Can you imagine telling some of those folks down there that land that's been in their family for hundreds of years doesn't belong to them? After great-great-granpappy stole it fair and square? I think I hear gunfire."

No question, the situation would get tense if there was a treaty guaranteeing a reservation. What if some locals were descended from the original inhabitants who were part of that treaty? Neighbor against neighbor.

St Pierre continued: "Anyhow like you said, a real long shot. Still, you never know. Every once in a while a previously unknown document shows up, misfiled in a neglected archive or tucked in someone's attic. Sometimes it's even genuine. Then the fun begins, maybe years and years of arguing in court."

It was all speculation. I asked if he knew anyone locally who might help me out.

"I don't know of any activists right there in that area. Some wannabes, but nobody real."

"There's a Capt Jack Thundercloud …"

"You're picking the winners. He's as much Native American as the Queen of England. Attracts the city kids. They have some kind of pretend tribe."

"Sammy, that's the one who –- one way or another – got killed, mentioned him in his notes. I'd say he considered Thundercloud a fraud."

"He's sure not alone on that score."

"Okay, what if there's nothing to the treaty idea; is there anything else that could put Sammy at odds with Zogby?"

"One of the main things that grated me about that book was how it didn't mention another way the original inhabitants left that area."

"And that was?"

This time, no doubt, the pause was for effect. "Massacre, mass murder." He fired the words at me like gunshots. "Once they'd taught the colonists how to survive there, the original people were viewed as nothing but trouble. They were in the way, moving around as they always had, hunting where they'd always hunted, fishing where they'd always fished. There wasn't much official law and order in those days so it was easy to trump up some horror or other, organize a neighborhood militia and go after Indians like wild game."

"There must be some record of that."

"There was one incident, probably not far from where you're staying. The remnants of the local tribe were invited to a feast and poisoned. Zogby doesn't even mention that one."

Awful, but what did it have to do with the case? "How would that relate to Sammy's death?"

"Was he a digger?"

I had to think about that one. "I guess you could say that. He was interested in artifacts."

"Well, suppose there was a big land sale pending, for instance, and this Sammy discovered the site of the massacre there, a previously unknown burial ground on the property? When development encounters a cemetery, everything stops, maybe for years, maybe forever. That could seriously piss off some folks. And it wouldn't have to be a massacre site, just evidence of a burial ground."

I thought of Scrap Blevins. "Happens I've met someone in just such a situation. Happens he is not someone you would want to piss off."

"Just a possibility."

A little light went on in my bat cave brain. "In fact, it reminds me of something ..."

St Pierre's speculation reminded me of a situation years before when I researched a story involving a huge suburban residential development. The question driving the story was how the project achieved zoning approval despite more than a few irregularities, and in the course of looking for an answer I visited the site and talked with the construction supervisor. He was more candid than was wise in the presence of a reporter and lucky that I wasn't the merciless sort who would hang him out to dry.

The site bordered the Potomac River at a bend with high flat ground overlooking water on three sides, making it an attractive location for settlement. As it turned out, Native Americans had noticed the attractiveness of the location long before modern developers. This fact became evident to the construction superintendent as workers turned up artifacts in the course of clearing and grading the land.

"I told them, just put that stuff right back in the ground and forget you ever saw it," the super said.

Why? Because the state would shut the project down for however long it took archeologists to assess the historic or prehistoric value of the site. Under certain conditions – say, the discovery of human remains – the whole project might be put in jeopardy.

Well, fortunately for the super, I was on the trail of possible bribery or some other mischief involving the developers, so evidence of Native American presence at the construction site wasn't a big deal to me.

But now, on reflection, I wondered if Sammy might have stumbled onto something similar, maybe not a burial ground, maybe just a significant settlement site, that could have threatened Scrap's sale of the land at the Point. But did that make any sense?

Scrap had handed Sammy that clamshell carving indicating Native American presence. What in the world was going on?

Having thanked and rung off with St Pierre, I called Wetherby.

"Oh, I don't think there would be a burial ground out there. Too near the water. There are Indian burial grounds, some of them substantial, known as pit burials. But that's floodplain there."

"So no burials."

"Not the sort you're talking about. Have you noticed any groups of rectangular boxes along the roadsides in your travels here?"

"Off hand I can't think of any."

"Well, keep your eyes peeled, you'll see some. Those are gravesites, some modern, some dating back to colonial times, above ground because if you dig down even four inches in the low country here, you'll hit water. Now, I'm no expert of course, but I have read a bit of history; I believe you'll also find above ground burial among the Indians. They did what are called sky burials."

"Sky burials? You're ahead of me on that one."

"Up on platforms, let nature disperse the body."

Wetherby's insights appeared to put a lid on the theory that Sammy had uncovered a burial ground in the conventional sense, but he could have been on the track of something along those lines. And there was the possibility that Wetherby was wrong. Or maybe he was right but Sammy found objects that indicated a sky burial site. Could be the corpse was put on a platform with special objects, like the carving, that fell to the ground and were buried by nature when the structure deteriorated. Scavengers took the bones but left the offerings.

Or another possibility was, for reasons yet unknown, Wetherby was blowing smoke to throw me off track. He was a likeable enough fellow and seemed fairly straight, but how many politicians, how many lawyers, accountants, church treasurers and so on, were both likeable and scoundrels at the same time?

As to why he might want to lead me astray, if that was the case, I had no idea. He was involved in politics, and that made him suspect. Even some of the most noble of that breed, with so many pies spread before them, have been known to jab a finger in now and then.

"Someone suggested Sammy might have discovered a previously unknown treaty. What about that? What if he found a basis for land claims by descendants of the original inhabitants?"

True, the 'someone' who suggested that was me, but I didn't need to add that. After a moment's thought Wetherby said the idea seemed unlikely.

"But possible?"

"It would seem far more possible that such a document, if it ever existed, would be destroyed. Surely those who might have taken the land would be powerful people who wouldn't leave anything lying around that could provide the basis for challenge."

"I guess you're right."

"Not so fast. Could be you guess wrong. It was standard practice to make several copies of those treaties. So, someone in Canada or Oklahoma could have found one in an old trunk."

If so, wouldn't it be big news? "Surely they would have come forward."

"If I were of a nefarious turn of mind, note that I say *if*, and found such a treaty, I might not go public with it at all. I might bring it to the attention of current landowners and suggest they could acquire said document – for a certain tidy sum – to do with it as they wished."

I said it was an interesting idea, but it didn't hold water if we were talking about Scrap Blevins. "My impression is, he's broke or close to it. Can't see him buying expensive old documents."

"You're right on that score," said Wetherby. "Any spare change Scrap ever had has gone for gambling, guns or tools. But what of those who want to acquire his land? A treaty wouldn't be in their interests, would it?"

Whoa. I saw the faint glimmer of a warning light. Wetherby's speculation sounded like he was priming me or spinning me for some reason. I needed to think about all this. I thanked him for his comments and rang off.

I was hardly half way into lecturing myself on how paying down my credit cards required putting aside the Sammy stuff and focusing on the *Here & There* article when a call came in from von Klonk. "What the hell have you got and where the hell is it?"

Word for the day, hell. "I've got this hellish little collection of bits and pieces so far, and the hell of it is there's no center to the story yet."

"What? Center? Forget center. Give me the bits and pieces. I need the damn story, Holliday. I could have had this done for a tenth of what I'm paying you. There's freelancers just want to see a byline, and they'd do it for free."

How could I wiggle around that? Play to his Stalinist inclinations. "Sure. But this way you've got absolute control, you're guiding the story every step of the way, you know? I mean, freelancers, what do you get? Lawsuits, misinformation, embarrassments, who knows what kind of trouble. You're getting the work of pro, tailored exactly to your specs."

"You're so full of it, Holliday."

"It's just that I need a focal point."

"Focal schmokle." That was all he had to say? I suppose he was weighing his options. "All right, I'm a patient, tolerant man, Holliday, probably a candidate for sainthood for what I've put up with from you. I'll give you a little more time and then, I swear, I'll bring charges for impersonating a journalist. You were supposed to write about chicken, so have you found the big chicken deal down there?"

Think fast, I thought. "Chicken festivals. You ride around, nothing going on, then suddenly there are thousands of people eating tons of chicken."

"All right, fine, get going and find a freaking chicken festival and get that damn story to me. You're on very, very thin ice."

"Right. Matter of fact, I was just going to swap my skates for water wings."

"What? Never mind. Listen, I've been thinking about something you said. I've warned you already but I doubt it sunk in, knowing you. Don't mention muskrats."

Here was a new twist. "No muskrats? But they're big around here, integral to the story. I mean, you want to get a conversation going, just start talking muskrats . ."

I could almost see the smoke pouring from his flared nostrils. "Muskrats are a negative, Holliday, a turn off. Don't mention muskrats. Ever again."

I had him going, a devilish pleasure I was reluctant to relinquish. "Sure. But, hey, don't knock it 'til you've tried it; isn't that what they say?"

"I don't give a flying flip what *they* say. I want to see what *you* say, and I want to see it tomorrow." The tail end of the sentence had a chop to it, like a robotic machine in a factory. I-Want-To-See-It-To-Mor-Row, whacka-whacka-whack.

What could I say?

I couldn't say anything, unless I enjoyed talking to dead air, von Klonk had hung up.

Chapter Twenty

What were chances, bright and early on a Tuesday morning, of finding a chicken festival in full swing along Rt 13? Probably near the chances there'd be of a rich widow standing along the road waving a sign, 'Ghostwriter Wanted, Money No Object.'

How do you go about finding a chicken festival? Think, think. Ah. Follow the feathers.

I didn't see any feathers. There were signs, mostly weathered to near oblivion, touting great deals on waterfront property, but no rich widows and no chicken festivals. So what? It was a great day for a drive, another sunny spring day. I'd now had a weeklong string of them with only afternoon showers.

Maybe I'd spot something scenic to pad out my article. There was a sprawled, dead deer by the side of the road. A victim of last night's traffic. Vultures hopped around the corpse, tearing off chunks of breakfast. Probably not von Klonk's idea of photo-caption fluff.

I shouldn't have taken the turn for Chincoteague, but it just reached out and grabbed me like some weird magnetic force field. I'd been warned; the island wasn't part of my article. I just wanted to have a closer look at the village I'd breezed through on my way to Assateague Park for that strange meeting with McCobb. A few minutes wouldn't matter.

On my left were the fenced acres of antennas and satellite dishes at the Wallops Island NASA facility, just before the causeway to Chincoteague. It was kind of eerie, a science fiction sort of setting, out in the middle of the coastal marshes, a huge, sprawling complex for monitoring weather and launching commercial and government rockets. Or so it was claimed. If you subscribed to the ideas in Sammy's notebook, it could be the east coast version of the notorious Area 51. I scanned the skies for flying saucers.

The long causeway is just a little ribbon of road across a wide bay separating the island from the mainland. When the weather is rambunctious the causeway is shut down and the island is on its own for the duration. That would usually mean a natural tantrum – hurricane or tropical storm, both all too familiar to the locals.

On the island, Main Street preserves a bit of small town atmosphere. There are shops, a fire station, a VFW hall and then a long residential stretch along the island's south side. Over the years, pricey new condos have gradually replaced the homes of watermen, or those homes have become vacation cottages, and fancy recreational speedboats bob where weathered skiffs and old diesel workboats once harbored.

There are plans afoot to abandon the ancient bridge at Main Street and redirect traffic so that entry will be on Maddox Boulevard, a strip of stereotypical beach town motels, restaurants and tee shirt shops leading up to the undeveloped thirty-seven miles long barrier island at Chincoteague's back doorstep. That would be Assateague, home of wild ponies, miniature deer and miles and miles of beach without so much commercial presence as an umbrella concession.

Much to my surprise I discovered several bookstores on Chincoteague. The main fare was beach reading – best sellers, romances, fantasy. But one shop featured classics, collectibles and quite an assortment of regional lit. And, lo and behold, on a shelf behind the sales station, a copy of *Pocomoke Diaspora: The*

Dispersal of the Indigenous Peoples of the Eastern Shore of Maryland and Virginia by Dr Morton Zogby.

"I'm sorry," said the clerk behind the counter, introducing himself as co-owner of the shop. "It's sold. I'm just holding it for pickup. Hard to believe but I can't keep a copy in stock. Being out of print, I can practically name my price, and still it sells."

I asked if I might have a look all the same. I took the time to browse the introduction, conclusion and index. Of course it was a difficult book, that's a requirement of scholarly tomes, but most often buried in a sea of big words will be a paragraph or two of what it's all about. The rest is show-off stuff, sort of like the pro wrestler strutting around the ring in a rhinestone cape before getting down to the real business application of *The Secret Ear-Twist of Sudden Discomfort*.

So, as I saw it, Zogby's secret twist was that, prior to colonial times, there was only one tribe occupying the peninsula now known as Delmarva. Those who claim otherwise (meaning renegades like Judge Wetherby) are misguided fools. In their delusion, the unbelievers believe that the strange names of numerous geographic elements – Pocomoke, Assawoman, Machipongo and so many more, particularly the names of rivers and streams – indicate independent tribes that lived in each area.

Not so! According to Zogby, all were in fact Nanticokes. And why does that matter? Because when the chief of the Nanticokes made deals with the newcomers, he represented all Native Americans on the peninsula and had the authority to do so. Accomac? Occahannock? Wicomico? There were those and others but it didn't matter, they were all Nanticokes, and the chief of the Nanticokes sold the land, and that was that.

Once the lands were sold the original inhabitants were branded troublesome, wandering vagrants, accused of various horrors and mischief. What were the colonists to do but take vigilante action — for the good of the community of course.

Made to understand, in one way and another, that they were no longer welcome on their traditional hunting and fishing grounds, the surviving Indians — in the Zogby account — packed their kits and moved up the Susquehanna to Delaware and Pennsylvania, and then on to New York and Canada. Or, in other cases, they crossed to southern Virginia and thence wandered on to Oklahoma. To some extent, my source St Pierre agreed.

He didn't agree, though, with Zogby's claim that by the time of the Revolution there were very few Indians, only some stragglers, left in Maryland, and, further, that before long even the stragglers had disappeared.

It was easy to see how the professor would be quite popular with those who wanted their forbears depicted as genteel, noble people of none but sterling qualities who had simply made the best of a bargain with the savages of the region. Killing off those who didn't understand the deal was glossed over as something like a sporting event. As for any remnants, well, there just weren't any.

I closed the book and thanked the shopkeeper "Do you know of someone named Thundercloud who has a shop around here?"

I wasn't laughing so I guess he was laughing at me rather than with me. "Oh, sure. You can't miss it, up on the Maddox strip. There's a big billboard of an Indian chief out front."

"You don't hold this Thundercloud in high regard?"

"I have, might we say, reservations regarding his Native American bona fides. But he does dress the part sometimes, war bonnet and all. Kind of pathetic; the bonnet flops one side to the other when he struts around, you'd think it was a big bird trying to carry him off."

"Putting on the Indian thing."

He glanced around the shop. "They say don't judge a book by its cover. All the same, that guy is as pale as a powdered geisha."

Indian Art and Jewelry. I fought my way through a swarm of hanging beads to get into the gallery. The atmosphere was thick with the cloying scent of incense. Glass cases offered silver and turquoise jewelry while weird, distorted images of bears, ghost dancers, warriors and wolves adorned the walls. It seemed there was nobody home.

A peek through another bead-bedecked doorway at the rear of the shop revealed a room with a massage table at its center. On the table, motionless as if asleep or in a trance, lay a naked form, obviously female.

Pacing around the table, muttering and slowly waving a feather, was a beanpole of a man with flowing white hair. His sunken cheeks hinted at dangerous drug use, though, as a mystical sort, maybe it was just a result of fasting. He could have passed for an aging rock star, one who hadn't made the mature move to clean-cut crooning. He glanced my way. There was a wild intensity to the look worthy of a zombie thriller. He put a finger to his lips, motioned me back into the shop. I backed up a bit, out of his view, and stood listening.

"Wawa-we-nah, wowo-we-no." Over and over again.

I turned my attention to the shop. There was something peculiar about the paintings, they were real but unreal.

If a little learning is a dangerous thing, a good journalist likely has a head full of dangerous things. Each assignment has the potential to add at least superficial knowledge of something new. Even when not on assignment, I'm often chasing down one rabbit hole or the other, looking for story ideas. Which explains how I happen to know something about over-painting.

A closer look at the paintings on the walls showed just that, photos and illustrations, painted over. It's a technique initially used for enhancing photos that goes back to the earliest days of photography. More recently it's become an art form in its own right, or so practitioners contend. Quite often it's hard to distinguish from graffiti. Basically the artist is just coloring or doodling over someone else's work. My guess was the pictures in the shop were blown up out of old books or magazines and then decorated, or should I say desecrated.

As for the jewelry, I'd bet most of it originated in China. That's no big deal, unless it is labeled authentic. Mislabeled it could be a costly big deal for the customer who bought a cheap import believing it to be the real thing. If an import is sold as Native American, the seller is violating federal law. A few pieces looked genuine. But even some jewelry attributed to an Indian artist can be a bit dodgy. Again relying on a tidbit picked up along the reporting trail, I recalled that if a Native American takes an imported polished stone and simply glues it to an imported finished setting, it can qualify as 'genuine' Indian jewelry.

"That will do for today," I heard the chanting man say. "We're making progress. Yes, we're definitely making progress."

A few moments passed and then he came through to the shop. "And how may I assist you, pilgrim? That poor dear is infested with psychic toxins, but we're getting her clear of them, slowly."

The poor dear had found shorts and a blouse. She blew past us in a rattle of beads. "You look as though you could use a good cleanse yourself. Lots of little karmic leeches clinging to you." He was coming toward me, still armed with the feather and the zombie stare.

I gave the air in front of me a palms-out push.

"Whoa." I explained myself as a magazine writer on a mission, that being to profile some of the more fascinating characters of the region. "Assuming you are Capt Jack Thunderclap, you come highly recommended."

From the look I thought he was about to challenge my flimsy credentials but he just wanted to set me straight. "It's Thunder-Cloud, C-l-o-u-d."

"Let me make sure I've got the name right, that's a fairly important element, isn't it?" I had my handy little pocket-sized reporter's notebook out, just to add some credibility. It actually had that in print on the front of it, Reporter's Notebook, very official, like it was issued by the governing body of journalism. "Okay, Thundercloud it is. The honorific? It's a military title, Captain?"

"You are not very familiar with this area, are you? Of course, there are many captains who own or operate boats, but it is a general term of respect. You don't actually have to be a captain to be called Captain. If others call you Captain, it's a sign of respect. I am a chief, but that would not be understood around here, so I am Captain."

The way he went about explaining it, I felt like a visiting kindergarten class.

"Got it. And Thundercloud, that's a family name?"

"It was given to me by my spirit guide, Washaquonasin."

"I'm going to need spelling on that one. Spirit guide … no

kidding? A ghost, something like that?"

He squeezed his face into a mask of mild pain, the anguish of the misunderstood missionary. "An entity from the other side who favors me with powers and visions. The paintings you see on these walls, they are visions channeled to me by my spirit guide. Being new to all this, as evidently you are, you could not possibly understand."

"But I need to understand if I'm to write this article."

"It will take a lot of time and a lot of work if you are to access the spirit world. Perhaps, though, I can provide shortcuts. There would be a consideration involved."

I feigned startled innocence. "There's a fee for your assistance?"

"Those who wish to join the tribe make donations as part of the initiation and continue to do so as members. Of course, there are rewards for members who bring in new recruits and further rewards if those new recruits bring in others, and so on."

"You're a for-profit prophet kind of thing, sort of."

"May I urge caution? The spirits do not take kindly to mockery of those they empower. Are you joining or not?"

I played the objectivity card, explaining that as a reporter I was required to maintain an independent perspective. I couldn't join the group but, for this article, which would undoubtedly generate an army of new recruits, I needed to know something about its activities and functions.

"It's a circle of students, really. Under my guidance."

"You meet here at the shop?"

"Usually we do bonfires on the beach."

I tried to picture it. "Bonfires? And you sing folk songs, roast hot dogs?"

He waved the feather as though brushing aside my comment. "Not *exactly*. We chant, dance, travel to the other side. We connect with the spirits of the original people and they teach us to use power."

"Power. Casting spells, cooking up love potions, that kind of thing?"

"Perhaps you could lay down the shield of skepticism and accept. Power includes many things, the ability to fly or to read the minds of others or to shift shape and become whatever being or object you wish." He paused, assessing his effect. "There is more ... there are levels of revelation."

He was, of course, right about the shield. I was sending skeptical messages and Thundercloud was reading them. He wagged a bony finger at me and announced: "Our path is not for everyone."

I was pretty sure that I was among those for whom it was not, but for the sake of conversation I asked: "So, can anyone attend these beach parties?"

"They are powwows, not parties. Invitation only. First, particularly in a case such as yours, you need to be deprogrammed. You are possessed by evil spirits, psychic leeches, ancient curses, and there is the problem of your own limited level of consciousness."

Ancient curses? An image of Sammy's clamshell came to mind. "Sounds like I need more than just a tune-up. Is there a sign-up sheet? What can a person do to get fixed?"

"Seek and ye shall find. Attending my workshops is a step in the right direction. You can earn your certifications that way."

"Certifying what, exactly?"

"It depends on the workshop. In the next one, if you were to fulfill all the requirements, I would certify that, like me, you are the reincarnation of a former Native American occupant of this region. I was a chief, of course, but there are many roles, warrior, hunter, shaman, priestess, many roles."

"Who was Sammy Sanchez?"

"Sammy?"

"Well, yes, was he a warrior, something like that, or an extreme case?"

"I've released that one. I have nothing to say."

"I guess you've heard he's dead. If it was you released him, you did a bang-up job."

Duck for cover, it's the evil eye. "Sometimes that is for the best. For some, it is the only cure. They need to cross over, permanently."

"Are you saying what I think you're saying? That's bizarre."

Perhaps he was consulting with Washaquonasin. After a moment he said he had another soul retrieval session coming up shortly and a few things to attend to first.

"Mind if I come back to continue our interview tomorrow?"

Another consultation with the great beyond. "I don't think so. I'm very busy."

"Chief, or Captain, like I said, this article is going to be in hotels, motels, restaurants, wherever tourists might pick it up. And they'll probably send copies home to their aunts and cousins and the local barber's shop and dentist's office. Doctor's office, too, maybe the vet's. I mean, it can do you a lot of good."

"Call me. I'll think it over." So saying he walked to the beaded curtain leading to the outside world and parted it for me. With a smile and wave that wasn't reciprocated, I re-entered the fresh air and sunshine of reality.

A new BMW pulled into a parking spot and a pair of tanned legs got out. Following their connections I arrived at blondeness framing a taut face that looked as though it was battling the effects of the years with surgical assistance.

Thundercloud had mentioned soul retrieval but it looked more to me like a case of youth retrieval. I smiled and nodded as a way of wishing her luck. The way she sped past left me wondering if I had acquired the power of invisibility.

I'd missed lunch and it was getting late for finding a chicken festival. I compromised, opting for fried chicken at the gas station across the causeway, no reservation required.

The gal behind the food counter looked like she could handle a Harley in a hurricane. And then she smiled and called me honey.

It was love at first bite. I could have hung around all evening, ordering and eating fried chicken. Not really, but it was tempting.

CHAPTER TWENTY-ONE

Serena had the evening off from her job at the pizza restaurant. She met me on the porch, looking good in jeans and a plain white shirt that probably wasn't chic enough to be called a peasant blouse. She had an odd bit of news.

Someone had come by looking for Indian relics. "He said he heard Sammy left some artifacts and he wanted to buy them. Creepy old guy."

"That's weird. What did you tell him?"

"I told him no, but he didn't believe me. He was very rude."

Relics? I didn't recall seeing any. Oh, yeah. "There's that clamshell thing."

"Sammy left it here for a reason, don't you think? Maybe he showed it to people, or told them about it, then got worried. He brought it here for safe-keeping."

"It's also weird that this fellow tracked you here. So how did you get rid of him? I imagine Miss Worple ran him off."

Serena shook her head. "She's away at one of those meetings. I thought the guy was coming through the door, he was all fired up. Zinker happened to be in the neighborhood, he pulled up and saw there was an argument going on. He ordered the man to go away."

"Sorry I wasn't here to be of help."

"Well, he's gone. Zinker checked him out. He said it was some college professor, strange name."

"Zogby?"

"Yes, that's it."

So. It was looking like my inquiry had stirred up some trouble.

"Well, now. That's very interesting."

"You know him?"

"I've had the pleasure, but only by phone. And only because I was going over those notes Sammy left."

"Then Sammy must have shown him the clamshell."

"Very possible." I was thinking about cause and effect. I'd called Zogby as a member of the press interested in what happened to Sammy. Next thing you know, he shows up at Bay Breezes, all belligerent and looking for Sammy's strange little artifact. What was up? I wished I knew more about that report Zogby mentioned.

Serena wanted to know the significance of Zogby's visit but I didn't have an answer, not yet anyway. "Honestly, I don't know. I called him after I read the notes. He didn't say much but it seems to have rung his bell."

Serena gave herself a hug. "Then of course Zinker wanted his reward as big hero. I don't know what he expected – well, I suppose I do. I said I felt sick, and at that point I *did* feel sick. He finally left."

"You don't buy Zinker's line that he just happened to be passing by?"

"Passing by to where? That road is a dead end, just goes to the mad artist. I don't think he is any pal of Zinker."

"What was he doing here, then?"

"Snooping on me. He's a stalker, that's what he is."

"Well, I do wish I'd been here."

"So do I. But I have to give Zinker credit, he got rid of that guy. I didn't know what would happen next, as wild as he was acting."

We sat on the porch as the day faded to gray and I told her about meeting Chief Thundercloud, or Captain Thundercloud – I had to wonder what his real name might be, could be some interesting history there. "I'll say one thing, your son sure had a knack for getting on the wrong side of some strange characters."

"Strange people do strange things, and he was so curious. I wish he had known you, Andy. Maybe you could have shown him how to turn that curiosity into a career."

We sat in silence. Serena couldn't hear the question echoing in my bat cave brain: "You call this a career?" She retreated at the sight of headlights signaling Miss Worple's return.

I didn't mind calling it an early evening.

Still, it took a good hour for the mental churn to slow down to where I could fall asleep. Who was who and what was what? Well, maybe some answers would turn up tomorrow. And there was the small matter of that article I was supposed to be writing . . .

The next morning I ambushed Judge Wetherby on the porch and began telling him about Zogby's visit. He interrupted. "Give me a minute."

Wetherby went inside. I sat in a rocker, telling myself to remember to ask if Wetherby knew anyone who was close to the professor.

There was, as might be expected, a breeze. I listened to wind chimes trying to make the most of it.

"Had to say hello and ask for coffee." He folded into an adjacent rocker.

I outlined what I knew of the professor's visit and asked about any contacts he could recommend.

"Wouldn't expect that kind of behavior from of a man of Zogby's stature, would you? But I've heard he can fly off the handle. Well, yes, I do believe I know someone in his department at the University. What do you figure he was so worked up about?"

"Serena said he was looking for artifacts, which makes me think of that clamshell Scrap gave Sammy. Funny thing is, he was fairly dismissive of anything to do with Sammy when I talked to him. Just being sly, I guess."

Serena brought a tray with coffee. There was cream and sugar, I supposed for the judge, and a bottle of Tabasco.

"Well, he has no right to that clamshell, or anything else of Sammy's for that matter." He paused, composing his thoughts and prompting a suspicion that he knew more than he cared to say. "As I said, I have a friend in Zogby's department at the University, perhaps he can shed some light. I'll give you his number. Are you of the opinion Zogby is involved in this Sammy situation?"

"I don't know what to think." And, really, I didn't. So I threw something up against the wall to see if it stuck. "If Sammy was killed by someone and I had to pick a possible culprit, based on my experience so far, it would be Biggers or Zinker."

The Judge had been staring off into the woods as we spoke. He turned to look at me. "Do you have any evidence to support your suspicions?"

"Nope. Just gut feeling. I wouldn't put anything past either one of them."

"Well, trust your gut a lot more than you'd trust those two. Our CD group has been discussing how to deal with them. We want them gone."

"Why is that?"

Again, that long thoughtful pause. "I'm certainly not saying either is a murderer. It's that they harass and disturb; they're up to no good."

"What kind of no good?"

"We have suspicions. We don't have evidence, so we're keeping an eye on them."

It seemed like he was holding back on what might be a useful clue. "What do you suspect? You think they're working together on something shady?"

"Holliday, I've been in public life for fifty years and I've had a lot of dealings with the press. I know better than to speculate. It comes back to bite you."

I could sympathize with his point of view. I knew reporters who were as untrustworthy as street-corner Rolex salesmen. But, except for a few minor slips, I wasn't one of them. "I'm not working on a story about Sammy, Judge. I just want to help Serena, and I'm personally curious, that's all."

"So you say now, and I believe your good intentions. But neither of us knows what twists and turns lie ahead. I've already been more candid than is my inclination."

One more try. "I didn't create the sources I had in DC by jumping into print with everything I knew. I've kept plenty of confidences. All of this is between you and me. Maybe I can help gather the evidence you need."

I wished I knew what he was thinking, or even half of it. As things stood, I was getting the molehill while he kept the mountain inside.

He opened up a bit. "Look, this isn't speculation on my part, simply one of the ideas floating around the community. Tie me to it, I'll deny it and do my best to run you out of here. Maybe they're growing marijuana or it could be they're helping move dope through the region. That sort of thing goes on. If it's anything like that, you want to be very careful with your inquiries."

"Well, if you find me in a ditch, you can add that to the evidence collection. Although I just had a run-in with that Thundercloud fellow. He'd be another candidate in the event of my demise."

Wetherby nodded. "Thundercloud and his motley crew are on our list as well. They're planning an event at Parkers Point, some sort of protest."

I had a vision of chaos. "From what I've seen and heard of Scrap Blevins, that's asking for big trouble. I'd think the authorities would intervene. There's likely to be mayhem."

Wetherby frowned. "The authorities are fairly sensitive these days. They don't want bad press over persecuting Indians."

"Even fake Indians? Well, I can't imagine Scrap will put up with it."

"That's the other side of the coin. We don't want those troublemakers around, but we don't want Scrap getting locked up for mass murder either. We'll come up with something, you can count on that."

I saw them in my mind's eye: Biggers, Thundercloud, Zinker. "Well, that's three possible candidates for blame around what happened to Sammy."

The judge held up an index finger. "And now you're ready to add Zogby to the list."

"You don't think he's homicidal?"

"I've heard he was escorted from a meeting after attacking a heckler. I'd call him dangerous, under the right conditions. Truly, from years on the bench, I think anyone is homicidal given the right circumstances."

There wasn't any right time to ask, so I just plowed ahead. "Pardon my curiosity, Judge, but would you happen to know who owns the store where Sammy was found?"

That drew a hard look. "As it happens, I do. Bought it at a tax lien auction."

"I'd heard you've bought *a lot* of properties at tax auction. Any chance Sammy was snooping around about that? I mean, there might have been some questions about conflict of interest, you being a judge."

"That was a little above his level of expertise. Very smart kid but it was other busy bodies stirred that up. There's no shortage of them around here."

"Was there a problem?"

"I might have had to step aside if certain cases had come my way. But may impress upon you the fact that I was in complete compliance with state and local public ethics laws."

Obviously, given the cold tone the judge had adopted, it was time to switch gears as far as questioning. "So you had Scrap clear out the junk there?"

"That's what Scrap does. You know, if you're really interested in my activities, I've got forty-seven file boxes of records back at the house. You're welcome to dig through them. Maybe you could write my biography."

"That's all right. I've got an assignment."

"You might be better off attending to it. Just a thought."

Chapter Twenty-Two

Vernon Putnam surprised me. Unlike his colleague Zogby he answered his phone without aid of an aide. Initially restrained, he warmed to the conversation after I'd introduced myself and mentioned Wetherby. I told him about the encounter with Zogby.

"Zogby can be a hot-head."

"That's what I was wondering; if he had a capacity for violence."

"I'm not telling what's not common knowledge. There have been times when he had to be restrained. You'll find that's a well-known fact."

"So what is his problem?"

"He's got a lucrative consulting business. Any threat to it could provoke one of his famous tantrums."

"Consulting? What's that about?"

"These days, before you can develop a building site you need to show that it is not archaeologically significant. If it happened to be, you could probably proceed at some point, but there would be a long wait while the site is investigated. Zogby is The Man in site analysis, certainly around here, and he's getting known nationally."

I briefed him on the situation regarding Sammy and told him that, as I understood it, Sammy was interested in Parkers Point. "What would there be to develop out in the marsh?"

"I'm not talking tract housing."

These were deep waters and they were going over my head. "So what are you talking? I thought perhaps Sammy had discovered a treaty or some other document that would show …"

Putnam interrupted me. "This has nothing to do with a treaty or anything of the sort. Zogby examined the site in question and found nothing of significance, no remains, no artifacts. So, unless we act on Wetherby's information, the project goes ahead."

"Whoa. What project and who is 'we'?"

There was a long pause. "I'm on the state's advisory committee on archaeology. I assumed you knew that. And, frankly, I thought you knew about the project. Are you sure Judge Wetherby recommended you call me?"

Thank you, Judge, for throwing me in without a life preserver. "He's not the most candid. Must be he thought you'd fill me in."

"I don't think so. I'm not at liberty to say more."

End of conversation. Beginning of bewilderment. Wetherby wasn't just holding back on a few details; he hadn't given me the first clue to what was going on. Questions floated in my mind's sky, billowy clouds of fluff trying to form into something that made sense.

How did Sammy's little clamshell carving fit into Zogby's findings of nothing found? Why had Wetherby let me make the phone call without briefing me on Putnam's role? What was all this stuff about a committee and development?

I'd heard the judge and Miss Worple talking. He was still around. So I sat on the porch and waited. What were chances he'd give me some straight answers? All I could do was ask. I didn't have any real leverage.

He stepped out, saw me, looked as though he was about to retreat. I stood up, making it clear he wasn't going to get away. "Your friend was helpful to a point but then he shut down when he realized I didn't know about some project at Parkers Point."

Wetherby shook his head, a gesture of despair that wasn't sincere enough to show on his face. "I can't help it if you didn't have sense enough to string him along, Holliday. Doesn't speak too well for your reporting instincts."

"The problem is, I didn't know I was on a fishing expedition, Judge. I assumed you'd told me all you know about whatever's going on."

"So much for your assumptions, eh? Well, it's politically sensitive, that's the problem. I don't want any of it attributed to me, so I gave you another source. You could have dug deeper."

"And found what? I'm still in the dark. Does this have anything to do with a report Zogby mentioned?"

Wetherby took his time, as though reviewing a variety of possible responses. "Look, I've had enough controversy in my time. I do not want any more, you understand? I put you on the trail and if you can't sniff it out, well, you're not the kind of dog you claim to be."

"Dogs? Look, you bring a city dog to the country, you think right away he's going to catch a country rabbit? Give me a break, Judge. I'm trying to figure out what happened to Sammy Sanchez. I need some help."

Wetherby massaged his chin. "Sit down then, it'll take a few minutes."

We sat, and he went on: "Yes, it has to do with a report. One of the big kicks these days is alternative energy. Grab a piece of that action and if it catches on you're on your way to owning the bank. Strange as it may seem from what you've seen here, you have by chance landed in the middle of one of the alternative energy hotspots."

He said it was all about wind farms, and an international firm, Cykco, that had vast holdings of that sort in Europe, was eager to get a foothold in the US. "Now, you know from your wanderings down that way that Parkers Point has one essential commodity in abundance, that being wind. There are other considerations, such as ease of access to the turbines."

"How does that go?"

I'd become more used to his reflective pauses. It was a style far removed from machine-gun chatter of my DC sources. I liked it better. "Generally the Bay is anywhere from twenty to two hundred and fifty feet deep. But look at a chart of the waters off Parkers Point and you've got a shallow depth for nearly a quarter of a mile, three or four feet at most, rising or falling with the tides. In the old shipping days that made it treacherous but in terms of this project, it's ideal for setting up and maintaining the towers."

Before he went on, I had a long moment to listen to a woodpecker, hammering like a carpenter framing a house. "Now, they aren't going to lower the turbines from the sky, they have to be erected, and once they are in place they require maintenance. Where do the barges and cranes dock? Where do they run the cables ashore? You need lots of infrastructure on private land. Most of the shoreline down there is state wildlife management area, scooped up dirt cheap from bankrupt landowners to provide hunting grounds for the citizenry. The only substantial site in private hands is Scrap's land."

I said it sounded like Scrap shouldn't have a care in the world. He could sell or lease his land and buy a small country with the proceeds.

"One problem. All this has been hush-hush, just the money boys and the politicians. Mulroney, of course, is right in the thick of it as middleman. Because Scrap needed money to pay off those gambling debts, Mulroney's got his name on a contract. Scrap didn't know he was signing away a goldmine. It's Mulroney and his cronies that will make the big bucks, Scrap gets peanuts unless the deal falls through somehow."

"And could it fall through? There has to be a public hearing, surely. Maybe when people learn of Mulroney's involvement, that will kill the contract."

He shook his head. "Doubtful. Nobody cares about Parkers Point except maybe a few birdwatchers and duck hunters."

"So Scrap is screwed."

"Maybe not. Enter Zogby. He made a bundle doing an archaeological assessment of the site. I mean, this was a name-your-price deal for him because he's at the top of the archaeology heap around here, the authority. He found nothing of significance, says there was nothing there but a dump for clamshells from the village up the way."

"So, like I said, Scrap is screwed."

"Hold your horses, Holliday. Zogby wouldn't be the first expert to come tumbling off his pedestal, would he? Suppose new evidence emerged to discredit his findings? The consequences are major. In the least, the project goes into limbo and Zogby loses credibility and standing. He gets sued to recover the assessment fee, somewhere way up in the tens of thousands as I hear it. Various agencies and academic interests might then want to know if he intentionally overlooked evidence. And, Zogby makes an enemy of Mulroney and the money boys, which would be very unhealthy in several ways."

An image appeared in my mind's eye. "Are we by chance talking about that little clamshell thing that Scrap gave to Sammy?"

Didn't he hear me? I asked again: "So Zogby found nothing but, thanks to Scrap, Sammy found something? And then some public spirited citizen got word of the clamshell to the state's archeological advisory committee?"

As was often the case, Wetherby thought his answer out before he spoke. "That certainly is a plausible scenario."

"But if all this has gone on behind closed doors so far, how did Sammy know about Zogby's report? I thought the comments in his notebook were referring to treaties or something else mentioned in Zogby's books, but it sure looks now as though he meant the report was bunk."

"I'd venture a guess someone tipped him."

Someone? Anyone sitting on the porch with me, by chance? "You've told me a lot. But I think you could tell me more if inclined."

"I sure as hell have told you a lot, Holliday."

"So why leave gaps? What did Sammy know?"

I was watching Wetherby as he talked but he was staring off into space. I followed his gaze. What was he doing, counting clouds? They were puffy little things, some Latin name I could never remember. As symbols, though, each one might represent another piece of the puzzle Wetherby was putting together for me. "Well, as far as the report, Sammy got wind of it somehow, he was a wonder at listening in on private conversations. He came by my office asking about it. My friend on the advisory committee had provided me with a copy. I got called away and inadvertently left the report on my desk."

I said I was shocked to learn that anyone could be so careless. That was good for rueful smile and a nod. I pushed the point: "But not so careless that you couldn't put the blame on some little snoop if any trouble resulted, right?"

A mock shrug indicated feigned innocence.

What did it all come down to? I thought I had a pretty clear picture. "And so, in challenging Zogby both personally and via the review committee, Sammy winds up poking his nose into a secret deal that might be worth a whole lot of money."

"Millions, Holliday. Around here, that's major. This isn't going to be a little local electric sort of project. Power generated here will be shipped to a National Power Grid distribution center up in Delaware, it could be sold nationwide."

I was thinking about reporters I'd known who'd met with serious accidents, even deadly violence, while asking questions about deals involving millions. And the investigative reporters I knew were experienced pros, not amateurs like Sammy.

Chapter Twenty-Three

There was a message to call McCobb. I was leaving my own message on his machine when he picked up. "Meet me at Jane's Island. Rent a canoe or kayak and follow the channel across from the dock until you hit sand, then hike over that dune to the Bay side. I'll be there."

I'd read of Jane's Island, a state park, partially on the mainland but mostly an island just offshore, not far from Crisfield where I'd had such a grand time in the company of Capt Lucky.

"Why would I want to do that?"

"I've got something interesting. You'll want to hear it."

I agreed to an early morning meeting. After all, Jane's island might be good for a few paragraphs in the article. A quick check with my guidebook advised that it was largely salt marsh, meaning, soak well in repellent.

In addition to several thousand acres of marshland, the park includes eight miles of beaches, much of that accessible only by boat.

In the course of breakfast chat – I breakfasted, she chatted – Serena asked about my plans for the day. I told her I was off on a boat trip to Jane's Island. As I was leaving she presented a brown paper bag and a thermos.

I kissed her cheek. She gave me a look of mock surprise and hurried back toward the kitchen.

Though described as salt marsh, the grounds visible from the entryway to the park looked like a fairly urban recreation area with picnic pavilions and ball fields. I found the boat rental station with no trouble and chose a canoe from among the variety of boats offered, including kayaks and motorboats.

The basics came back to me fairly quickly. Paddle too much on this side you get headed for that side. Balance, that was the trick. Maybe I should write about the zen of paddling your own canoe.

On the waterway leading to the mainland beach tourists in rental boats fished or tried their luck at crabbing with small pots or chicken necks on string. It was their outfits – foldaway fishing hats like the one I'd picked up, photographer vests, khaki pants with seventeen pockets – that identified them as tourists. The standard uniform of the local watermen was jeans and tee shirt, baseball cap, maybe a sweatshirt if the weather was cool.

I wondered if McCobb slept in his trench coat and fedora. Maybe not the fedora. Or maybe he didn't sleep. A half-mast wave of his hand passed for greeting. He stepped close, producing a micro-cassette recorder from a pocket. I asked why we had to meet way out here.

"You never know."

Naturally, my eyes followed the recorder as it disappeared back into a pocket. "You never know what?"

"You don't want to know. I checked you out, Mr So-called Holliday. Wasn't long ago you were on a lot of watch lists."

"That's not news, exactly. It says more about you than about me. You have access to watch lists."

We were walking the shoreline. For once I was grateful to Cole for his suggestions; my feet got wet but I was wearing tennis shoes, so it didn't matter much.

McCobb picked up a shell. It was a clamshell, similar to the one Sammy had but without the carving. "The watermen bring clams up along with the oysters they're after. Just a few, not worth selling. Shuck 'em and eat 'em, right on the spot, fresh as can be."

"You've tried raw clams?"

"Sure. Chewy. Briny."

"Thing is, McCobb, what's this all about?"

"This? Say, I liked that story of yours a while back on diplomats using immunity to smuggle antiquities. A real wonder that one didn't get you killed. And the secret CIA contract with the escort service to entertain visiting dignitaries? There's hell to pay over that one. You had credit card receipts that traced to the strip in Baltimore. Somebody was sure stirring up trouble. I truly believed they'd have to pick you up with tweezers after that came out. Charmed life. But you sure got suckered on that last one."

I couldn't figure out where our conversation was headed. But it was obvious McCobb knew a lot about me, too much for the average newspaper reader.

"I thought I had solid sources. They came across good as gold, I would have bet on it. And now it's as though they never existed."

"They definitely used good bait. But what's so surprising? My guess is it was payback for something you'd written. The Agency has a long memory and, unofficially of course, a tendency to settle old scores."

I didn't like the sound of that. "So are you one of the score-settlers?"

"Not where you're concerned."

Seagulls shrieked and swooped above us, apparently just joy-riding in the coastal breeze. Off in the distance, out on the Bay, a freighter bound from who knows where plowed water toward the port of Baltimore.

I figured I might as well act as if I knew what I didn't know. Sometimes that works. "So you're still associated with those people? I got the impression you were retired."

McCobb's smile came and went in a flash. "Those people? From rumors I've heard, you never really get out of that game. Except the hard way. As a retirement present, I got set up in a little import business, just wandering off to Africa or the Caribbean to inspect coffee crops, you know what I mean? It was a decent cover. But somehow, I wound up in a stinking hellhole jungle jail. Had to send in the Seals to get me out. Well, two Seals. The extra one was just in case."

"I'm surprised you're telling me so much," I said. "You guys don't usually talk about your trade unless you're seriously drunk."

"Us guys, is it. Well, Holliday, seeing as you're screwed as far as credibility, I'm as safe talking to you as if I was talking to a lamppost. Safer, these days."

"Thanks a lot."

"You know damn well it's true." McCobb studied the horizon and the few fishing boats bobbing out on the Bay. He surveyed the big dune I'd crossed. He looked up and down the shoreline and then at the sky. I took all that for dramatic gestures. There was no way he could actually tell if some big-ear satellite was tuned in on us. "You blundered into a lot of great stories, right?"

"True. Seems I was, as you say, charmed. Fate steered me to the right place at the right time, something like that."

"You were spoon-fed."

"By whom?"

"You'll never know."

McCobb must take me for thick as a brick. Of course I knew, to some extent, but the benefits outweighed any urge to be overly curious. No need to get defensive about it though, might as well play to his perception of me as useful idiot. "Come to think of it, I'd been running into some strange people, time and time again. There was this foreign colonel with kind of a German or Russian accent and an acrobatic wife ..."

"Too obvious. You're pissing in the wind, Holliday. You'll never figure it out. In DC, the bartender is Mossad and the taxi driver is KGB. It's hopeless to waste time guessing. Half the staff of that news outfit you worked for was plugged in somewhere; our guys or their guys or both."

I tried to look shocked and appalled. He fished out the microcassette player from a trench coat pocket. "So, here is what I have for you. It's a little recording I made the other night. Listen."

He held the recorder close to my ear. I heard a bird.

"That is Chuck Will's Widow, big night bird, not as big as a hoot owl but big. Sounds like a Bob White but there's more to its call, more complexity."

"You brought me out here to listen to a birdcall?"

"No, just keep listening, more to come."

The bird completed a three-verse serenade and then came a human voice. "You stupid old sot. You're drawing too much attention. They're gonna catch on."

McCobb clicked off the recorder. "That's Zinker, the rent-a-cop." He held the thing up again.

Then a different voice, slurring: "By God, you're not gonna run roughshod over me, dammit. We're partners. You got some of my deal, I get some of yours."

"I got no partners, specially not some damn drunk that can't be trusted. Watch yourself, you'll be ..."

The next few sentences were inaudible.

This time I recognized Biggers' voice, something between a mutter and mumble. "What you so damn worried about, nobody's on to us."

And then Zinker: "That nosy writer. You can't trust writers. Anything goes on, scribble-scribble, next thing they're writing it. Then ever-body would know."

"Chickenshit, that guy. I shot his lady friend's dog an' he didn't raise a finger."

"Your brain is a brick, Biggers He walloped you good and you don't even know it. And what's this lady friend stuff? Serena? He lays a hand on her ... You just get rid of the evidence, like I said, and be quick about it."

"First you cut yourself in on my business, now you're giving orders, trying to cut me out of my share of your stuff. You can only push me so far, sorry-ass phony cop."

"I can push you into a jail cell for a long, long time, buster. Do as I say."

McCobb shut off the recorder. "Then they walked away, still talking, but that's all I got."

"What do you figure they're up to?"

"A thing or two, but who knows what? Sounds like Biggers had something going and Zinker cut himself in. And now Zinker's got something going, Biggers wants a piece of that. Maybe a pot farm out in the marshes somewhere. Maybe a meth lab."

"And nobody stumbles on it?"

"If they do they forget it, for health reasons. But I've heard your friends Wetherby and Worple are out to lower the boom on those two, some way or other."

"They haven't said anything specific."

"Wouldn't. Not to a journalist."

"Funny thing is, if I found somebody was packaging crack cocaine as baby formula, *Here & There* wouldn't print it. Well, maybe, if the dopers took a big ad."

"That rag has no credibility."

"You're saying it's a good match up?"

"I'm saying, you want the tape?"

"Keep it. Something happens to me, send it to somebody who might get some use out of it."

"And who would that be? Next of kin?"

"I was thinking more like the state police."

He didn't have to flippantly wish me good luck. His look handled that, eyebrows raised and upside down smile. He turned, about to head in the direction of the big dune. He must have had a canoe or kayak stashed, but I hadn't seen it.

"One thing, McCobb. Are you part of this wind farm deal?"

"Wind farm? What the hell do I care about some damned wind farm?" He tossed down the clamshell he'd been carrying and walked away.

After returning the boat I sat on a bench beside the canal and enjoyed a lunch somewhat reminiscent of brown bag school lunches of long ago – salami with cheese for sandwiches, a packet of celery and carrot sticks, a small bag of chips, two oatmeal cookies – great fun. I thought I should give Serena another kiss, but maybe not. One thing leads to another.

The bonus was that she had included a bottle of hot sauce. A few drops from the small bottle put some kick in the still-warm coffee.

I asked a park ranger about a shortcut to Chincoteague. I'd had to go a long way north in order to hit a place where I could turn south to Crisfield. She smiled and asked where I'd parked my helicopter. But then she added that I could take a right at Marion Station and head over through Frogeye, cutting about twenty miles off the route I'd taken coming in.

Of course, I had no business going back to visit Thundercloud. I had enough information to mention him in the article and my remaining questions had nothing to do with the *Here & There* assignment. Besides, he'd asked that I call before coming by. But I doubted there would be an invitation.

I eased my conscience with a few stops at little shops and restaurants along the way, collecting business cards from a fish market featuring real fish that you could look in the eye rather than those unrecognizable frozen slabs from the supermarket, a busy bait and tackle shop where the owner actually seemed genuinely interested in each customer's request or question, and a farm and garden emporium so extensive it could have been an arboretum. I struck out on the Mexican restaurant, a look through the front window left me wondering if it had served its last taco.

There were several cars parked in front of Thundercloud's shop, and two bicycles close to the building. Inside, I heard singing.

We love the creatures of the forest,

We love the birds in the sky,

We love the fishes in the deep blue sea,

Let's share our hugs with all the bugs,

There's no need to ask why ...

Through the second beaded curtain I saw a group formed in a circle, doing a hopping, swaying sort of dance as they sung. The circle was all women, of various ages, the youngest likely a teenager in cutoff shorts and a bikini top, and the eldest probably a grandma, in Bermudas and a tie-dyed tee shirt. In the center stood Thundercloud, singing along but also making motions to illustrate the song, flapping like bird, wiggling like a fish, embracing himself and nodding approval as he met each pair of eyes.

My first instinct was to run. It might be contagious.

I stood and stared.

Thundercloud caught sight of me and grimaced. "All right, my precious ones, that will do for today. Don't forget the Saturday powwow, and those who aren't paid up be sure to do so beforehand. Scoot along, now, scoot along."

Several of the women scooted past me as ordered.

"… He's so inspirational, it's like hanging out with Buddha or Jesus …"

"… But he's so much more fun than those guys, I mean, really, don't you think so? …"

"… I could just hug the whole planet right now …"

Two women remained, fixated on Thundercloud as if he had just descended from the sky on a golden stairway, and apparently asking questions I could not hear. "Not now, not now. See you Saturday night, be sure to bring candles."

I waited, browsing the display cases of faux Indian jewelry. Actually there were a few nice pieces tucked among the junk. A few big turquoise-studded rings that looked hand-worked, not assembly line castings. Two hefty squash blossom necklaces. A couple of nice inlaid buckles.

The two women joined the scooters. Thundercloud greeted me with a distinct lack of warmth, arms folded, no hand offered. "I do believe I asked that you call me."

"I happened to be in the neighborhood. The door was open."

"The door is always open. Even when it's closed."

"A commendable policy. Well, I had a couple of questions."

"You know, I had a look at your magazine, whatever it's called, a waste of pulpwood, not the sort of thing I'd want to be seen in."

I manufactured a smile. "That's why they brought me in, Chief. I'm the fixit guy, hired to brighten and beautify those tired old pages. And you can be featured in the story that blazes the path in that new direction."

He closed his eyes, meditatively. "The way I see it, Holliday, this is your last stop before cranking out fillers for fortune cookies. But I'll play along for a few minutes. What's on your mind?"

Of course I felt defensive, but what was there to defend? He had the magazine pegged, in my humble estimation, and me as well. "I'm sure readers would want to know how to become members of your club."

"It's not a club. Don't be ridiculous. We are spiritual seekers, dreamers who make our dreams real. We are a tribe. Of course, those who are accepted are encouraged to assist financially. There are expenses."

"Sure, that makes sense. So, what's it cost?"

"For you or generally?"

"I'm not looking for special consideration, Chief. On the other hand, I do represent our army of readers, coast to coast and border to border."

"I wasn't thinking in terms of special consideration, at least not as you interpret the phrase."

"OK, so what's the deal?"

"The deal, as you term it, is that an approved initiate can enter the outer circle for a donation of one hundred dollars ... seventy-five cash."

"And the inner circle?"

"The initiate progresses through the various circles gathering greater and greater powers, the innermost is restricted to a very select few and so there is bidding for those spots."

Bidding? That was a new one on me. I tucked it away for later. "Well, another thing; I'm not sure how we establish your credentials as an Indian. You have to admit, you look, I don't know, maybe out of a Russian fairy tale."

"Put that in your article and I'll have your scalp. Reincarnation is a marvelous process. Once you discover who you were in a former existence you can reconnect with that spirit."

There comes a time when you've just got to get down to business. I gave it a shot: "I found some comments in Sammy Sanchez's notebook that I don't think would have been to your liking. He says you just make things up and pass them off as historical or spiritual truth."

Thundercloud grimaced and glanced around. It crossed my mind that he might be looking to see if there would be witnesses if made good on his scalping threat. "Sammy? I tried my best to help him and he as much as spat in my face with his false accusations."

"I got the impression he thought you were scamming, that you want Parkers Point for a carnival style Indian theme park, maybe a casino resort."

He spoke like the cop who was one step away from swinging the nightstick. "I warn you, Holliday, and you do not listen. There was a time when an enemy of the tribe would have been tied to a stake and roasted."

"Or beaten up and tossed in an abandoned refrigerator?"

"That's outrageous. My message is one of peace and love."

"You haven't convinced me of that."

Was his every move part of an act? The next moment, he relaxed and smiled. I swear I thought he was about to hug me. I'm sure I looked toward the front door, instinctively mapping my escape.

"Holliday, I do believe your talents are wasted. You're a smart guy, how about coming into the winners' circle? We could use a savvy writer to help promote the cause, might be some real money in it."

"In 'it'? I'm not sure what you mean, 'it'?"

"Well, Sammy was on the right track, he just had the wrong attitude. Strictly confidentially, if we can get that land at Parkers Point – the sacred home of our ancestors, you understand – we can fill in the marsh, get investors, put in a resort, condos and all that. Of course we'd stay true to the Indian theme, change the name to Pocahontas Point. How's that sound?"

"You'd have gambling?"

"By all means."

"But if it's sacred land?"

"Wise up. Once we get it, it's up to us, we'd be sovereign. Besides, the original people were big on gambling games."

"So Sammy was right. Isn't that something? And he was going to expose your scheme to grab the land, turn it into a casino resort."

"I'm not getting through to you, am I, Holliday? I thought you might have real potential. Too bad. Well, I think our interview is concluded."

"Whatever. I guess I've got an interesting story, Thundercloud claims property as sacred so he can build a casino resort."

"If I were you I wouldn't approach it that way. You notice that the spirits did not deal kindly with Sammy, could be there's a message there for you."

"I'd love to stay and listen to more threats, Chief, but I don't want to hold you up. They'll be missing you from in front of the cigar store."

Chapter Twenty-Four

I woke up with at least a temporary urge to act responsibly. With a little actual work I could wrap up the article over the coming weekend and clear out before it was too late, too late to avoid getting tangled up in intrigues and in the lives of other people.

Somewhere in the region would be an event to focus on, I didn't really care what, but something featuring chickens or crabs would be ideal, and I'd even take an art show, concert, flea market, boat race or parade, whatever. All I needed was a glance at the calendar in a local newspaper.

As I made my way to the nearest convenience store, it occurred to me that it might also be a good day to ambush Zogby. I know, I was going to clear out, not get involved. But I was involved, and the questions would follow me if I fled without answers.

A surprise appearance at Zogby's office might shock him into a revelation. It would just take a few minutes time. And then I could go off in search of festivals.

I was some ways from the university so, in a rare display of foresight, I called Zogby's office to make sure he was in.

"He is working from home today."

"I need his address. I have a big, fat check for him."

"Sorry, his orders are that he's not to be disturbed. You can leave the check here at his office."

"It's too big to leave lying around, madam. I have to deliver it personally. And I'm leaving town this afternoon."

"I don't believe a word of it. You're that snoopy reporter who called the other day." Click.

Losing my touch? Found out before I'd even got to the door. A bad omen. I sought solace in coffee.

The two ladies behind the counter at the convenience store were deep into an assessment of a third party whose sins, apparently, would have brought a blush to a bawdyhouse madam.

My transaction, paying for coffee and a newspaper, was completed without even a break in the hot gossip. Upon inquiry, a telephone book thumped on the counter accompanied by "... and you know what *she's* like, the little tramp."

No listing for Zogby.

I called his colleague, Vernon Putnam, whose name Wetherby had given to me. Our last conversation had ended abruptly. When he answered, I immediately apologized for being ill prepared when last we talked.

I told Putnam that Wetherby had clarified a few things for me, now I needed to confront Zogby but couldn't find a home address. He asked me to hold the line for a moment.

"Here it is. Twenty-three Fawkes Lane."

"Twenty-three Fox Lane, got it."

"Fawkes."

"Fox."

"Listen carefully. Fawke as in gawk."

"Oh, Fawke."

"You're getting there. Fawkes."

Really, when you think about it, Fawkes is a tough one. Of course there's the "aw" sound, but it depends on who's making the sound how it comes out; talks, socks. Smallpox.

That's what I thought about as I hunted for Zogby's number on a side street that probably hadn't changed much since horse and carriage days.

There were great piles of brick in the solid old colonial style, with columned entrances or half-acre porches, others done in clapboard like their country cousins, the farmhouses, and some sprawling in the 'big house, little house, kitchen' arrangement. The rule was manicured lawns and gardens. And then there was one that broke the rules.

Why Zogby's neighbors tolerated the tangled shrubs passing for a front lawn and the shabby exterior, its former yellow mostly faded to mottled mustard, I could not guess. It was a cottage, a good-sized first floor and then little dormers above, bedrooms I assumed, where small windows provided a peep at the outside world. As for being a neighborhood nuisance, no sense going to court to have the place torn down when it soon would tumble of its own accord.

I knocked on the front door, shaking loose a few chips of old paint. The door opened only enough to display a large nose and hints of a small man attached to it

"Whatever it is I don't have time for it."

"I'm working on a magazine article. Mind if I come in for a minute?"

"Oh, you. Indeed I do mind. I'm on my way out for an important engagement. May I suggest that you make an appointment?"

"I'll be glad to. Can I come in and discuss it?"

"Absolutely not." He was still speaking through the barely open door.

"So how do I make an appointment?"

"Go to the devil, make an appointment with him and keep it." He shrank back to give himself leverage in slamming the door. It must be a local ritual. I'd encountered the same treatment on my first visit to Bay Breezes. I put myself at risk of serious injury by planting a foot on the sill. It was time to play hardball.

"I think Sammy was murdered. You're withholding evidence."

"A preposterous supposition!"

"Sammy disagreed with your findings on Parkers Point. I need a response from you for my article."

At least now I had a clear view of him. I could imagine that, wrapped in robes and topped with skullcap, he might look like an overfed, pompous prince of the church. But he wasn't bestowing blessings. "I need not respond to the provocative fabrications of a know-nothing nobody. Go away or I'm calling the police."

"I'm giving you an opportunity to tell your side of the story. This is going to look bad in print."

"You will look bad behind bars for trespass. Now, clear off."

"You're making a mistake."

"We will see who is making the mistake. I would be well within my rights to shoot you. Out, out!"

What could I do? I doubted that a nosy stranger in a small town would fare well if Zogby complained to the police. It seemed highly unlikely that von Klonk would foot my bail. The mood he'd been in, he'd try to add to the charges.

I sat in my car and wondered what next.

I'd crawled through a few windows in my day. In pursuit of truth, you understand, not for personal gain. Well, yes, I might have gained personally if I'd found the truth. But that was then. These days, I had a clearer notion of consequences. A prison cell might solve my housing problems but it would also put a very solid lid on my trashed reputation.

"Holliday, you've been dodging my phone calls." Yes, it was von Klonk again. I could have told him that his calls were like listening to a sadistic weather reporter who invariably forecasts rain. I didn't.

"I was too sick to come to the phone. Nobody warned me about salmonella poisoning. I followed orders and went to the chicken festival. It's taken me days to recover. They thought I was a goner."

"You are a goner, Holliday, but first I want the story. By the way, the ad guys are on me about, who is it, Chief Thundermug. What are you doing poaching on the boss's territory, Chincoteague? You're asking for big trouble, as is your apparent penchant."

"I was nowhere near Chincoteague, I was on the approved, specified pathway when suddenly –- Cowabunga! –- there he was, this guy in a war bonnet, demanding to be included in the story. I had to deal with him, I was in fear for my life."

"Cowabunga, Holliday?"

"It's Indian talk."

"Sure it is. You're certifiable. And I don't believe a damn word of your bonkers excuse. But now you've got the ad guys worried. Seems Thundermug isn't taking an ad because he thinks we're going to do a hatchet job."

"Fair turnabout since that's what he threatened to do on me. Capt Jack Thundercloud – that's who you mean – don't worry, I'll calm him down."

"Do that. *Here & There* doesn't do bad light. I thought I made that clear."

"Absolutely. In fact I'm working on a profile that spotlights him as the second coming of Hiawatha, the noblest of the noble savages. I'll have it wrapped up in the next couple of days."

"Couple of days? Get it done and get your ass out of there. Looks like there's a hurricane going to smack into you. Are you aware of that?"

"Hurricane? Really?"

"Don't you listen to the news? LouLou, that's its name. Coming right at you."

"You're concerned about my welfare."

"Not in the least, but I want that damn story. Get a move on, Holliday."

I probably should have gotten a move on, but I felt stalled out. I roamed the empty house. Serena was at work at the pizza restaurant; Miss Worple was off on some mission. I looked through the door of Serena's room. The picture she'd showed me of Sammy was propped on the bureau. A proud looking young fellow, sporting that fancy belt buckle his father had left behind.

Fortunately, Barney Cole called with an invitation to dinner. "Meet me at Ray's Shanty on the road to Chincoteague. Great seafood."

There was a carnival parade of towed boats, from skiffs to sailboats and big powercraft, on the main road, an unusual sight that I first thought might indicate a festival in the offing. But then, let's see, could it have to do with the hurricane? The boats were in retreat.

I pulled into the crowded parking lot. The building would have been easy to pass by if it hadn't been for the sign. From the outside you could have taken it for a warehouse or small factory.

Inside, old ads and artifacts adorned the muted brown walls, bits of local seaside history. Heavy wooden tables and chairs added to the rustic feel of the place. The booths were genuine enclosures, not just back to back seating separated by a headboard. As I studied the menu and munched hushpuppies, Cole rattled on about the crab cakes, oysters, fish in a variety of fried, broiled and baked variations. "Take your pick, you won't be disappointed."

Ever the contrarian, I picked the prime rib.

A platter arrived, something with shells. Cole explained: "Appetizer. Oysters on the half shell."

I guess I've led a sheltered life. Oysters in a stew, yes, but raw? No, haven't been there. Did you ever look at an oyster really close? They look like something left over after surgery, the doctor says "Don't worry, Mr Holliday, we got it!"

Watching Barney, I tried to follow his lead, loosening the beast with a little fork before chugging it. I learned later that his was the style of the true aficionado, no cocktail sauce, no lemon, just appreciate the real flavor. To my uneducated palate, about as appetizing as a gulp of seawater.

Hopefully I'll never swallow my tongue, but I can say I had some practice while on the Eastern Shore. That's what eating raw oysters felt like. I made my way through three and left the rest for Cole. He accepted my apology for not being a big fan of uncooked mollusks and emptied the tray with great enthusiasm.

The prime rib didn't disappoint. It wouldn't have disappointed two people. But if asked I wouldn't have shared. I didn't know when I'd see the next meal anywhere near as good.

At the same time, I could have swapped plates with Cole, his piled with clams, mussels, rockfish and shrimp.

I was listening to Cole, answering his questions about how the article was coming along in ways I thought might please him. But my third ear, that mystical device which often provides reporters with information they might otherwise miss, was tuned to surrounding conversations.

People were talking about Hurricane LouLou, what to do, where to take their boats, the history of disastrous hurricanes thereabouts.

"Isn't it early in the season for a hurricane?" I asked.

"Maybe you'd like to take that up with Mother Nature. It's true, tropical storms are more the norm this time of year, though it is officially hurricane season. A tropical storm can be just shy of hurricane strength, and pack near as much wallop."

Cole said he wanted to meet with me because he thought it would be best to clear out for now and come back another time. "The way they're predicting, the storm's coming right up the Bay and smack into us. Hurricanes can make a mess of things. You should take a break and come back when it's tidied up."

I'd already heard von Klonk's demand, wrap up the article and clear out. No doubt there was wisdom in that. Unfortunately, I hadn't got started writing it quite yet. "Where's a safe place if I do happen to get caught here?"

"Do you know anything about hurricanes, Holliday? They like nothing better than to make a mockery of the very idea of *safe place*. Get across the bridge, and go soon because there'll be a monumental traffic jam, and then they'll close it."

"Close the Bay Bridge? How will anyone get out then?"

"They won't. There are other ways out, further north, and those will be gridlocked. Personally, I'm heading for my sister's place in Baltimore, soon as we finish here."

"I don't get the panic. There are houses here – and I'd say Bay

Breezes is one — that have stood for hundreds of years. That's many a hurricane season."

"What you don't see is the houses that aren't here. Read your history. And just because the house survives is no guarantee the occupants will. There've been hurricanes kicked up tsunamis, gigantic walls of water. Left some solid buildings standing and drowned every living thing in them. They found bodies seven and ten miles from where the person stood when the water wall came through. It's no joke."

I passed on dessert. I just wasn't in the mood.

Cole must have known that this time I was ready to claim I'd left my wallet back at Bay Breezes. He covered the bill and the tip without comment. As we parted company in the parking lot, he asked if I'd given up on the notion that Sammy was murdered.

"Nowhere near. I really want to know what happened."

"You're better off forgetting it, Holliday. A wild goose chase if ever there was one."

"Good of you to be concerned, but I'll probably keep poking around. Thanks for the dinner and the hurricane warning." I didn't mention that he still owed me for our last dining experience.

"Hate to see you wasting your time," he muttered, walking away.

Chapter Twenty-Five

I stopped at several motels out on the main highway. They weren't particularly busy at the moment but each of the clerks I talked to said they expected to be booked solid in short order, thanks to the approaching hurricane. Not that they were on high ground, exactly, but they were higher and more inland than a lot occupied places on the peninsula.

It occurred to me that as a travel-writer I should give a critique of the motels, but what to say? Maybe there was a book on how to critique a motel? Maybe a university offered a course I could monitor? "This motel is habitable, does not appear to be infested with bugs, and has clean rooms and a pool. The pool looks fairly inviting, you can see bottom. In the corridors are several vending machines."

Could be I just wasn't cut out for travel writing. Truth be told, I had only a vague idea what it entailed. Magazines I'd seen in dentist or doctor offices, I'd reviewed mostly for the pictures. As for the freebies like *Here & There*, I might have glanced through that sort of thing on a trip, checking the ads for a burger stand or pizza shop. Topless bars with bottomless drinks? Scary.

The thought that pestered me between stops was of Cole's continued efforts to steer me away from the story behind Sammy's death. Could it be Cole had something to hide that might turn up in the course of an investigation?

Somehow that made me all the more determined to find out what really happened to Sammy. But was it really such a great idea to stay and ride out a hurricane? I'd never been in an actual hurricane, but from what I'd seen in the film, *Key Largo,* it wasn't an event I'd care to experience. Flooding. Wild wind. Debris flying around.

But, look on the bright side. In the end, the sun came out. All was well, generally speaking. Except for those people who got drowned.

On my way downstairs in the morning I heard Serena talking to someone at the front door.

"Mandatory is a command, Serena. Now, pack up and I'll get us somewhere safe. It's a mandatory evacuation."

"I am staying right here."

"You'll be on your own."

"I *am* on my own. Thanks for the offer, but goodbye."

She gave the door such a slam that pictures and mirrors rattled on the walls, knickknacks and vases danced on little tables.

And then I heard Miss Worple. "What's all the racket? Who was that, Serena?"

"That pest Zinker. He wants to evacuate me."

"Is that so? And you told him?"

"To get lost, of course. I'll have nothing to do with him."

Miss Worple folded her arms and fixed her eyes on the door that had just slammed. "We'll be doing something with him, soon enough, don't you worry." She saw me, standing at the foot of the stairs. "Sorry about the noise. These Latin types, you know, they have such tempers."

I didn't know, except as stereotype, but it was far too early in the day for getting into it. "A lot of people have tempers. Shouldn't we all be leaving? The hurricane may come right through, the last I heard."

Miss Worple shook her head. "The Worples don't run from

hurricanes. Those men who do the yard work, they'll be around to sandbag the doors and close the shutters."

"You barricade yourself in?"

"We can still come and go through the kitchen. This old house has ridden out many a hurricane, Mr Holliday. It's not going anywhere just because LouLou is coming through."

The phone rang. Serena answered and looked at me. "For you."

She couldn't know that I didn't want to speak to von Klonk. What would I tell him? I'm about to leave because of the hurricane, but I'll have to come back later to finish the article? He'd go ballistic.

Not to worry. I had to think for a moment when the caller identified himself as Vernon Putnam. It was the colleague of Professor Zogby, the one who had been surprised at how little I knew of the Parkers Point controversy.

"Wetherby wants me to pass this on to you. Zogby asked that I take his class while he's off on an errand. He seemed highly agitated. I couldn't get a lot out of him but I'm fairly sure he's going to Parkers Point. He thinks if there are any artifacts there, the hurricane might reveal them."

"So he can pitch them into the Bay before anyone else sees them? Sounds like he's desperate. As I hear it, the Point will likely be flooded."

"Desperate is a good word. But he's right, storms do sometimes reveal what has been hidden. Anyway, that's all I know."

I thanked him. But I wasn't so sure about thanking Wetherby. There was now a big problem. Should I do the sane thing and clear out or head for the Point and see what Zogby was up to?

Well, they say the best reporters are those whose instinct is to run toward the sound of gunfire rather than away. I wanted to be counted among the best, didn't I? Well?

I stepped out on the porch to survey the situation. The atmosphere was warning of trouble brewing. In the dreamy, pale light it seemed as though the sun had not yet risen, as though the illumination was done with neon. The wind was a loud whisper, like traffic. You could smell the humidity in the air.

Miss Worple joined me.

"LouLou is down around Norfolk according to the television. If you're leaving you'd better go now. All indications are it's headed right toward us."

"I thought it would be more ferocious."

"The calm before the storm. You can never really tell about a hurricane. Some tear the place apart, some sail overhead and are no worse than a hard rain. Are you leaving or not?"

Time to make up my mind. "Well, if you're going to tough it out, I guess I can as well."

"You should be safe in the house. I have to run over to meet quickly with the Judge and some friends. A little problem has come up."

"A little problem. You mean LouLou?"

"More than that. You've heard us talk of Thundercloud?"

"The fake Indian. We've met."

"That crazy man is bringing his mob here. They're planning a ceremony at the Point."

"A ceremony? When?"

"As the hurricane arrives."

"They must be nuts."

"All the more reason we've got to deal with it. The handout he's spread around says they'll be calling upon ancient spirits to halt the hurricane. Our fear is mischief they'll cause and blame on the storm."

"You're going to try to stop him?"

"Try? We'll do better than that."

The road in front of Bay Breezes is seldom disturbed by traffic, a lane so quiet that a passing car is an occasion for comment. In the rare event of passersby, Miss Worple or Serena were often drawn to a window to see if the vehicle contained friend or foreigner, and though unable to sort tourist from local, I sometimes joined in the surveillance game.

One or the other was bound to say: "Where do they think they're going?" After all, the road dead ends at Scrap's patch of marsh. Basically it goes nowhere.

The appearance of a caravan of eight vehicles was, therefore, as unexpected as a fish in the bathwater.

They traveled at a snail's pace, apparently lost.

Miss Worple had left for the meeting of the Civil Defense group. Serena heard the sounds and joined me at the window. "I wonder if that's Thundercloud's bunch."

She shook her head. "No idea. Mad people, with the weather coming."

"I'll go have a look."

"Don't go. Might be a gang of bad people looking for trouble. You don't know."

"I need to know what's going on."

"Then you're as big a fool as them."

I followed the crowd on foot.

They parked in wide spots along the road's edge near the Point. After initial twists the road is arrow straight, so at some distance I could see as from each vehicle emerged six or eight people, wrapped in plastic ponchos and wearing headbands adorned with feathers. They were forming up in marching order. It looked like a parade of large birds.

I caught up with the last of the end of the line. "What's going on?"

"We're going to stop the hurricane."

"You're with Thundercloud?"

"He's leading a ceremony."

Above the wind – it was now setting the treetops dancing – the marchers raised a weird chant: "Ho Ah Ho, Hey Ah Hey! Hurricane must blow away. Woooooooo!"

Up at the front of the formation I could see Thundercloud in his floppy war bonnet, raising his fist in time with the chant. He waved them forward and they were off, ponchos and feathers flapping, heading toward the Point.

I tagged along at a discreet distance. Down along the line of marchers came a shout. "The game warden has a poacher! The game warden captured a poacher!"

"Cruelty to animals!"

"Slaughterer of wildlife!"

"Let's get the poacher!"

Oh, marvelous. Now what? The crowd broke into a trot. Although I had long ago decided running was an activity indulged in only when chased, I lumbered along behind.

Past the rustic bridge and the No Trespassing sign, the gate lay bent and crumpled, and just beyond it was the apparent battering ram, Biggers' truck. He stood beside the truck, pistol in hand, and facing him, holding a spade like a baseball bat, was little Zogby.

I could see that the two were yelling at each other but the words were lost in the wind and the chatter of Thundercloud's mob. From the looks on their faces, though, it was an easy guess they were not exchanging courtesies. I was witnessing a Zogby temper tantrum.

Thundercloud's crew formed up at the battered gate, awaiting orders from the faux Indian-in-chief.

Biggers turned toward the assembly, his pistol wavering in their direction. Zogby careened over to where I was standing, some distance apart from the group. "He's crazy. He thinks I'm some kind of investigator out to get him. I haven't the vaguest idea what he's talking about. What in blazes is going on here?"

"They think this is sacred ground. Things are liable to get nasty."

"That's absurd. This is a dump, I've proven that."

Biggers was slouched against his truck with the pistol still carelessly aimed at Thundercloud and his war party. He was ranting, but not at anyone in particular.

The sky was turning stormy black. The wind drove a salt mist off the Bay where leaping waves sported frothy white caps. The muck at our feet had turned to slime and the slime was turning to water, water everywhere.

"We come as friends!" Thundercloud roared.

Biggers peered in Thundercloud's direction as though the world ten feet beyond his nose was a blur, leaning forward as if the gain of a few inches might clarify the view. He lurched around and clambered aboard his truck.

After sitting for a moment in apparent confusion, he raised a bottle to his lips for a long pull and then fired up the engine, gunned it a time or two and shot forward, sending the flock diving from his path. He tore across the bridge.

The wind was picking up, the sound like a big engine approaching from the Bay side. And then there was a slightly different sound, the grumbling rumble of an ATV. It was Scrap, coming at us full throttle out of the marsh grass. He slammed to a stop in front of the assembly and raised the big, ugly shotgun. Three explosions rang out.

"Open season on hippies, yee-haw!"

As one, the crowd froze.

Zogby had eased around behind me as if I might serve as a shield. I was going to suggest that it might be a good time for us to clear out, but when I turned to say it, there was no Zogby. I glanced toward the road back to Bay Breezes and saw him hurrying along at a waddling run across the bridge.

All eyes were on Scrap. No one paid attention to Zogby's exit.

Thundercloud began walking in Scrap's direction. "We come in peace. We are going to stop the hurricane."

"Stop it in your own damn backyard, buncha clowns. Get the hell outta here."

A half dozen more explosions rang out. Scrap had lowered his sights though he was still firing over the feathered heads. The rear ranks of the gathering broke as braves and bravettes fled toward their vehicles.

Thundercloud turned back toward his flock. "Face your fears! He's bluffing!"

His flock was in flight.

Scrap got out of the ATV. He advanced, shotgun at the ready. "You got ten seconds to change direction, feather-head." He fired a round into the muck just ahead of where he stood, sending up a splatter of mud in Thundercloud's direction.

Thundercloud threw down his war bonnet and bolted through what remained of his flock. They folded in and followed at a run, their chanting now exchanged for squawks like disturbed geese.

I was the only one left.

"This ain't no bus stop. *Move* I told you!"

"Ease up, Scrap. I'm not one of that crowd."

"Oh, it's you. Wetherby's pal." I guess that was a good thing because he put the shotgun back behind the seat of the ATV. "Didn't bring your walking on water shoes? Well, we gotta get out of this mess. The tide's rising. Come on."

Just then Serena came running toward us, sloshing through the rising water, rain poncho threatening to become a kite. "I was worried. There are cars all over the place stuck up that way, nutty people running up the road."

Scrap didn't seem the type to ask divine assistance, so I suppose when he looked up at the heavens he was gauging the storm. The wind had risen to a roar, grasses were bending low, and the water was rising around us. "Both of you get in, now or never. We'll find a way through."

Serena looked at the two-seater, shrugged and climbed on my lap. Sometimes even a bad day has its moments. I put my arms around her middle, a human seat belt.

The stream under the bridge – Scrap called it a gut –had blended with surrounding rising waters. Scrap stopped and got out, wading forward. I couldn't hear exactly what he shouted but his grim look telegraphed trouble. "The damn bridge is all tore up."

The rain was lashing us two ways, down and sideways. The wind tossed debris like darts. Talking meant yelling.

I had a question that I thought might be pertinent. "Will this thing float?"

"You better hope we don't find out. With no guidance, we'd be out in the Bay, probably upside down." He spun the ATV around and headed into the marsh grass. "We can hole up in the lighthouse. Pray we don't get a surge."

The wind cranked up to a shrieking banshee howl and the rain was hitting like bullets.

At least the wide stairway leading up to the main floor was still intact. We made it inside, though there didn't seem a lot of difference between in and out. Large areas of roofing were missing and the second floor and the lantern room above were fairly much collapsed into the first, but up against the walls that hadn't lost siding, away from the doors and windows, there was some shelter.

Still, the place was flying apart, trembling and shaking in the gale. There was no talking. Serena would have been welcome to huddle against me but she stood stoically, back to the wall, looking out through a gap across the room where once had been a window.

Not that there was much to see other than the next gray wall of driving rain. Oddly, there was no thunder or lightning, just the roaring, rolling wall of wind-driven rain. We watched as bits and pieces of the building flew away. And not only bits and pieces, whole sheets of metal roofing that had been slapping in the wind tore loose and sailed off into the storm.

I wondered if the others were tormented by thoughts similar to my own, that at any moment we could be whisked away to oblivion. Scrap looked steely, as though, if we were whisked away, he would damn well ride it out to wherever. Serena had a blank, shut down look, as though her mind wasn't working at all.

Above and around us was a sound like a fleet of speeding trucks and a squadron of warplanes. I yelled in Scrap's ear asking how long it would last.

"Maybe an hour until we're in the eye."

What was there to do? There was nothing to see. The whole world had turned stormy gray. We were all soaked. And, I suppose, each dealing as best we could with the prospect of very possible doom. And yet, it was exciting, in a roller coaster sort of way. I was experiencing nature's wildest power, up close and personal. The sense of wonder certainly didn't negate the fear but it took some of the paralysis out of it. No doubt it sounds crazy but I was thinking, if I'm going to die, at least it won't be in some half-assed way, lying in a bed with pneumonia or sitting on a couch in front of a TV clutching my chest.

How long will this thing keep coming at us?

Somehow, we endured, and so, fortunately, did a sufficient portion of our shelter.

The calm came gradually, at first just lighter shades of gray and then more and more real, honest-to-goodness daylight.

Scrap had a look at the situation from the outside walkway. "It could come back twice as bad, no telling if this place will hold up. We've got maybe twenty or thirty minutes."

I didn't see the ATV. Scrap said it had gone under, but it was tied up so it would be there when the water subsided. "But probably ruined by the saltwater. Anyway, the ATV's no good to us, water's too deep now. I might get us out the back way, across the tumps and hummocks. We'd be swimming, some of it, maybe most."

He'd stumped me. "What do you mean, tumps and hummocks?"

"I mean, you got to learn to read the marsh. Patches of solid ground, little ridges where you can get a footing, and damned tricky. Step wrong and you're in a bog."

Looking around from the walkway, I saw nothing but water, not the least hint of a tump nor hummock. There was water in all directions, decorated by jutting bushes and grasses up to the edge of the woods and continuing on into those woods.

The only island other than the lighthouse was Scrap's huge tangle of metal junk, piled up as an artificial hill – everything there was twisted and rusted but if you looked real hard you could make out the skeletons of crab pots, bed springs, panels from vehicles and appliances, siding, barrels and gallon-sized cans, coolers, a wheelbarrow, even a skeletal bicycle or two. Surrounding it were strange welded constructions, more like components of a train-wreck than sculptures.

I said that at least his pile of junk wouldn't be going anywhere.

"Don't be too sure. A rush of water can pick up a car and carry it out into the Bay. It's happened.'

It was quiet now and we could talk. "Looks like you cleaned out behind every barn and shed on the Eastern Shore."

"People leave stuff lying around. They move on, die, whatever, there it is. I got a use for it, that's all."

There it was. And there we were, with part two of a hurricane headed our way.

Just then we heard the roar of an outboard motor. Scrap recognized the boat. "It's the Sheriff's rescue boat. Come on."

The boat was good-sized outboard with deep sides and a canopy over the steering area. We climbed down the steps and aboard. The uniformed officer at the controls said Judge Wetherby had figured out where we must be and called for help.

"You're lucky he got through before the phones went out. We won't get all the way up the road," the officer said. "I need a few feet of water."

We whisked across to what had been the road. The deputy idled the engine. "You'll have to wade from here. It's about knee deep. Take it slow. I've got to get this thing back to the dock or we'll lose it when the storm kicks up again."

Scrap asked to ride along to the dock.

I climbed out and helped Serena over the side. The trip to Bay Breezes wasn't easy. We took each step with care. Rushing water wanted us to go its way, not our way.

I kept an arm across Serena's back. She plowed forward with grim determination. I felt almost euphoric as we got to Bay Breezes, as though we were lone survivors of a ferocious battle. And then I remembered, the battle was only half over.

Chapter Twenty-Six

"Well, aren't you a pair of wet hens."

Thank you, Miss Worple, for the warm welcome. She and the Judge were sitting at the kitchen table having coffee and tea, as though it was a quiet, normal afternoon.

I said I thought they would be out rescuing storm victims.

"We're in reserve," huffed Miss Worple. "They called out the National Guard. So we'll wait, head out later and locate the ones they missed."

Serena and I changed to dry clothes. She was back in her housekeeper role and I sat at the table, welcoming hot coffee and sandwiches, uncomfortable that Serena didn't join us. I dosed the coffee with hot sauce and recounted the day's events.

"We had plans to deal with Thundercloud and his motley crew," Miss Worple said, "but by the time we got here, they were scattering hither and yon."

"Scrap gave them a good scare."

"We were ready to do the same, you can bet on that," she said. "And we're ready to mobilize should they return."

Outside the wind resumed an eerie serenade. "The back side of LouLou lost force coming up the Bay," the Judge said. "They're saying it's down to a tropical storm, but there's a good deal of damage south of us, and, as you've noticed, serious flooding around here."

I asked the Judge if he knew what had prompted Zogby to head for the Point at that particular time.

"Well, I might as well tell you. It's damn well off the record, though, you've got that?"

I gave my most sincere nod.

Miss Worple excused herself. "Serena and I should check the flashlights. There's no telling if the power will hold. We've been lucky so far, except for the phones."

I could understand the Judge's reluctance; he had no real assurance that I wasn't just another journalistic snake in the grass. All I could do was state what was obvious to me, he could be passing along the scoop of a lifetime and I had nowhere to go with it. "As I've said all along, the magazine I'm working is phobic about controversy. If it's dicier than a question of which way to turn at a crossroads, they wouldn't touch it. So what's this all about?"

"Zogby is in a panic over renewed interest in his report. But he needn't be. It will stand."

"Despite the presence of artifacts?"

"Here's what happened." He said that after Zogby's report came out denying the presence of any artifacts, Scrap decided to throw a wrench in the works. "All right, I admit, he had a little help with the idea. He was getting shafted and I didn't like that. So, at my suggestion, he salted his property."

"Salted it? Planted and found relics where there weren't any, you mean? You damn near shafted me, Judge. I was pitching that burial ground story to national magazines."

"It was for the good of the community."

In my mind's eye I was watching the last few nails being driven into the coffin of my career. "Which doesn't include me. Thanks a lot."

"We all have to make sacrifices."

"I didn't see myself climbing on any sacrificial altar." But what was to gain by bitching? Wetherby viewed the world from

Wetherby's perspective. "Well, how did you pull it off?"

"Wasn't difficult. His property was basically a shell midden, a dump, but just up the way on state land was the village site. Scrap being a beachcomber, he had found a few things up there."

"So he gave the clamshell to Sammy and said he'd found it on his land?"

"Got it in one. Knowing, of course, that Sammy was likely to stir up some trouble over it, and that would require a re-evaluation of the site. And that, in turn, could mean a long postponement of the wind-farm plans, and maybe, if the commission ruled that way, Scrap's land would be declared an archaeological treasure, off limits for commercial use."

"That wouldn't solve Scrap's money problems."

"The ruse only needed to go on until Mulroney got out of the picture. He was the man in the middle, cutting a secret deal with Cykco while screwing Scrap out of a small fortune. But we knew, put enough pressure on him, he'd bail. Or get bailed."

"So, let's see, you were no doubt seriously alarmed when Sammy showed you the clamshell, realizing that it might reflect badly on the integrity of Zogby's report. Something like that?"

"I was astonished, and of course somewhat embarrassed for poor Zogby."

"And a scandal involving the report would splash over onto Mulroney, exposing his secret deal and then that would reflect on Cykco. It would make Cykco look like a partner in defrauding Scrap."

"A perhaps unwitting partner, mind you. But your conjecture seems plausible."

"So you felt an obligation to forward news of the find to your friend on the state commission?"

"You know, the public has a right…"

I interrupted to make the point that Wetherby and Scrap could be responsible for Sammy's death. "People get totally ruthless when there's huge amounts of money at stake."

"Of course they do, but I don't see that anything of the kind occurred. The commission got in touch with Cykco about the possible need for re-evaluation of the site. Cykco raised hell with Zogby and then dug into the Mulroney deal, found that Mulroney was playing games and dumped him."

"And he just stepped aside, no fuss?"

"Honorable politician that he is, he withdrew to avoid any appearance of conflict of interest. But of course in politics that means he was afraid he'd get caught with his hand in someone's pocket."

As an old Washington hand, I could hardly argue with that analysis. I asked if Cykco had backed out of the project.

"Not at all. The professor, once he calms down, will be happy to learn that his report still stands, that there was no village on Scrap's land. I've withdrawn the challenge presented to the state archeology commission. I told them new information had come up about the find and it turns out the artifact came from state land after all. And the company, now that it knows what's what, will deal directly with Scrap."

"So he'll sell to them?"

The Judge said Scrap would likely lease the site to Cykco. He'd get money up front to settle his gambling debts, and then have a long-term guaranteed income.

"And you don't think Sammy got caught in the middle of all this somehow?"

"Why on earth would he? He had a minor role, passing the clamshell from Scrap to me. If anyone was in the middle of it, it was me, not Sammy."

I reminded the Judge that Sammy had challenged Zogby.

He thought about that. "I don't know Zogby. You've had dealings with him, and you have suspicions?"

"I've met him twice. This last time he was in a panic, no telling what he might have done. Was he like that when Sammy confronted him? I don't know."

I rarely sleep late, but then I hadn't had occasion to spend a day getting slapped around by a hurricane. Recovery called for extra rest. I thanked the lizards, spiders, spooks and any other creatures that might be sharing the room for their consideration.

After breakfast I sat on the front porch looking at the disarray left by the storm – trees uprooted or seriously injured, limbs downed, natural debris and trash wherever the receding waters had dumped it. A forest green truck pulled up. I thought about going inside for a gun but it wasn't Biggers who got out.

"I'm Sergeant Brad Cummins, Environmental Services Police, looking for Mr Holliday?"

"Present and accounted for."

Cummins had the broad shoulders and square jaw that would look good on a cereal box touting its health benefits. If he hadn't gotten through college on a sports scholarship it was not for lack of physical qualifications. "Good. I understand you were a witness to an incident yesterday when one of our wardens held a certain Professor Zogby at gunpoint?"

"I saw that from a distance. A lot of others were closer."

"The others have scattered. We'll try to track them down."

I'm knee-jerk helpful to law enforcement when they're in good-cop mode. "The leader calls himself Thundercloud. He has a shop on Chincoteague."

"Did you overhear any of the confrontation?"

"There was that small matter of a hurricane brewing. I could see it was an angry exchange. Later Zogby told me Biggers mistook him for an investigator. I have no idea what that was all about, nor apparently did Zogby."

Cummins was armed with a clipboard and he glanced at it. "Biggers says he was cautioning Zogby, who then became abusive and threatening. ESP sometimes assists in apprehending those who dig illegally for artifacts, and it appeared to Biggers that Zogby might be doing so. Or so he says."

"That isn't state land, is it? I thought Scrap Blevins owned that land."

"It's state land on either side. Biggers said he was confused about the line. I know it's a bit fishy, that's why we're interviewing witnesses. Now, regarding Mr Blevins, is it true he fired a number of shots at people gathered there?"

"He just fired a few warnings, well over their heads, and they were trespassing." I didn't mention the splattering shot he'd taken at Thundercloud, hoping it would be forgotten by all concerned.

"That could result in assault charges – but it would be a state police matter. Both Biggers and Zogby had left by that time?"

"Biggers had, and Zogby was making tracks. You can also report that Blevins subsequently saved my life, as well as that of Serena Sanchez."

"That speaks well of him, certainly. I'll make a note. Blevins isn't of primary interest to us. Zogby has made a complaint about

Biggers. So, we're mostly checking out Biggers' story. Will you be in the area for a while in the event I need a formal statement?"

"My editor wants me to pull out. You could call him and tell him you've impounded me."

"You like it here?" He glanced around at the storm damage.

"I'm fairly much a city slicker but I've got some interests here."

"Well, thanks for your help. Call me if any more details come to mind." He handed me a card.

"I'll also testify Biggers belongs at the target end of the firing range if that will help."

Cummins tried to squelch a sympathetic grin. "Would you qualify as an expert witness?"

"Officer, I'll go back to school and get whatever credentials it takes to qualify."

He gave a little wave of the clipboard and headed back toward his truck.

I had every intention, or at least some, of getting on with the article. And yet I sat enjoying the morning calm. A team of groundsmen arrived, but even the roar of chainsaws didn't rouse me. I felt heavy in the enveloping wicker chair.

In the twilight zone between wakefulness and dozing, I pictured the bikes I'd seen on Scrap's scrap pile. I wanted a closer look. I pried myself loose of the wicker clutches and found Serena in the kitchen.

She said Sammy's bike was a Schwinn. "A black Schwinn. I loaned him the money to get it. That's why he was taking jobs with the watermen. Why?"

"Just curious. You said before that the bike wasn't found at the site, but it has to be around somewhere."

The phone, working again, interrupted us. It was von Klonk, fuming and whining as usual. What did he think, I was some pulp-fiction writer cranking it out by the yard? Maybe I should go on strike; 'withhold my excellence' as the young journalists, the college grads, are coached to threaten when feeling unappreciated. Let him deal with *that*.

But he might.

So I explained about the weather, perhaps just a little imaginatively. "It's rained a gusher for three days and nights. This place is a disaster area. There's no electricity. I'm amazed there's a phone line."

Yes, I lied about the electricity. Everybody lies a little, don't they? It's a matter of degree. It wasn't like I had a degree in lying. Von Klonk was silent. I filled the dead air with a few rounds of hello-hello, a fitting chorus for the disaster drama.

"Candles, Holliday? Have they by any chance heard of them, down there? I was told in school that once upon a time there was no such thing as electricity, and people actually wrote by candlelight."

"It's the flooding. We've burned all the candles and can't get to town for more."

"You're a pro, or so you allege – write in the dark."

"I fully understand your frustration, but you've got to make allowances for acts of God."

"It's an act of some sort, that's for sure. By the way, I got a call from Barney Cole complaining that you're stirring up trouble, raking up muck. Whatever that's about, knock it off."

Cole, you don't know who you're messing with. "You know what it is? Cole is obsessed with muskrats and irritated that I won't write the story his way: 'Eastern Shore – Mad About Muskrats.'"

"Cole says that? You're pulling my leg."

"I wish I was joking. But, you know, they're all kind of nutty around here."

"You must feel right at home."

"The thing is, Cole's planning a specialty restaurant, McMuskrat. Even offered me a franchise. Of course, it's out of my league. Maybe you'd be interested."

"Get real, Holliday."

"Anyway, he says we're obliged to promote muskrats since he's arranged this tour, tit for tat kind of thing."

"You tell him *Here & There* won't be bullied. No tits, no tats. We have integrity and, what's that other stuff, objectivity."

I'm on a roll, Cole. "Well, of course, that's exactly what I've insisted ever since he first began putting the pressure on. I said you were seriously anti-muskrat, that you wouldn't go for it, no way. So now he wants to win you over with a crate of frozen muskrat burgers. Shall I give him your home address?"

"I don't want any muskrat burgers, not even one." Holliday, just write the damn story and forget the damn muskrats. Tell Cole I'm vegetarian, tell him the story is done."

"Will do."

"Will you? That would be a first. You're actually going to do something I asked?"

Click. He was gone.

Let's see. What to write about? Fishing. I hadn't really looked into sport fishing. I could probably get a few paragraphs out of the *what and where* of fishing. So far I'd only come as close to bait and tackle as a visit to one shop, plus that bonkers trip on Capt Lucky's floating wreck.

I was about to check the index of my guidebook when there was another phone call. It was McCobb.

"Meet me at the fishing pier in Saxis."

"I've got work to do. Can't we discuss whatever it is by phone?"

As I hoped, he was adamant. "Phones aren't secure."

At least it had something to do with fishing if I was to meet him at the fishing pier. And then there was the small matter of finding it. I'd been a lot of places in the region, it must be near one of them. But according to the map, Saxis sits off by itself beside the Bay, you don't get there by way of anywhere, you go to Saxis and that's it.

Turns out, Saxis is among the last of the true working commercial fishing villages on the Eastern Shore. It's on a slip of sand between a vast marsh and Pocomoke Sound, with a residential main street, a few side streets, a wharf edged with shacks and sheds. There's evidence of glory days, closed stores and weathered warehouses. And a grand fishing pier, built as a tee, a long walkway ending in a cross-section. And there at the far end stood my informant. I assumed if there'd been anyone fishing on the fishing pier, he'd booted him or her into the Bay.

"I thought East Westerly was off the beaten path. This place is teetering on the edge."

We were close enough for easy conversation but he stepped closer. "It's isolated, all right," he said in what was nearly a stage whisper. "Good and isolated."

"Okay, so what's up?"

"Some of the boys saw Biggers loading a boat."

"Hardly sounds like news. Everybody around here is either loading a boat or unloading a boat. With what?"

"Don't know. It was those big bank traps, a couple of them, stuffed full of something."

Bank trap. It sounded like an economic term. "That fellow Lucky mentioned bank traps, what are they again?"

"Big cages, they use them to catch peelers, soft-shells. There's money in it."

"So maybe Biggers was going crabbing."

"You don't go out with your traps stuffed full of something. And they're set close to shore, not out where he was headed. I don't mean to put ideas in your head but you could stuff a body in one of those things."

We watched a small boat pass slowly by, heading toward the piers and pilings of the main dock, a lone fisherman almost idling his motor to avoid wake. He waved, we waved back. I should have hollered, asked him for an interview. I could see fishing rods but not his catch, if any. "I take it you think this has to do with Sammy?"

"Whatever he was dumping, it was something he wanted hidden. Sammy, the way I hear it, was into finding what people want to hide. You following me?"

If I was following him it was at considerable distance. I tried to catch up. "That's really speculative. But maybe you're onto something."

"It's a long shot, but you don't have anything better, do you? Biggers went out with a boatload. He came back with nothing, just a nearly empty bottle of rotgut, that's what I was told."

"Well, if he came back empty, we'll never know, will we?"

McCobb had been more or less talking to my chest. He raised his eyes to mine. "You a diver?"

"Capt Lucky already tried to pull that one on me. No way."

"OK. So, if you can't go to the traps, then, it seems obvious you have to get the traps to come to you."

This guy should host a game show, he talked in riddles. "Sure. Just whistle?"

"ESP wants to get the goods on Biggers, and maybe this is their chance. They've got sonar, they can find the traps."

"And they're going to search the whole Bay, right?"

"I've got friends at Wallops Island, space cadets; they have satellite imaging of everything that goes on hereabouts. Of course, that's only daytime. They're working on something to see through clouds or at night, but they aren't there yet. So the drug runners know to work at night, hide out during the day."

"There are drug runners on the Bay?"

He gave me one of those "You're hopeless" looks. "I can see how they had an easy time pranking you."

"Pranking? You're talking about the bastards that turned my life upside down? And who is *they*?"

"*They* is whoever they were, that's all. Anyway, if I give Wallops the approximate time Biggers went out, they'll figure out where he went."

"Find that out and I'll pass it on. I've got a contact in the ESP. And maybe you can just give me a call, skip the mystery meeting stuff?"

A jet passed overhead, far overhead, a slow moving commercial job, not one of those Navy hotshots that sometimes, contrary to policy, explode through the sound barrier, rattling and even breaking local windows. The jet added its contrail to others, the hieroglyphics in the sky, streamers left by flights bound for Washington, Baltimore, Philadelphia, Charlotte, Atlanta and other big cities far beyond Saxis, and not just in miles.

"I'm not knocking your connections, Holliday, but I might have more luck getting some action."

"You know some people at ESP?"

McCobb shifted posture to chin up, shoulders back. "Can't say as I do. But I've done a few favors for the governor. He owes me."

I walked back to my car. McCobb was still standing at the far end of the fishing pier. He waved. To me? Probably to his friends at Wallops Island, via eye-in-the-sky satellite.

It was intriguing. Here's a guy who spends a lot of time prowling around at night, and he tells me that's when drug runners cruise the Bay.

What was his game, anyway? First he's recording bird music, then he's got access to watch lists that include me among the watched, now he's pals with the governor and can get his hands on satellite data? Was he putting me on the track or throwing me off?

You meet his type in Washington, mostly at cocktail parties. Secret agents. Cryptic. Enigmatic. Most of them harmless fakers, playing roles, pumping hot air into the balloons of their own egos.

Not all of them though.

Sometimes they're the real deal. But by the time you know they're real, you don't want to know.

Chapter Twenty-Seven

I parked before the little bridge, now just a plank walkway due to the destruction wrought by the hurricane. An array of pilings and timbers lay on the far side, indicating Scrap was going to rebuild it.

Crossing with care, I made my way along a wide trail back to where Scrap was working on one of his strange junkyard assemblages. He shut off his welding torch and pushed up the visor of the safety helmet.

"I want to take a closer look at a bicycle on the heap there."

"What's the deal with that?"

"It could save you being invaded by a herd of cops."

"I don't need any favors."

"Look, if you have trouble here it could screw up your lease arrangement, okay? Just get the bike."

He seemed about to make some sour comment but thought better of it. He scrambled up the heap to the bike I pointed out. He brought it – the crumpled remains of it, anyway – to where I stood in the clearing that served as his studio and gallery. He shook his head. "Takes some work to twist them up like this."

The rear fender and tire rim of the bike were nearly doubled forward, the drive chain hung loose, the front handlebars were well out of alignment.

"And you found it along the road? Near here?"

"Just up the road. If I hadn't picked it up, someone else would. Lots of people on the lookout for junk. I figured it was just dumped."

"There was no sign that it was wrecked right there?"

"I didn't think about it, just hauled it back here."

It was a Schwinn.

"It's Sammy's bike. I'm fairly certain of that from Serena's description. Look, there's a different color paint on the fender. No question, someone hit him. And it wasn't you?"

"Hell no, it wasn't me. That's gray paint. I don't drive anything gray, now or ever."

I have to admit, I was surprised it wasn't green paint, matching Biggers' truck. He seemed the most likely candidate for running someone down on the roadway. Zinker's car was tan. There remained plenty of possibilities. In the general vicinity there might be thirty or forty gray vehicles.

"Scrap, this bike has been smashed hard. Looks to me like somebody sideswiped it, whacked it off the road. There's a good chance the impact would have killed the rider, and I believe Sammy was the rider."

Back at Bay Breezes, I called Sergeant Cummins, the officer with the ESP who had visited me to ask about Biggers.

"My interest is in Biggers and I don't see how this fits in. Probably a job for the state police."

"I'd just as soon let you handle that, okay? I want to be helpful but I don't want to spend hours explaining things to cops I don't know. Meet me at the entrance to Scrap's property."

"I guess I'm obliged to have a look since you've called me. No promises on keeping you out of it, though. I'll see you there in half an hour."

Cummins was waiting in a green pickup parked at the little bridge leading to Scrap's domain. When he stepped out I again noticed the contrast between him and Biggers. They wore basically the same uniform, but Cummins's gray shirt and green trousers bore signs of recent laundering and military pressing. His baseball style cap hadn't served as a pigeon roost, and he was either a natural baby-face or he'd shaved that morning.

We walked in the direction of Scrap's outdoor studio and junk heap. There was no shotgun wielding welcoming committee; Scrap must have been off collecting junk. Cummins surveyed the bizarre metal sculpture gallery with a bemused half-smile. "I'd heard about this but never seen it. They might tag him for operating an illegal landfill, but I guess he'd beat it, claim to be an artist."

"I'm with you, I don't get it. But, you know, once sculpture gets beyond naked women and generals on horseback, my interest fades to black."

"At least now I know why they call him Scrap. I thought maybe it was about picking up road-kill."

"People do that?"

"You kidding? They can have shooting wars over venison that isn't all tore up."

"The road-kill killings... I like it, but I think my editor would blow a gasket, if he has any gaskets left."

I told him Serena had said Sammy had a Schwinn.

"Man, somebody got hurt bad when this happened."

"I'd say somebody got killed when that happened."

"You may be right. Unfortunately, at the moment your guess is as irrelevant as mine. Interesting. But not much forensic value there, moved from the site, ... raises some questions, though, that's for sure. Mostly about Scrap, I'd say."

I pointed out the gray paint. It was a good time to put in a word for Scrap. "Blevins has been seriously helpful. I'm hoping we can move all this forward without any problems for him."

"Keep you out of it, keep Scrap out of it. My job's to enforce the law, not hide people from it." Cummins folded his arms. I took that as a reluctance to commit to any particular course regarding Scrap. "He's probably in the clear, only trouble comes if he's concealing a crime rather than reporting it. From what you say, doesn't seem he intended to conceal anything. Now, where did this incident take place, assuming there was an incident?"

I told him what Scrap had told me about finding the bike. He said he'd have a look, and meanwhile the bike should be left as found. "It's a matter for the sheriff and the state police. Sort of wish it tied to the Biggers business. We need all the whack we can get. But it doesn't look that way."

"I heard there was a fresh lead on Biggers."

He squinted like a rifleman. "That's confidential."

Thinking it might raise the level of candor between us, I told him what I knew about Biggers' recent boat trip with the bank traps.

"Sounds very close to the intelligence we got, but that came from way on up the ladder. You could say top rung."

"It seemed the best way to get attention."

That generated another skeptical squint. "You're saying … well, you're right, anyway. It came down as one of those 'get it done yesterday' missions."

"So did anything come of it?"

"Like I said, it's confidential."

"I could remember your name next time I'm talking to friends in high places." A bit of bluff, but I genuinely could ask McCobb to pass a comment along to his pals.

"I'll make my own way, thanks. As for those traps; we found them full of deer hides, a few trophy heads."

My city-trained brain didn't process that one. "Hides? Heads? What's that all about?"

"Money. The meat's a no-brainer. People need to eat and store-bought is expensive. Lots of folks around here lived many a year on venison steaks and stews."

"But you said hides and heads?"

I don't know what Cummins was thinking but I guessed he was framing a simple answer, considering my ignorance of the subject. "There are markets for hides, they're of course leather, might be worth messing with if you're moving a quantity through the buyer's back door. Head mounts with a big, wide antler rack would be the big deal. They're worth a lot as trophies."

"People want trophies that they didn't hunt themselves?"

"Well, by the time it's hung on the rec room wall in the big city suburbs, they'll have cooked up quite a story about how they bagged it. You've got to admit, making up a story is a lot easier than getting eaten alive by greenheads, chiggers and mosquitoes, maybe getting soaked in a storm or lost in the marsh, not to mention the risk of getting shot for a deer by some other amateur from the city."

"So there's money in trophy heads?"

"A legitimate mount sets you back a few hundred, at least. If it's illegal, a great rack, a fine specimen, I've heard a thousand, maybe two. But we're talking about a market where price isn't a big deal, these rich city guys don't mind paying top dollar for bragging rights."

"So, why was Biggers dumping the stuff?"

"That's what we're working on. The way I hear it, some of the locals are fed up with the guy and ready to turn him in."

"I also heard he was hooked up with Zinker in whatever was going on."

"I'm beginning to wonder what don't you know. Yes, that's how it looks. I figure Zinker was the link to the guys who bought the trophies; he does have the big-money connections. But we've got to prove it."

Cummins said he'd try to stir some interest in the bike and went on his way.

It was a day that couldn't decide which way to go, clouds, sunshine, clouds. I stood where we had parted company, thinking, listening. I knew I had to be careful about coming to conclusions.

Poachers seemed like a good lead as far as what became of Sammy. But what about ill-tempered Zogby or greedy Thundercloud and his cult or all the others who had a grudges big and small against a snoop? I tried to clear my mind by focusing on where I was, what I was seeing and hearing. I was in a clearing, underneath a changing sky of light and dark, looking out over an inlet from the Bay, with marsh and woods on either side, and, behind me, a sand road that eventually led to civilization as we know it.

There were a few ducks on the inlet. All was still. I found the stillness disturbing. In the noise and hustle of the city you have a defense against deep thoughts that arise in stillness, such remembering that quote from Thoreau: "Most men lead lives of quiet desperation."

The closer I listened the more I realized the stillness was in my failure to hear. There, a distant crow cawing. In the woods, a nattering squirrel, upset by some intrusion. And now the tap-tap-tap of a woodpecker at work.

It is strange and maybe I was just feeling frustrated or stressed, but it seemed nature was trying to tell me something. Nature is wild, but not in the sense of the word as used in the city. It's not craziness, it's... what is it? ... a different sort of sanity. In the city everyone is busy trying to force something to happen. Nature just happens.

I have to admit, the Eastern Shore can put on a sunset. It almost makes you want to write a poem about it. There was more to that Thoreau quote, wasn't there? Oh yeah. "... and go to the grave with the song still in them."

The next morning I told Serena about the bike.

"I'm going to shoot Scrap Blevins."

"Serena, I'm sure he just found the thing along the road. This may be what we need to get the cops back on the case. Give it some time."

"Maybe so." She didn't sound convinced.

I surprised myself with a terse response. "No maybe. It's no solution if you go getting your ass thrown in prison."

"You're crude."

"You'll know crude if you wind up in prison. Ask Miss Worple about the bad stuff goes on there, I heard she used to be a guard."

"Used to be? I don't think she ever quit."

"Just wait. We're on the track of the answers you want. Meanwhile, there's something else..."

"What?"

"I need to borrow your picture of Sammy. Just for a couple of hours, I'll get it right back to you."

"You need to see if someone recognizes him."

"Something like that."

Thundercloud was alone in the main room, packing boxes. His sneer didn't exactly invite me in but I ignored it.

"You're clearing out?"

"Bad vibes around here, man. I'm heading west."

"Don't be in too big a hurry. The cops may want to talk to you."

I walked over to the display case where I'd seen inlaid belt buckles. He watched me, scowling.

"The belt buckle in the center there, where did you get it?"

"It's vintage, old Mexican work. These migrants, they sell things."

"That one didn't come from any migrant. It belonged to Sammy Sanchez." I showed him the picture.

"Ridiculous. There are lots of belt buckles in similar styles. You're just making trouble, Holliday. I warned you against that."

"Well here's a warning for you. That buckle links you to Sammy's death and you're going to have a lot of questions to answer when I tip the cops."

He scanned the room as if looking for an escape route. Or a war club to shut me up. "Wait a minute. I remember now. It was some guy, three sheets to the wind, wearing a green uniform. Don't know who he was, haven't seen him before or since."

"Aren't you supposed to keep records of purchases?"

"Come on, Holliday. I keep records when I have to, like any other business. That guy wanted twenty bucks, probably for a bottle of booze, I gave it to him, no big deal."

I pulled out my wallet. "Here's your twenty. Give me the buckle."

"What about my profit?"

"Where's the profit in, at best, receiving stolen property? It can get worse, if your story doesn't check out about the guy in green."

He opened the case and handed the buckle to me, then helped himself to my twenty. "Take it and clear out, you're nothing but trouble."

"You haven't seen trouble ... yet."

I was on my way through the door when I heard Thundercloud bark: "I only gave ten for the damn thing."

I spent the afternoon driving the side roads, looking for a green pickup truck. I checked out a lot of dead ends, figuring that would be where I'd find Biggers. I didn't find him. What if I had? Getting a straight story out of him would be a good trick. I'd have been better off calling Cummins to tell him about the buckle.

Probably, if I'd found Biggers, I'd have gone for the throat. In my mind's eye a vision kept playing of that green pickup careening down the road, plowing into Sammy on his bike. Was that how it went? It seemed plausible.

Serena came back early from the restaurant. "We weren't busy."

I showed her the buckle and told her what I knew about it.

She grimaced. "I'm going to shoot Biggers."

"Serena, we've been through that one. Nothing's solved by shooting anyone, it just leads to more trouble. I've got this fellow Cummins interested in the case, let me show him the buckle, it'll add fuel."

"Nothing is ever solved anyway, it's just one kind of trouble leading to the next. At least I will have avenged Sammy."

"Think about what he'd want, Serena. He sure as hell wouldn't want his Mom in prison."

"You are right about that but that doesn't make you right." She left and went to her room.

Chapter Twenty-Eight

Later that evening as I sat at the little desk in my room, typing and balling up pages of false starts on the article, there was tap at the door. It was Miss Worple, looking worried. "Serena's gone. So is my .32. It was in my purse and it's gone."

"You keep a .32 in your purse?"

"The .45 takes up too much room."

"Where did she go?"

"I heard her sweet-talking someone on the phone and thought that was really strange because she's not like that. I think I heard her say the firehouse, behind the firehouse."

It was a short drive. I pulled around to the back and saw Biggers on the ground. Zinker was standing over him.

Serena had the .32 trained on both of them. When I got closer I could see Biggers was bleeding from the mouth, just a dribble running down his stubbly jaw.

"What's going on?"

Zinker raised a fist in my direction. "Stay out of it, hotshot. Crazy bitch, drew on me when I got here. I was trying to help her."

Serena's face was set in anger. "Zinker followed me. Now I have to shoot them both."

I raised my hands, palms out. "You don't have to shoot anyone, Serena. Put the gun down."

It was like something out of a movie – except, if things got just a little out of hand those wouldn't be celluloid bullets flying around.

"Damned if I will. At least I'm shooting Biggers. Out of the way, Zinker."

Zinker stood his ground. "I rescued you. I rescued you from this old bastard and this is what I get?"

"Stand aside or this is what you'll get." She wagged the pistol at Zinker. "I lured him here. He killed Sammy."

Biggers raised himself to one elbow. "Hold on, lady. I didn't kill nobody, must have been this asshole. Though he's not much at killing. I've had worse mosquito bites."

"Zinker?" She was pointing the pistol at Biggers but raised it toward Zinker.

Biggers sat up, holding his blood-streaked jaw. "Nutty kid of yours turned in a drug runner to Zinker. Couldn't get much dumber than that. Just gave this bastard ideas."

Zinker kicked Biggers in the side, toppling him. "Shut up you goddamn idiot. Wasn't me. I didn't kill him. I have no idea what happened to him."

Serena moved toward Zinker. "What about a drug runner?"

Zinker lit up like a kid who got his Christmas wish. "We'll be rich, Serena, you and me. Mexico. We can leave tomorrow. There's a delivery coming in tonight, people I know will take it off my hands. We'll be rich."

Suddenly the firehouse siren began screaming.

Zinker looked at the alarm tower in alarm. "Somebody called in a damn alarm. The volunteers will be here any minute. Come on, Serena. You'll live like a queen."

Serena turned the pistol back on Biggers. "You had Sammy's belt buckle. If you didn't kill him, how did you get it?"

"That damn thing? Found it when I was searching Lucky's truck. Figured it might be good for a few bucks so I pocketed it."

The pistol swayed back and forth between Biggers and Zinker.

I know enough Spanish to know Serena wasn't delivering compliments. Zinker made a dash for his car. He peeled out in a spray of gravel.

The siren stopped as suddenly as it had started.

Biggers wobbled to his feet. He muttered something about Mexican whores, which seemed fairly suicidal under the circumstances.

The circumstances were that Serena was hunched down with the .32 pointed at him. She held the pistol in one hand, her other arm out from her side as if for balance. It wasn't marksman form as I knew it, and yet it looked as though she knew what she was doing. And I had to stop her before she did it.

I grabbed her arm and forced it down. She tried to twist away and then gave up.

It didn't occur to me in the heat of the moment, but, upon reflection, you could get killed trying to stop someone from killing somebody.

She let me take the pistol.

Biggers climbed into his truck and tore off.

As he careened out, a car pulled in. I didn't want an encounter with the volunteers, but too late.

No, it was Miss Worple.

"What's going on with you two; don't you know it's getting late?"

I said we knew. "There's been some trouble. We've got to clear out. The siren just went off. I'll explain later."

"Of course the siren went off. I called in a false alarm. It's time someone took a stand, people marauding around all night."

I handed the pistol to Miss Worple. "Maybe you should try a

shoulder holster, less chance of losing this thing."

"I've got one. Serena said it might bother the guests so I quit wearing it."

Serena was shaking. I guessed she was angry with me for interfering with her vendetta. But she didn't flinch when I put an arm around her shoulder and pulled her to me. She was crying.

Miss Worple slapped the side of her car. "Get her out of here, Holliday. I called the switchboard back, told them there's no emergency, I was just having a nightmare. Still, someone might be along any minute."

I bear-hugged Serena. "You get back to Bay Breezes."

"All right. And where are you going?"

I wasn't sure. I walked her to her car. "You looked like the gunfighter back there. Do you know about shooting?"

"Sure I know. In this country you are hunters, there is all this ready-aim-fire. Where I come from, you are more likely the hunted –- bandits, cartels, revolutionaries –-so there is no ready, no fancy aim. That's how I learned; point, shoot."

"Thank goodness you didn't get to the second part."

"You didn't answer me, where are you going?"

If I was on the right track, the answer might launch Serena off on another mission, pistol in hand. I told her to get back to Bay Breezes and we'd talk later.

The right track? What business was it of mine, all this stuff with guns, drugs, dead Sammy, illegal Serena, poachers, political deals, wannabe Indians, a corrupt professor, a half-wild hermit with a shotgun-machinegun? None of it had to do with a puff piece travel article.

One more day, spent in the library, I could wrap up the

article, clip and paste, be done with all this. Why should I care how all the craziness was playing out?

The trouble was, I did care. Isn't that always the worst thing? There it would be, in my head, hiding out until the small hours of some dark night when it would come back to take payment in lost sleep, the haunting memory of another person, place or thing I had walked away from, another retreat.

There was no sign of Biggers' truck along the road. He was probably holed up somewhere numbing the pain, nursing himself into that stupefied alcoholic daze that freed his demons to make trouble for others. Well, a time would come to deal with him, if others didn't get to him first.

There was good reason not use the phone at Bay Breezes, risking being overheard. Besides, the drive gave me time to clear my head. What did most to clear my head was watching for deer. What in the world goes through their minds, what compels a creature to dash into the face of a roaring steel menace with lights blazing in the darkness, why not run the other way? Maybe getting smashed by a car or truck was preferable to a bullet or an arrow. The image brought thoughts of Sammy, out on that dark, lonely road. As for preferences, the deer would undoubtedly choose to live if it had a choice. Same for Sammy.

The big tourist rest stop on Rt 13 was lit up like a football stadium on game night. I sat in the car for a few minutes, pondering. It was just a hunch, but the way I put it together Sammy had worked for Lucky Brevard and discovered something about dope running. He went to Zinker with what he knew. Zinker kept the information to himself, maybe mentioning it to Biggers — who was his partner in some scheme involving poaching. Someone thought Sammy needed to be hushed up. Now he was dead. And Zinker was bragging to Serena that he would soon be rich.

I used the public telephone to call Brad Cummins. I didn't tell him about the firehouse hassle, focusing on what might happen next. I gave Cummins my best guess.

"I believe Lucky Brevard is picking up dope that's delivered to his crab pots. I don't know where it comes from or where it goes. He's probably part of a relay to Baltimore or Washington. I'm fairly sure he'll be going out to haul in another delivery, probably at first light because he doesn't have working lights on his boat."

"And you just figured this out, all by yourself? Come here for a few days, get a handle on something the homeboys haven't cracked in years of patrolling the Bay? Come on. Lucky Brevard? You better check the mushrooms in your spaghetti sauce, Holliday."

It wasn't a time to get into what I'd deduced from Zinker's pitch to Serena. "Look, I understand how you see it, and that's how most anyone would see it. But I've heard some things that convince me otherwise. Come on, you can catch him if you get moving."

"It's a Coast Guard job."

"There's no time. Harvesting drugs in crab pots isn't of interest to your outfit?"

"Coast Guard."

"You want to make this difficult? What's the name of your commanding officer, Cummins? If I get the Governor to give him a call, maybe then you'll listen?" He still didn't know it was actually McCobb who'd got the Governor involved. There was no reason he would ever know. I'd let him assume it was me, and that's how I left it.

"Now, never mind that, Holliday. I know you can pull strings. But I need a little more than a theory about some old crackpot and his crab pots."

"I'm telling you, you can catch him in that act. You're the one to do it."

"Dawn's a few hours yet. Meet me at the boat launch there beyond East Westerly, five-thirty. I might need you at the helm if there's trouble."

"Doesn't he operate out of Crisfield?"

"For charters. If he's crabbing he'll be at the commercial pier not far from where you're staying."

I found the pier and dozed, waking as Cummins pulled in towing a Boston Whaler. To me, not knowing my fore from my aft, it looked like a small boat for this kind of work. I'd guess an eighteen footer, small but with a motor on the back about the size of a washing machine.

The hazy gray of earliest light grew brighter as a rim of rose decorated the horizon. Lucky's old gray box truck was there. Cummins scanned the boats and empty slips along the pier. "He's pulled out already."

"Couldn't have been too long ago. Like I said, he hasn't got lights. But he must be in a panic, heading out before break of day."

"That's good to know, about the lights. That's enough to tag him for right there."

Cummins expertly backed into the launch ramp, got out and released the winch cable to lower the boat from the trailer.

"Hold this line while I park the truck."

We got in the boat. I was having some doubts. "Lucky's long gone, it looks like. Can we intercept him?"

"There's a little chop to it today, not bad but there'll be some bumps. Hang on."

Cummins stood at the center console. We pushed off. The engine caught, trembled, growled its eagerness. We whipped across the water. Any more throttle and we'd be airborne.

Lucky's boat was sitting idle near a line of buoys used to identify the location of pots. We were close to the cove where Parkers Point jutted out. I had a "so that's it" moment. Chances were, Sammy's night visits to the Point were to watch for deliveries.

Cummins pulled in beside Lucky as skillfully as a rodeo cowboy closing on a steer in a roping contest.

Brevard was suffering a seizure. His face beet-red, his arms flailing, jittery as ice on a hot griddle right before the meltdown. "Did you guys get my stuff? You've got to give it back! I'm a dead man."

Cummins played it cool. "What stuff, Lucky?"

"You don't have it? Had to be that bastard Zinker. I warned them about him. Too late now. I'm a dead man."

Cummins casually put a hand on his holstered pistol. "Settle down, settle down. Now, let's have a look at your cargo."

Brevard scanned his boat, his eyes wide with desperation. "Ain't no cargo. That son of a bitch Zinker's got it."

"I'll just have a look." Cummins tied up to the side of Brevard's boat and climbed aboard. Less gracefully, I followed. Cummins pulled a package about the size of two bricks from one of the crab pots on the deck.

"That's all I found," Brevard moaned. "There should be a hundred. He got 'em."

"My bet is you're facing a lot of jail time, Lucky, just for this packet. Now, tell me exactly what's going on and you might get a break for cooperation."

Lucky blurted and sputtered hysterically. "Some hard guys from Baltimore, some of Pitbull's gang, they offered me a chance to make big money."

I didn't like the sound of that. I had more background on the case than Cummins so I took the lead asking questions. "According to Serena, Sammy's last job was working with you. Was he in on these drug deals?"

"Damn snoopy kid. He caught on about night deliveries coming up the Bay. He was playing all superior, warning me, said he kept watch down at the Point. That's how I knew where we'd find him."

"So you found him and killed him."

"I had to tip the gang that Sammy was onto the deal. This big monster of a guy took my truck, forced me to go along, to point him out that night."

"Keep talking, Lucky. The bike was all smashed up, how did that happen?"

"It wasn't my idea. He just slammed right into the kid, on the dead-end there by Bay Breezes. Those guys are ice cold killers."

I asked if the impact killed Sammy right off.

"There was no blood, he was kind of icy blue and looked, I don't know, cracked, broken. He was dead all right."

Cummins shook his head. "You're an accessory."

"What was I supposed to do? Can't just bury him, water table like it is. The big guy left the body in the truck, said it was on me to get rid of it."

Cummins asked for the name of the big guy.

"*Trouble*. That's all I ever knew for a name. They all had nicknames, mostly like that, Trouble."

"What's coming to you is pretty much out of my hands but I'll see what I can do. So Zinker's got the stuff. Where's he gone?"

"Don't worry, the Pitbull crew will find him. After Sammy caught on, he told Zinker, next thing Zinker is blackmailing me, wanting a cut. I passed the word to Pitbull's gang. They're sending some guys down today to pick up this load and deal with him."

"You're a mess. Come on over in my boat. I'm calling headquarters and the Coast Guard. This is going to be a major operation."

Lucky was breaking down, teary and trembling. "All I wanted was a big new boat so Ingrid would see I wasn't a laughing stock, that I was Capt Brevard, with a big new charter boat."

Cummins unsnapped the case on his belt that held handcuffs. "You sure blew that one."

"Just let me get Ingrid's picture from the cabin."

"Who's Ingrid?"

"My true love. I wanted to make her proud of me."

You couldn't help but feel sorry for the poor guy. He looked pitiful. "Get it and come on."

I'd been standing to one side, staying out of the back and forth. Cummins said we'd have to wait on his backup and the Coast

Guard. They would impound Brevard's boat. "We'd handle it, but if this stuff is coming in from offshore we need the Coast Guard involved. And the state and sheriff for the crew coming from Baltimore."

Neither of noticed when Lucky came out of the cabin and headed toward the front of the boat. Cummins glanced that way. "What's he up to?"

We looked forward to see Lucky wobbling, hugging the anchor with the rope draped over his shoulders and around his neck.

He toppled over the side. There was a loud splash. We ran forward. Well, Cummins ran, I moved faster than usual, watching my step on the slippery deck.

"Crazy son of bitch." Cummins peered into the murk. The waves weren't big but it was rough enough so you couldn't see where Lucky went in.

"I know he can't swim."

"Show me who can with fifty pounds of anchor."

Cummings stripped off his shirt and trousers. He dove but was up in thirty seconds or so. He climbed back aboard.

"Visibility two feet down there. Nothing we can do until divers get here."

I looked in the wheelhouse and saw the empty frame. Ingrid had gone down with the captain.

Cummins crossed to his boat and got on the radio. I followed, feeling useless and a little dazed.

Hopeless as it was, we watched the nearby water as we waited for the Coast Guard.

It must have been fifteen minutes before the red and white

response boat, not a whole lot bigger than Cummins' Whaler, came barreling toward us.

Cummins told the officer in charge that he had been showing me around when he spotted Lucky and decided to do a safety check.

The two conferred out of my hearing. Cummins waved me over. "The Chief here might want a statement from you later, but right now he'd just as soon I took you back to shore."

I didn't have any problem with that. A larger boat and a helicopter appeared as we pulled away.

At the pier I thanked Cummins for keeping me out of the Coast Guard encounter and asked what he thought would happen next.

"They don't know what they've got yet, I don't either really. Sure surprised me, you being right about Lucky. He had lots of people fooled."

"There's still the problem of Lucky's Baltimore connection."

"You heard him mention Pitbull? That's the guy runs the inner city dope syndicate up there, owns some clubs with backroom gambling, and a lot of other businesses."

"I'm guessing that among those other businesses are so-called escort services. I got close to him, I guess. Somebody slipped me a bunch of receipts that made for a good story. Thing is, I never found out who was behind the services, the front-men who wouldn't talk."

"I don't doubt it was Pitbull. He's probably the last of the old time racketeers. It's a gang, but more like a mob syndicate, not like the younger crews trying to move in. All his boys dress like they're on their way to Sunday church. Anyway, he's well known to law enforcement. Just haven't made the case yet."

"He sounds smart."

"He's truly clever, in an evil way, deliveries by kids on bikes. They've got no idea who they work for, and they won't do serious time when they're caught. Just as smart about runners, the mules. We've just witnessed a prime example. Who's gonna stop an old cracker like Lucky, in a beat-up truck headed up Rt 13? Not likely if he minds the rules."

"Well, Lucky won't be testifying against him."

"He wouldn't have, anyway. You can bet Lucky never met Pitbull, never even saw him or talked to him. Some big black guys in suits cut a deal with him, he assumed it's a Pitbull deal, maybe heard a little talk. He didn't know anything for sure. Pitbull's lawyers would have ripped him to shreds."

"What about Zinker? Lucky seemed sure he has the dope."

"That's for the state police and the sheriff. I told headquarters what we'd heard. They might need more than the wild talk of a dead man. But if Zinker's got it, our guys will get him."

Maybe so. And maybe not, if those Baltimore heavies get to him first.

Chapter Twenty-Nine

What I needed was a good rest I wasn't law enforcement, I'd leave the Baltimore crew to the sheriff and state police. Cummings had heard Lucky's confession, maybe that would be enough to nail Trouble for Sammy's murder. And if the bad guys figured out Zinker had their dope, there might be another murder to hang on them. The trick would be to keep the news about Trouble from Serena until he was under lock and key. She had a tendency to try to settle things on her own.

Back at Bay Breezes, Miss Worple blew by me like a hurricane as I came through the front door. Serena stood in the hallway.

"What was that all about?"

"Someone heard news of gangsters on the police scanner. Her defense group is meeting at the firehouse."

That sounded like a ridiculous idea. "They should leave it to the sheriff and the state police. The way I hear it, those Baltimore boys are cold-blooded killers."

Serena clenched her fists. "She's not my favorite person but I don't want her killed. Or the Judge, either. Go stop them. They won't listen to me but maybe you can do something."

"Me? Not my job, Serena."

Her face darkened, reflecting inner fire. "No, of course not! You're the guy on the horse in that book, on to the next windmill, right? Into people's lives, jot some notes, mount up and off you go to the next windmill. Miss Worple and the Judge are going face to face with killers but it's no business of yours."

I wished I had pulled over on the road and gotten some rest. I was in no condition to calm her down. More likely, I'd say the wrong the thing. "That's the truth, Serena. I'm just here to write a feature story."

"Aren't they friends? But forget it. Go write your stupid story."

I felt like a wounded knight, I wanted to say, "After all I've done for you!" But of course she was right. To a large extent, journalism provides a defense against real involvement. You might venture into a conflict situation but the notebook is a shield, jot your notes and clear out, leave others to deal with hard parts. On to the next story.

I didn't curse. I heard it coming, barreling up out of my injured ego, and shut it up. "All right, I'll see what I can do. But don't get your hopes up."

"Wait a minute." She disappeared into the kitchen and came back with a cup of coffee. I took a sip. In an instant the pores at the top of my head were shedding tears.

"Holy Toledo, this stuff is half hot sauce."

Her smile was forced, mocking. "Gives you balls like a bull."

"It's giving me a damn heart attack. Enough." I handed the cup back. "I'll make the best of the balls I've got, thanks."

As a result of Serena's elixir I was very wide awake as I headed toward the firehouse. Even my brain woke up, and that produced thoughts. Like, why would these people listen to me? I didn't even speak their language, based on my experience with *merkle bush* and *free chicken*. But I'd committed myself to action. What to do?

Where was the flash point in all of this? Where would you have to intercede to head off the violence? Zinker. It was a long shot but if I could get Zinker to turn himself in, the Pitbull crew wouldn't have a target. And if they backed off, the Civil Defense crowd could go back to practicing the capture of Cuban submarines or whatever. Or was I too late, had Zinker already lit out for the border or been taught a terminal lesson about stealing from the Pitbull gang?

His address was on the card he'd given me at our first encounter, that would be a place to start anyway. Maybe he was packing up for his get-away.

My plan? I tried to think of one. Start with what you want to achieve and work your way back from there, voila, you've got a plan. What did I want to achieve? I wanted to calm the Civil Defense group, and I wanted the Baltimore boys locked up so Serena wouldn't go hunting them on her own. Hopefully, one of them would be a guy named Trouble.

My plan was a work in progress.

I stopped at the little East Westerly post office, the small building with a flag that brought to mind a government outpost in frontier days. I asked the lady at the counter for directions. From the back of the room a radio preacher offered to wash away my sins. I take it he carried a big bucket.

"That was Miss Ruthie and Miss Ada, their house, before it got taken away. They had to go to a home. Used to have dogs, and those dogs had chairs at the table just like you or me."

"Is it far from here?"

"New fellow, that Zinker, he hasn't kept it up like they did, doesn't care about the trees and flowers. Comes in here like he owns the place. I've had to set him straight a time or two. Doesn't do any good."

"Up the road, down the road?' I even pointed the directions, hoping to prompt a useful reply.

"You need to slow down a little, Mister. I'll pray with you if you like. That's how I slow down when things get too hectic for me."

"I don't need a prayer, I just need directions, that's all."

She had been leaning forward on the counter. She drew back and straightened up. "Sorry I got to talking, didn't realize this was a life or death situation." Her tone was stern, as though I'd violated the rural post office code of conduct by being in a hurry.

"I don't mean to be rude. But it *is* most likely a life or death situation. Kind of urgent."

Her eyebrows went up. The 'you must be kidding' look became 'you must be nuts.' One eyebrow came down, then the other, and I sensed a decision to send me quickly on my way. "A mile down this road toward town. Left on Saw Mill Road. You come to Cinnamon Run Baptist, you gone too far. Half a mile, maybe a little less, just an old farmhouse sitting back from the road, used to be white, kind of gray now, that's it." She headed back toward the comfort and safety of the radio preacher's sermon.

I called out thanks and she gave a wave that looked like she was erasing me from a chalkboard.

Zinker's car was out front but so was another, a big black boat of a car.

I turned around, drove past again, pulled off and parked on a logging road a short ways from Zinker's place. I'd cut the engine when a black Cadillac Fleetwood blew by, one of the last big V8s. I'd seen it around. Despite having my view blocked by tinted windows, I knew it contained trouble. Maybe even a guy by that name.

I pulled up in front of Zinker's, wishing I had company, preferably company with guns. There wasn't much I could do but take my chances. A peek in the window showed Zinker in a big armchair, a fixture due to being securely wrapped in his own duct tape. I didn't see anyone else, so, taking a deep breath, I went in.

"Looks like they used all your tape. You got more, I hope."

What I could see of his face went red. Without any particular gentleness, I pulled the tape from his mouth. I'm sure a stubbly growth of beard didn't make the experience any more pleasant. There were signs he'd been worked over. His face was bruised and one eye was nearly closed.

"Cut me loose. They'll be back." He struggled with the ties that bound him, shifting this way and that with very little effect.

"They?"

"That gang from Baltimore, buffaloes dressed like preachers. Three of them. I think they shot Biggers. They'll be back for me."

"Was one of them named Trouble?"

"Yeah, I heard that name."

"Where's Biggers?"

"They dragged him out behind the house and I heard a shot. Crazy son of a bitch. Came busting in here, drunk as usual, raising hell about his share of the loot. He thought the Baltimore guys were buyers. Gave them a lot of lip."

I went out back to look for Biggers.

Biggers was sprawled in the grass with a Rorschach of blood framing his head. There might have been some brain matter mixed with the blood. I only locked close enough to see he was beyond repair.

Back inside, I asked Zinker why they hadn't shot him as well.

He stared off at nothing, undoubtedly pissed that I wouldn't unwrap him.

Was it going to be like pulling teeth to get him to talk? That was an idea. "You want to get loose, Zinker, you better come up with some answers."

"They caught on that somebody had their dope, thanks to Biggers. I told 'em it was Scrap raided the pots. Makes sense, Lucky had 'em placed just off the Point. They didn't even know anyone had got to the pots, just came to warn me off of cutting in on Lucky. They'll be back when they find Scrap hasn't got the stuff. Maybe they'll go after Lucky first."

"Lucky drowned himself, Zinker. But not before telling Officer Cummins you've got the dope. So they went after Scrap?"

"Yeah. They know him from his gambling debts, he's into them deep. They bought that Scrap was stealing their stuff, gonna sell it to pay them back. His way of getting even. Sounds like Scrap, don't it? Now come on, cut me loose."

"Interesting. And they're going to find out you lied and come back to do some serious damage. I sure wouldn't want to be in your shoes, or anything else of yours."

"I let you off when you were beating on Biggers. Give me a break. I said you could have half."

"Half your trouble? I don't think so. Where's it stashed? Don't tell me. It's in an old freezer out behind one of your sheds."

"How'd you know that? Come on, cut me loose."

"If I do, here's the deal. You take that stuff and get yourself down to the sheriff's office. Tell them you seized it as evidence and were going to turn it in when those gangsters showed up. You say it's the result of your investigation. And you forget about me being here. I don't want to have to explain about finding you and not reporting Biggers sad demise. You'll be a hero."

"That's ridiculous. The stuff's worth a fortune!"

"Do as I say and you might come out of this alive. It's not just Pitbull's crew after you. I have a feeling the Civil Defense crowd is coming for you as well. If you do as I say maybe you'll stay out of jail. The Baltimore boys probably run the jails, you'll be dead meat."

"All right. Probably the only way out of this mess."

"There are other ways but they're fairly unpleasant. Is it true that Sammy told you Lucky was the middleman in the dope deals?"

"Yeah. I told him I'd handle Lucky. But I figured, why not cut myself in for some easy money?"

It sounded like the truth. I cut him out of the duct tape. "Don't pull any crap, Zinker. If you don't keep your word, I've got a tape of you and Biggers talking about your various crooked deals." True, I'd left the tape with McCoob, but I could get it if needed.

He wobbled trying to find his legs.

I left Zinker to work out his salvation. He was a bully and didn't deserve any consideration. It was his greed that got Sammy killed. But he was the one who could put Trouble and his pals away; I had to take the risk. Could be I'd let a viper out of a pit. No one but myself to blame if the viper bites the hand that freed it.

I needed to warn Scrap. I drove toward the Point but parked some distance from the little bridge Scrap had rebuilt.

After taking a quick shower in repellent, I made my way through the thicket along the road. The three toughs from

Baltimore were standing outside their car just before the little bridge. From what I could tell, they were arguing over their next move. There was no getting past them.

I backtracked to where I'd seen an old rutted farm road heading off into the woods. The entry was obvious enough, but from there it just disappeared into wilds. Still, worth a try. If I couldn't get past the bad guys directly, maybe I could get around them.

The track was overgrown and littered with forest debris, the ground was soft and damp, but the well-worn ruts were still visible and I followed them.

I was walking a mat of rotted leaves and pine needles, so there was no great worry about the give-away crackle or crunch like walking in upland woods. Plus, I could see that the path skirted the entrance to the Point and, as I had hoped, headed for the lighthouse.

I was concentrating on avoiding detection, but still, I could imagine some youngster of long ago treading this same path, maybe carrying a fishing pole or maybe a basket of eggs and pail of milk for the lighthouse keeper's table.

Closer to the Point, tall marsh grass lined the sides of the path. The cover assured that I wouldn't be visible, but at the same time obscured my view of the area where I had last seen the Baltimore delegation.

Would there be a problem with the stream that ran under the little bridge? Not to worry, the path stayed to the landward side of it.

Scrap was working at his sculpture, sparks flying as he welded one pipe to another. The flame of the torch sputtered and he pulled off the welding mask. I told him about the Lucky and Zinker and the gangsters.

"Sammy got killed because he was keeping an eye on Lucky's crab pots, that's where the deliveries came in, just out there off the Point."

"So that's it. I'd noticed his pots were getting raided at night, at least that's how I saw it."

"You didn't check it out?"

"What, and be target practice for whoever was doing it? I don't think so, none of my business. Just Lucky's bad luck."

"Speaking of bad luck, there's those three gangsters down by the bridge."

"Well, they'll probably come in and try to kill us. Three, you say?"

"Rough characters. I thought I'd better warn you."

"Thanks."

"You don't seem too bothered."

"It's just another war."

Maybe so, but this one involved me. "Wouldn't we be safer up in the lighthouse?"

"Not hardly. They stand underneath and shoot into the floor; sooner or later we get hit. The scrap pile is a ready-made bunker. We'll hide out there." He picked up his Streetsweeper shotgun and led the way.

It was a precarious climb but we got up to where we had a view of the entrance to Scrap's property. I was glad of a hideout but worried about tetanus as we scrambled over rusted auto and boat body parts, large appliances, plumbing apparatus, industrial and farm equipment and other salvage.

I'd guess we were fifteen feet up, a few feet over the marsh grass. We were in a cleft in the debris, hidden from those approaching but exposed to our rear.

Three men in black suits appeared on the trail from the little bridge. Scrap pushed me down among the heap of metal. The men moved slowly, pistols at the ready, scanning the path ahead. They stopped momentarily to gape at the strange sculptures.

There was a brief conference as one pointed his weapon toward the junk heap. He moved forward and began to circle the pile. As he came around to the back, he would see our position.

Scrap rose to a crouch and seemed ready to fire. With twelve rounds to loose in a couple of seconds, he could solve our problems very quickly.

He pulled at the trigger. Nothing happened. He flattened out beside me. "Shit, the damn cylinder's jammed. We're toast. You have a gun?"

"Nope."

"Ever-body should carry a gun."

"Those guys seem to agree."

"Make like a mole. Dig down."

The man who was circling the heap called to his companions. "Over here!"

And then I heard thunder, but it wasn't thunder. It was a rumble of disciplined yelling, but I couldn't make out the words, just Buh-Buh-Bum! Buh-Buh-Bum!"

It got closer and louder. Was it Thundercloud's cult coming back? Lambs to the slaughter.

A female voice sounded like it was coming over a loudspeaker.

"Stomp the Evil! Stomp it out!"

The three men looked in the direction of the racket.

From our perch I could see a golf cart. I kid you not, a golf cart.

The driver and a passenger were decked out in bright orange jump suits and white safety helmets. The passenger chanted into a bullhorn. The voice was familiar.

"Stomp the Evil!"

Behind the cart came an army of what looked like road workers or utility repair personnel, twenty-five or thirty strong, similarly attired, and all marching, stomping, their booted feet pounding the soft earth.

Those who weren't carrying rifles or shotguns had other armaments, pick handles or baseball bats.

"Stomp the Evil!"

One of the Baltimore gangsters turned and started down the path, deeper into the marsh. The other two hesitated just seconds, staring at the approaching mob as if stunned. Then they turned to follow their comrade.

It was pure madness but I had to know. I stood up and shouted: "Hey, Trouble!"

One of the fleeing gangsters turned, a perplexed look on his face. He fired a wild shot in my direction and resumed his retreat.

All three broke into a full tilt run.

The parading newcomers moved slowly, as if they had been frozen and were not quite thawed.

From the golf cart came the eerie command, "Stomp the Evil!"

From behind the cart a resounding chorus: "Stomp it out!"

It was the army of the bizarre, the drill sergeant calling commands and the troops counting cadence.

"Stomp the Evil!"

"Stomp it out!"

"Stomp the Evil!"

"Stomp it out!"

I looked at Scrap. "What in the hell?"

Scrap shook his head in mock dismay. "That, my friend, is the county Civil Defense squadron, and that's the honorable Judge Wetherby and his sidekick Miss Worple in the chariot out front."

"What's with the fires?"

"Fires?" Scrap groaned. "Aw, shit. Now look what they've gone and done, setting fire to the marsh."

"Why?"

"Scares out the rabbits. Or in this case, those bozos from Baltimore."

"We should show ourselves, let them know we're all right."

"You don't want to mess with them right now. They get in a mood, it's kind of a mania. Best not to interfere."

"Well, then, don't you think we should get out of here?"

"That's not a bad idea. Gonna be a lot of shrapnel if my propane tanks go."

The area down toward the little bridge was ablaze and thick smoke blew our way. "We'll have to take the back way," Scrap said.

"Tumps and hummocks, right? Never mind that. Come on, I'll show you how I came in."

We clambered down from the junk pile and climbed into his ATV, the crazy chant indicating we were just moments ahead of the arrival of the marchers.

I directed our retreat with hand signals.

"I'd forgot about this old trail. You're a regular Daniel Boone, Holliday. Up to a point. I mean, not that you'll die at the Alamo."

"Wasn't that Davy Crockett?"

"Some old guy. It's not important."

We got out of the smoke and into the woods. A glance back showed a big patch of the marsh smoldering in a dense black cloud.

I was on the lookout for the Baltimore crew but didn't see a trace. I asked Scrap what he thought would become of them.

"Not likely they'll go back through the smoke and face the Civil Defense bunch. Maybe swim out and drown. If they make it to a road, probably get collared. All this stuff with Lucky and Zinker, the place will be crawling with law."

Scrap pulled up to where I'd left my car. I was puzzled. "Won't there be trouble over burning the marshes?"

"Could be a little trouble, maybe, since they're not professionals."

"It takes a specialist to burn a marsh?"

"Used to be us ignorant country folks did it, like I said, hunters scaring out rabbits, but also because it was good for the muskrat trappers, keeps the grasses down, and good for the marsh, made for new growth. Now it's all fancied up, ecology, smart people doing the same damn thing but with rocket-science reasons why. Lot more screw-ups these days."

"Screw-ups?"

"Yeah. Scientists, they go to burn a hundred acres and it turns into a thousand, or they don't watch the wind and the fire goes to town, stuff like that. Scientists screwing things up."

"Reminds me of a story by Flaubert."

"Who's that, Flawbear?"
"Some old guy. It's not important."

Chapter Thirty

It was a beautiful Chesapeake afternoon, blue sky, cottony clouds and warm sunshine. I'd asked Serena to join me for a walk, just a little stroll down the dead-end lane toward Scrap's bridge. At first she refused, saying Miss Worple wouldn't approve. I said I'd take the blame, I'd tell Miss Worple I needed the names of some plants I planned to mention in my article. "Miss Worple doesn't have a clue about plants. She couldn't argue if I turned to you for answers."

We'd walked a few yards when I decided to get down to it. "Serena, I'm going to find a way out of this rut I'm in. I'm going to quit the magazine, head back to Washington and find a real job. When I get myself set up, maybe you could come up and join me?"

She didn't speak right away. "That's quite a compliment, very unexpected." Another pause, then she continued: "The problem is, we are both trying to figure out what to do next in our lives. I don't want to be cornering you in a certain way."

"In other words, no."

"In other words, do what you think is right for you. I'll do the same. We'll keep in touch, and just see where life takes us."

I'd lost my head. It happens, some people never learn. I wasn't considering whether we shared a passion for each other, or whether, even if the passion was there, we could get along the other eighty percent of our togetherness. I wasn't considering the habits of a lifetime, the necessary generosity and tolerance of each other's way of doing things. She had her ways, I had mine, and togetherness often meant a clashing of ways.

I was in love-conquers-all mode, a foolish place to be. She was being practical. Why did she have to do that? Still, it wasn't a total brush-off, was it? Though I didn't feel exactly encouraged. She turned and hugged me. I returned the favor. And I have to say, it wasn't a goodbye hug, more of a getting to know you hug.

Why stop there? Because, that's where she stopped. "I think you realigned my chakras, Serena. Hopefully, I'll be thinking more clearly."

"Well, the truth is, we hardly know each other, do we? I mean, from what I've seen, you're not exactly a homebody. I think you could be happy living out of a camper if you had your typewriter and a story to chase."

"People change."

"I want you to be who you were meant to be."

She was right, of course. I'd gotten way ahead of where we were in reality. We hadn't even shared the physical intimacy of a one-night stand. This was no time for fantasies that might dissolve into disillusion, maybe even pain.

And that was quite an order; she wanted me to be who I was meant to be. Who was I meant to be? Is there a test you can take? Maybe there's a scientific machine that they strap on your head, you get some kind of biofeedback? It whirrs and beeps and then you get a printout of your who-you-really-are reading.

But you just have to figure it out for yourself, don't you? And many of us follow a path of chance and happenstance, envying the few who don armor, mount the white horse and charge ahead on a charted course.

Back at Bay Breezes she headed to the kitchen.

"You're looking a bit lost." It was Judge Wetherby, sitting in a wicker chair on the porch.

"Disoriented, maybe."

"You got more than you bargained for, coming here to write an article on a forgotten corner of the Peninsula."

"No argument there." I wasn't going to sing the blues for Wetherby so I changed the subject. "I tried calling McCobb. He has a tape I'd like to turn over to the cops. His phone is disconnected, no information available."

"Really? Well, I heard he had some business to take care of in Baltimore."

"You heard that?"

"Somewhere. Might have been on the police scanner?"

"Sure, they're always spilling the beans on sinister, clandestine operations on those things. Never mind, I don't want to know."

We thought our separate thoughts and listened to a berserk chorus of crows, dressing down an owl or a cat. The judge shifted in his chair. He massaged his chin. "In regard to McCobb, some of what I heard involved that fellow Pitbull, the one that runs drugs and prostitution, among other things, in Baltimore."

"McCobb and Pitbull? I'm listening."

"Seems this Pitbull is a very ambitious and ballsy sort, trying to blackmail a government agency."

"An agency. Maybe one that used him to provide talented escorts for visiting dignitaries? Maybe he recorded some of those events?"

"You seem to be on familiar terms with the tale."

"Just a guess based on what I do know. So possibly McCobb was gathering evidence for a counterpunch, smash the guy's drug business. Payback time."

The Judge patted his coat pocket as though he might have forgotten something. "Care for a cigar?"

"No thanks." It was a fairly sore subject. It seemed to me chances were good that the outfit behind McCobb had been behind the phony story that got me in hot water. Maybe yes, maybe no. I didn't want to dwell on it. "I'm guessing they caught the hoods who were after Scrap?"

"Oh yes. There'll be something on TV in a few minutes; the reporters were all over this one, it's big news."

We moved to the parlor and the television set. I noticed that Sammy's clamshell was still on an end table.

"Too bad that's fake. It would be a nice attraction in a local history display."

Wetherby looked at the carving. "Actually, Holliday, it's not fake. Scrap did indeed find it on his property."

"This is bonkers. So there should be a dig to find out what else is there."

"No. Things should proceed in the direction they are now going. For the good of the community."

"It's for the good of the community to learn about it's past, it's history."

"It's for the good of the community to have jobs, to revitalize, and to let the dead rest in peace. If I went to your hometown and commenced digging up the bones of your ancestors, would you approve? Why shouldn't these people get the same respect? Is it respectful to disinter the dead for the sake of curiosity, to pad out a Zogby book or provide a novelty for museumgoers to gawk at? It's macabre entertainment in the guise of science."

"But to some that land would be sacred ground."

"Maybe it's all sacred ground. We walk on the bones of those who have come before, the dirt is the dead, the rotted remains of ancient ancestors going back further than most minds can fathom, our ancestors' remains mixed with decayed animals and plants. That is the earth. That is what your fingers feel when you grub around in the garden. As for burial places, they don't endure. The tombs of the great are pillaged for profit or in the name of science. The graves of the lesser are building plots for those to come."

If I was an enlightened scholar perhaps I could come up with a dazzling reply. I'm not, and I held my tongue.

As we waited, an idea began to take shape. The events I'd been part of could be the makings of a book, maybe even a screenplay. With luck, that could be my ticket out of this rut. I could score a big fat advance. Serena and I would live happily ever after. I could see light at the end of this tunnel!

Good afternoon, I'm Roger Jolie and this is WHOT News. In the news today, arrests in two murder cases and a related drug bust in Wannapeake County. Police say three Baltimore men have been arrested on suspicion of murder and other charges. Wannapeake Bureau Chief Helen Highwater has more details:

Good afternoon, Roger. Authorities in Wannapeake County are not releasing the names of three suspects arrested in connection with the alleged murder of game warden Clement Biggers. They are also implicated in the killing of Sammy Sanchez, a young man from East Westerly whose death was previously thought accidental. A source in the Sheriff's Department told me the men are from Baltimore and are believed to be associates of a major drug ring with international connections.

Adding credence to the drug gang connection is the related seizure of a large quantity of cocaine and heroin. Police credited Luther Zinker, a private security guard employed by landowners in the East Westerly area, for assisting in the drug confiscation.

It appears that the warden, Biggers, was killed when he interrupted the gangsters who had taken Zinker prisoner. Details are sketchy at this point; we hope to have more in our next report.

The Baltimore men were apprehended after they allegedly set a marsh fire to divert pursuing authorities. An officer told me the men deny setting the fire, but the property owner, a Mr. Blevins, says he witnessed the act of arson. Members of the Wannapeake Civil Defense Squadron were first responders.

Police and sheriff's deputies found the men huddled in an abandoned lighthouse on the Parkers Point property. A source tells me the men may have been high on drugs and hallucinating. They claimed to have been chased to the lighthouse by, quote, "a bunch of swamp demons." More details as they emerge. Back to you, Roger.

Thank you, Helen. In related news, a Hollywood film company, Amene Productions, has announced the purchase of a film treatment from local entrepreneur Barnard Cole. It seems probable that the film, tentatively titled "Whatever Happened to Sammy Sanchez?," may be shot locally. Cole was en route to Los Angeles to discuss revisions based on the latest developments, and a possible book deal. He was unavailable for comment.

So much for my big ideas; that weasel Cole got there first and he's got the connections. Maybe I'd be smart to hang on to the *Here & There* job a while longer.

Although word processors were coming into use, I still worked with my trusty old portable Remington. I wrote about chickens, I wrote about crabs, and through that I wove mentions from sightseeing brochures plus lists from business cards and the telephone book. Motels, restaurants, antique shops, farmers' markets, gas stations and garages ... there, the ad department should be ecstatic. I topped it with the opening I had written before arriving, correcting the heron error. It was an epic piece of puffery.

I drove to Cole's office to use the fax machine and to leave a note. But his office was closed and dark. I slipped the note under the door.

Barney: I sure want to apologize for letting slip to the media about your plagiarized brochures. It would be just dreadful if a bunch of angry publishers and writers sued you for every last nickel. Hoping for the best, Andy.

It wasn't true ... not yet, anyway. But it made me feel a little better.

I found a fax machine at a nearby motel and sent the story off.

And then later came the expected call from von Klonk, although I was surprised by his opening comment.

"Don't bother coming back."

Hell's bells, fired after one assignment. Just when I'd decided I'd better keep the job. "What about the trial? You said thirty days and it's only been two weeks."

"And I'm a man of my word, Holliday. Integrity personified. I've got another assignment for you."

I'd come up with a suitable moniker, thanks to Thundercloud. "Lay it on me, *Chief*. Swim the Amazon? Barefoot across Borneo?"

"Keep smiling. I need you to go to Appalachia, pronto. We're behind schedule."

"Appalachia? Excuse me, I know something about Appalachia. It's shoot-first-moonshiners, abandoned coal mines, snake handlers and desperate poverty, have I got that right?"

"An image for you to dispel, Holliday. Advertising believes there is an untapped goldmine there."

"No one has found it so far."

"You will, Holliday. See to it."

Well, according to my bank, a meager sum masquerading as a paycheck had been deposited in my account. So, whatever the game, I was game. "You know, Chief, Appalachia runs from north Georgia to southern Pennsylvania. And there's an associated trail goes all the way to Maine. Is there anywhere in particular I should start?"

"Start when you hit mountains. Give me a call. I'll figure something out. Get a move on, Holliday. I need that story yesterday. Tick, tick, tick"

Isn't that the sound of a device made by a lunatic who is about to blow something up?

"How was the piece I sent in?"

"Fine, fine. Needed some tweaking, cut out all that poetic crap, put a new lead on it. But you got the length about right, after I trimmed it by half."

"So how about we skip Appalachia, run the second half next issue?"

I didn't like the tone of his reply. It was the dial tone.

Serena asked several of us to join in a memorial service for Sammy. There were only five people gathered that afternoon at the tip of Scrap's property – Serena, me, Judge Wetherby, Miss Worple and Scrap. It was high tide, going out.

We each had our say.

Serena scattered Sammy's ashes into the receding waters.

Judge Wetherby turned away from us for a moment. I'd swear he took something from his pocket and pitched it to where the tide was carrying Sammy's ashes out into the Bay.

Serena and I walked back up the sand lane toward Bay Breezes.

"You'll be leaving now?"

"I have to make a living."

"Did you ever think of doing something different?"

"Lately, quite often."

Her look was sharp. "And?"

"Not much to draw on. When I was much younger I played drums ..."

"You didn't keep it up."

"No. Actually, it was my left hand that didn't keep it up. It couldn't keep up with my right."

"Sounds awkward."

She had that right. "Yeah. That's how it felt."

"I guess that's important."

"What's that?"

"How something feels to you."

I let it slide. "Sure."

So.

With sundown coming on, I drove the sandy lane to the Point. Had I said proper goodbyes? I don't know. I was never very good at that part.

I parked at the rickety bridge and stood there, saying goodbye in my own way.

In the distance, the darkening cloud-banked horizon was streaked in burgundy.

Nearer, a Great Blue Heron glided above the wide, calm Bay.

*Enjoyed **Murder By Bay Breezes**? Here's what you can do next.*

If you loved the book and have a moment to spare, I would really appreciate a short review on the page where you bought the book (or Goodreads, or Librarything, whatever works for you). Your help in spreading the word is greatly appreciated. Reviews make a huge difference to helping new readers find this book.

You can find more information about this and upcoming books on The Andrew Holliday Facebook page

www.facebook.com/AndyHollidayMysteries

or to get in touch with comments or enquiries via email:

andyhollidaymysteries@gmail.com